D1713869

SANDOVER BEACH MEMORIES

A CHRISTIAN BEACH ROMANCE

EMMA ST. CLAIR

2019 Kirsten Oliphant

A different version of this was previously published as Sandover Beach Memories in 2018. This book has significant changes, but also keeps much of the same storyline and characters.

Cover by Bobbie Byrd

Editing by Cindy VanSchalkwyk

Warning: All rights reserved. No part of this book may be reproduced aside from small excerpts used in a review. Please contact Emma for permissions: emma@emmastclair.com.

This is a work of fiction. All characters, names, and occurrences are a product of the author's creation and bear no resemblance to actual people, living or dead. Any incidences resembling actual events or people are purely coincidental.

ACKNOWLEDGMENTS

The characters in this story are fictional and not based on anyone I know. The events are also fictional...with one exception. I absolutely DID get stuck in a Nag's Head beach house elevator, though with two girls I hardly knew and now call friends. And yep, the fire department did come rescue us. (Read more about this in the Note from Emma at the end!)

Fiona and Heather—I STILL don't know why I opened the elevator door while it was moving, but I'm really glad you still like me. Even after we had to be rescued by firemen. I won't forget that time!

Ginny—thanks for making that beach weekend possible! You had NO idea the impact it would have on me! But, to be completely cheesy and truthful, your friendship has impacted every part of my life since. <3

Rob. Everything in my life would fall apart without you. And no, I'm NOT being dramatic.

CHAPTER ONE

"I KNOW it's right in front of me, but I just can't see it."
Jenna muttered to herself as she pushed a cart slowly through the empty wine aisle of Bohn's Island Grocery. Monday morning was too early for wine. But she had come to the store desperate for coffee and decided to stock up on some other necessities. After her recent divorce and her mother's death, this meant chocolate, cheese, wine, and the one thing she couldn't find: a corkscrew.

When Jenna arrived back on Sandover Island the night before, she hadn't thought to check her mom's kitchen for food. In the back of her mind, she thought maybe there would be some non-perishables in the pantry or frozen meals. Instead of doing something practical like seeing what she might need at the house, Jenna had driven straight to her favorite beach access. She longed to hear the comforting roar and hiss of the ocean and feel the sand under her bare feet. The ocean tugged at her soul the way the moon pulled the tides. It always had. How had she lived three hours away for so long?

The sight of giant homes lined up along the beach made her feel sick. Jenna had seen the new builds along the beach front, but still hated them every time with as much venom as the first time she'd seen them. Three-story McMansions on stilts, painted absurd colors like pink and turquoise. Vacation homes.

The real estate agent in her noted all the features: the prime location, the square footage, the many balconies and large windows, protective storm shutters. Properties were still a bit cheaper here than the more popular beaches along the North Carolina coast, but growing exponentially every year. There were fewer and fewer of the historic, weather-beaten beach cottages along the coast. Some were taken by big storms, but more were demolished to make room for the ugly mansions.

Despite the presence of the massive house next to her, the ocean had done its work. Her soul felt lighter and the heaviness of the past year lifted, even slightly. Jenna might have stayed longer, staring at the moonlight on the water, but had caught sight of a man on the dark balcony of the house. From the shadows, he had waved, and she practically ran back to the car. The last thing she needed was to be hit on by some guy looking for a good time on vacation.

Despite creepy watching guy, the few minutes at the beach calmed her enough to face her mother's empty house. When she arrived, she had collapsed into bed in her old room, not bothering to unpack her car or check the kitchen for food.

Which left her groaning this morning as she realized there was no coffee. After the funeral a few months before, her sister, Rachel, stayed for the weekend to start packing up. Naturally, she started in the kitchen. There wasn't so much as a coffee filter in the cabinets. The fridge held only a box of baking soda, probably added by Rachel for freshness.

Jenna almost cried at the sight of the little orange box. Her mother had never kept one there. Neither did Jenna. Why was it that these small details and memories of her mother could send grief surging through her? When the wave of emotion passed, Jenna pulled some boots on over her yoga pants and headed to Bohn's, the only grocery store that On Islanders used, pointedly leaving the Harris Teeter for the tourists.

She should be thankful to Rachel, really. With an entire house to pack up, having any room cleared was a help. But all Jenna could think about was coffee. And finding a corkscrew, since Rachel had emptied the drawers of all silverware and utensils.

Jenna's cart now held two bottles of white wine, a box of trash bags, chocolate cookies, milk, Community coffee, fresh bread, and a stack of frozen Lean Cuisine meals. She had thrown a roll of duct tape on top. Because you can never have enough duct tape.

"Need some help?"

With her eyes still fixed on the shelves in front of her, Jenna could see the blue of a Bohn's apron as an employee pushing a cart filled with cheese stopped next to her. She must be looking right at the corkscrews but could not find one.

"Yes! Please. I know it's here, but I can't find a corkscrew to save my life." She ran a finger along one shelf, seeing mixers, decorative shot glasses, and cocktail shakers. Nope, nope, and nope.

A muscular arm moved right in front of her, and she stepped back as the man pulled a corkscrew right from the middle of a shelf. He held it out to her. "You were looking right at it. This one is pretty basic but will do the job."

She looked up at him, a "thank you" dying on her lips as she recognized his square jaw, golden-brown eyes, and tousled brown hair. A tiny shiver of something moved through her stomach. It couldn't have been attraction, despite his handsome face and playful smile. No, any feelings she might have had for this man shriveled up years ago—not that she had ever admitted that she had feelings at all. Nope. Never happened. You can't have feelings for someone you despise.

"Jackson Wells." His name even sounded like a curse on her lips.

He pretended not to notice and gave a little bow in his blue Bohn's apron. "At your service, Jenna Monroe."

She grimaced slightly hearing her maiden name. It felt both familiar and new. Jackson wouldn't know that she had only recently changed it back. She stood blinking at him, knowing that she should say something else. Coherent words escaped her. She blamed the lack of coffee.

Certainly not the way his broad shoulders looked in the button-down white shirt underneath the apron. Or the dusting of stubble on his jaw, the only real difference in how he looked since the last time she saw him. He still had that roguish bad boy thing going on, but with Jackson, it wasn't just a look. He had always been the bad boy. Probably still was. Leopards don't change their spots, her mom had always said.

Last she heard, Jackson had flunked out of business school. Now he was sporting a Bohn's apron and passing out corkscrews on a Monday morning. Fitting retribution after what he had done to Rachel. Someone—Jackson, she always assumed—had started rumors that Rachel and Jackson had hooked up at a beach party. It humiliated Rachel and seriously ticked off Jenna.

Jenna remembered holding Rachel as she sobbed. "He's the only one who would have said anything. And it's a lie, but no one believes me. Because what girl wouldn't want to be with *The* Jackson Wells? So now I'm the super-slut of the sophomore class. You should have seen the looks I got at church."

Jenna had been furious. Still was. But she also felt the ugly prick of jealousy that Jackson had tried hooking up with every girl in school, even her little sister, but never *her*. Jackson had never so much as flirted or asked her out. She couldn't remember having a conversation with him. Which had to be some kind of record.

Sure, most of high school she had been with Steve, but her whole senior year she was single. That was the year Jackson tried to get together with Rachel. Was Jenna more upset about the rumor or that he had gone for Rachel instead of her? This wasn't the first time she had wondered this, but the question came back up as she stood a few feet away from him.

It was an ugly train of thought, making her feel angry and sick. His smirking face before her brought to mind descriptions lifted from the pages of historical romance novels: cad, scoundrel, rapscallion. Modern words just wouldn't do for someone like him. It wasn't fair that jerks like Jackson Wells could be so attractive. He'd only gotten better with age.

Stop thinking about how hot Jackson is!

His deep voice interrupted her silent battle with herself. "How about some cheese to go with that wine? I've got Gruyere, aged White Cheddar, and some super stinky Gorgonzola."

Jackson held up three wheels of cheese from his cart,

wrinkling his nose and shaking his head when he got to the Gorgonzola. His wide smile infuriated her. He wanted to talk fancy cheese?

"No cheese. Just the corkscrew. I'm surprised you're still working here. Do they give raises to people who have passed the twenty years of service mark? Or maybe they give you a raise so you finally get above minimum wage?"

That wiped the smile from his face. It also made Jenna feel like the very worst person in the world. She may have been bitter and slightly depressed, but she had never been mean. Jackson scratched his chin, staring through the front glass windows of the store. "Unfortunately, no awards or raises. Just an apron."

"That's too bad. That could have topped the list of your life accomplishments."

As the words left her mouth, Jenna already hated herself. She was being petty and mean. There were plenty of things she regretted from high school. Wasting so much time dating Steve, the boy next door, for one. He was a cheater, just like her husband turned out to be. But she didn't sit around obsessing over her regrets or the people who hurt her. Why was she still holding this over Jackson's head? Rachel, happily married with two girls, certainly wasn't still hung up on the rumor. Next month would be their twenty-year high school reunion. Jenna shouldn't be carrying around this much negative emotion. But she wasn't about to apologize either.

The look on his face made her feel even worse. Jackson had gone from staring out the front window to staring at the floor. His shoulders hunched with something that looked like acceptance, like he thought he deserved the darts she threw at him. Jenna wanted to apologize, but couldn't bring herself to say the words. This wasn't like her, to be openly rude to someone. Was this because of her grief? Or because of the last few terrible years, struggling with her marriage and losing her mom? Had she turned into the kind of person who verbally attacks a guy in his late thirties working a minimum-wage job? That was low.

His haunted eyes met hers. Jenna's mother would have been so disappointed. She would have quoted that verse from Ephesians that had once been so familiar, "Do not let any unwholesome talk come out of your mouth, but only what is helpful for building others up according to their needs." This memory struck her harder even than the baking soda in the fridge. Her throat felt thick with rising tears.

Jenna had to get away from Jackson before she became a sobbing mess in front of him.

"Thanks for the help." She began to push her cart away.

"Good to see you again, Jenna."

As she worked to swallow down her tears, Jenna tried to think about the last time she had seen Jackson. Honestly, it might have been high school. As small as Sandover Island was, in all the years Jenna came home to visit her parents and then just her mom, she hadn't seen Jackson once. Until now, she hadn't really thought about him either. Not much, anyway.

Now she couldn't stop thinking about him: the sad look in his eyes and the resigned set of his jaw. The way his hair had that rumpled quality that no hair product in the world could fake. The way his smile turned up on the left side, looking more like a flirtatious smirk than a smile. Had he been wearing a wedding band? She hated herself for even thinking it. She needed to stop thinking about Jackson.

But the feeling that she had wounded him stuck with her, making Jenna feel sick as she reached the checkout. Jenna had been more than rude; she had been cruel. The words soured in her mouth. The woman behind the register eyed her cart and gave her a look, the kind locals usually reserved for Off Islanders. "I'm sorry, hon. You can't purchase wine until after noon."

Jenna groaned. "You're serious? That's still a thing?"

The woman smiled. "Bohn's store policy. I can re-shelve them for you."

Jenna wanted to scream. She was thirty-eight and couldn't buy a bottle of wine. Not because of a liquor law (though North Carolina did have some odd laws about that), but because Bohn's never sold alcohol before noon or at all on Sundays. She handed the two bottles over to the cashier, feeling like a child who had been chastised.

This whole morning made her feel like she had time-warped back to high school. Jenna had, like so many On Island kids, moved away as soon as she could. It was too much of a small-town. Jenna had briefly toyed with the idea of keeping their childhood home rather than selling it, but she hadn't made it twenty-four hours without being visited by ghosts of the past. The beach might soothe her soul, but the people on this island and her own personal history was simply too much.

CHAPTER TWO

JACKSON BARRELLED through the double doors at the back of Bohn's, sending them crashing into shelves on either side. Once inside his windowless office, he threw his apron down on his desk. His breath came in short pants and his fists were almost vibrating with the need to punch something. Instead, he closed his eyes, slowed his breathing, and spread his palms flat on the desk.

Let it go. Let it go. I can do all things through Him.
Let. Go.

Even though he saw Jenna the night before on the beach access below his house, Jackson hadn't been prepared to run into her this morning. Especially not when he was wearing a Bohn's apron, restocking shelves. No wonder she thought that he was a minimum-wage employee, not the owner of Bohn's and about half of Sandover Island.

Would it even have mattered to her? Jenna was hardly the shallow type. She probably wouldn't be impressed with his beach house or care about the fortune Wells Development had amassed for him over the past fifteen years since his father retired. She probably wouldn't even care how much of his salary Jackson donated every year to various charities. Jenna's opinion of him formed some twenty years ago and was clearly stuck there.

Why had he thought that might change?

Jackson had been waiting for Jenna to return to Sandover since her mother's funeral. Because of Wells Development, Jackson kept up with real estate and knew her mother's house still sat empty. He assumed Jenna or Rachel would come back to pack it up and put it on the market. He had even driven by a few times, noting that someone still took care of the lawn, though the house itself was dark. After the weeks turned to months, Jackson wondered if he had been wrong to think Jenna might come back.

And then last night, there she was. Jackson had wandered out to the balcony, letting the ocean soothe his restless thoughts. Like a dream, Jenna stood on the beach access below his house, looking as beautiful as ever. Heart thumping in his chest, he had simply admired her in the moonlight. Her hair had grown out a little since he saw her at the funeral. She had always kept it long in high school: a golden brown with the slightest wave to it, more if she spent time on the beach. Short hair suited her, framing her heart-shaped face beautifully in the moonlight as the wind whipped it over her cheeks.

Even from a distance he could sense the sadness that still clung to her. She had just lost her mom, but Jackson also heard somewhere that she had gotten divorced. No details, just that her marriage ended. She crossed her arms tightly over her chest, her shoulders low and stiff.

Jackson felt like a coward watching, when all he wanted to do was run down all three flights and hold her. Instead, when she happened to look up, Jackson simply waved. He opened his mouth to call out, but Jenna hurried away. The way she practically ran back to the car should have prepared him for the disdain that dripped from her voice this morning.

Like a fool, he had hoped to get a second chance with the one girl he had always wanted. You weren't supposed to fall in love when you were sixteen and carry that love, unrequited, until you were a few years shy of forty. Not that Jackson hadn't done his fair share of dating. He had. But Jenna stayed with him, mostly in the back of his mind, until he saw her again at the funeral. Then it was like that high school crush fanned into hot flames of something much deeper. He didn't want to really think about the feelings he had for Jenna. Especially since they were clearly not returned.

Jackson sank down in his office chair, feeling deflated. His anger still hummed under the surface, but for now, he wasn't going to punch a hole in something. For years, Jackson thought his attraction stemmed from that whole wanting-what-you-can't have thing. Jenna was always with that jerk Steve, at least until their senior year when she finally wised up. After the breakup, Jackson had asked her out, but she said no. Stupidly, he tried to hook up with her sister Rachel to make her jealous. That not-so genius plan backfired and led to one of the moments he was most ashamed of.

Jackson didn't start the rumors about him and Rachel or even confirm them, but the story spread anyway. The whole school thought he slept with Jenna's sister, when he hadn't so much as kissed her. He did find the source of the rumors and put a stop to it, but that wasn't enough. Rachel and Jenna both got hurt and he knew that they blamed him. He should have done more.

What he had planned to do when he talked to Jenna again was to apologize. The year before, Jackson had gotten to apologize to Rachel when she and her husband visited Mrs.

Monroe. He had pulled Rachel aside in the parking lot as she walked with her family to the car. It had been awkward, but Jackson let the apology tumble out. Through experience he had learned that apologies were best when sincere and unplanned. You couldn't ever contrive the right words. It had to be from the heart. Rachel had surprised him with easy forgiveness—and a hug.

Rachel may have forgiven him, but obviously Jenna didn't. She made that more than clear this morning, cutting him down to his knees dressed in yoga pants with sleep-ruffled hair. Despite her cruelty, Jackson found her unbearably attractive, even in her messy morning state. He wanted to run his hands through her hair.

Jackson groaned. Why had he talked to her about cheese? Why didn't he start with an apology?

"Everything okay back here, boss? You look like you've seen a ghost." His store manager, Mercer, stood just inside the doorway of his office, as though she could tell he needed a little space. He hadn't even heard her come in.

"Something like that."

"Do you ... want to talk about it?"

Jackson smiled at the hesitation in her voice. Usually Jackson was the one asking her if she needed anything. She never did. Mercer was only twenty-two and he had become something of her mentor. Sometimes he suspected that she saw him as a father figure, even though there was only sixteen years between them. His best friends were her age, but the distance seemed greater between Jackson and Mercer. He didn't mind, as the last thing he wanted was to blur professional lines with any hint of attraction.

As proficient as she was at her job, Mercer kept a bit of mystery about herself. A few months ago, she had showed up at Bohn's looking for work. Jackson took one look at her and got the impression that she was running from something. And if he used so much as the wrong word, she would run again. Jackson remembered her deft avoidance of questions about her past when he interviewed her. He recognized this because he was always trying to avoid talking about his own past. He gave her a job, half-expecting her to leave in a few months without telling him.

Mercer started as a bagger, then moved up to cashier. When Jackson started noticing small improvements around the store, it took him a week to realize that Mercer was responsible. The produce section was rearranged in a way that had customers thanking him. His office was suddenly clean, his files organized. Hand-lettered chalkboard signs appeared around the store. Jackson had promoted her to store manager and Mercer continued to surprise him. She still hadn't opened up, but he could tell that she had started to feel safe here.

"I don't want to talk, but I appreciate you asking. I'll be fine. What's happening this week?"

"One of the produce shipments was delayed, but that's fine. If we need to, I can send someone Off Island to a produce stand. They always have a great selection."

"I like staying local. If we run low, do it."

Mercer pulled her lip between her teeth, a tell that Jackson had come to recognize. Usually a great idea followed. "I was thinking ... Actually, maybe this isn't a good time."

"No, tell me. I have a moment." And it would take his mind off Jenna. At least for a few minutes, anyway.

She hesitated. In his current state, he just wanted to yell at her to spit it out, but he had learned with Mercer that if he waited, her answers were worth it.

"I was thinking maybe we could have a section of the produce department sourced locally. The farm stands along the road coming onto Sandover have had a hard time staying open the last few years. This would help them and appeal to locals On Island."

Those farm stands had been around for as long as Jackson could remember. He and his mother used to drive out at least once a week to buy juicy watermelons and tomatoes so sweet you could eat them like apples. The recent growth and development of the island had led to North Carolina building an interstate, which meant that the farm stands were easily passed over.

Sandover would have developed with or without his family's company, but Jackson felt guilty because of the negative impact on the community. He had done his best to develop the island ethically, keeping things as they had historically been wherever possible and fighting the high-rise hotels that were eager to bulldoze over historic homes along the beach. The houses there—like his own—were bigger than the historic homes that still stood, but were much better than having twenty-story hotels.

Mercer picked up steam as she talked. "Another option might be to bring the stands to us. Maybe on Saturdays, kind of like a farmer's market? We could sell their produce in-store during the week and then out in the parking lot with actual stands on the weekend. There might be other local vendors interested as well."

"That's brilliant. You want to run with it? Talk to the farm stand owners about both ideas. Are you comfortable doing that?"

She smiled, looking thrilled. "Absolutely. I'd love to."

"On Islanders will love it and I bet it will really help the farms. It's a great idea, Mercer."

Under his praise, she turned shy again and Jackson sensed he needed to back off. He never pressed her. If she wanted to talk to him, she knew he was there. She had connected with some of the other young singles at Hope, the church Jackson attended. Hopefully they were enough of a support system for whatever she was working through.

Jackson stood. "I'm heading home for a bit. You can call me on my cell if you need to. Thanks again, Mercer."

"Before I forget, I found a cart full of cheeses needing to be restocked. Someone abandoned it over by the wine. Do you know anything about that?"

He groaned. He knew *all* about that. "That was me, actually. Kind of a long story. Would you mind taking care of it?"

"Not at all, boss."

Jackson went out through the back to his Jeep. The abandoned cart of cheese had him thinking back to Jenna's face when she recognized him. Before disgust had colored her gaze, Jackson thought he caught a flash of something else. Surprise and ... appreciation? If not for everything that came out of her mouth after, he might have even thought it was attraction. Clearly not.

Jenna still saw him as the jerk of a womanizer he'd been in high school. He had been the guy with an anger problem who had failed out of business school. His past was a stain. It didn't matter how much he had changed, no matter how many millions he donated to charity or service projects he took part in with the local church, he couldn't remove it. He felt like he was constantly chasing his own shadow, trying to erase it, but finding it always right there behind him. Even after coming to believe that Jesus had taken his sin away, Jackson struggled to really *feel* that he was clean.

The anger started to build again, making his chest feel tight. He needed a release. The punching bag that hung underneath the bottom deck of his house served just this purpose. The sound of the ocean roaring as he connected again and again with the unflinching weight of the heavy bag was therapeutic. It kept him from putting his fist through any walls.

Using the Bluetooth feature, Jackson called Beau. Just hearing his friend's voice often calmed him. Beau had that kind of effect on people. "Jax! I thought I might be hearing from you today."

"Have you developed the gift of prophecy overnight?"

Beau laughed. "More like, I heard that Jenna was back in town."

"Right."

Despite becoming more of a tourist destination, Sandover still had a very small-town feel, especially to the year-round locals, who referred to themselves as On Islanders. It made sense that within twenty-four hours, people already knew Jenna was home. Jackson gripped the wheel, trying to work out what exactly he wanted to say now that he had Beau on the line. "I saw her this morning. Actually, last night too, but I talked to her this morning."

"I take it that things didn't go well?"

"If I said 'bad,' that would be too generous. She thought I worked at Bohn's, like as a bag boy or something."

Beau began to laugh. Jackson wanted to be angry, but Beau's laughter drew out a smile instead. If he hadn't been so busy having his feelings hurt, it *was* funny. "In her defense, I was wearing an apron and restocking."

Beau's laughter now roared through the car speakers. Jackson was laughing too by the time he pulled into the parking spot under his house. Like all the houses along the oceanfront, it was on stilts. He didn't move to get out of the Jeep yet.

"I'm sorry for laughing, but that is a great story. I can't wait to tell Jimmy. Can I tell Jimmy?"

"Of course. Tell the whole fire station. I'm sure the On Islanders will all know within the hour anyway."

At least once a week, Jackson met for what Beau called Breakfast and Bible. Jimmy, another firefighter, also came and sometimes Cash, a police officer. The other three were in their twenties, but the age difference didn't seem to matter. They were Jackson's closest friends, the best he'd had in his life. Their breakfast talks hit him harder than the sermons Sunday mornings.

Beau's voice had more concern in it when he spoke again. "Seriously, though—how are you doing?"

"I came home to get out some aggression, if that tells you anything. Thought maybe you could talk me down a bit." Beau knew all about his anger issues. His counselor had recommended finding a person who could help Jackson calm down and move away from the path of anger.

"Anything in particular about the conversation that got to you?"

Jackson rested his forehead against the wheel. There were a lot of things about the conversation that hurt, but picking the part that hurt the most was easy.

"Jenna only sees who I used to be. I'm not ever going to be able to escape that guy—the one who had shallow relationships and flunked out of business school."

"Jax, look. You don't stop struggling when you become a Christian. You struggle more because you see the things you're doing differently. You have a sense of conviction now that you didn't then. It's always going to be hard to look back. But you are not your past. It shaped you but doesn't have to define you. Your actions don't simply disappear, but you can't let shame over things you've done poison you. Even if Jenna sees your past when she looks at you right now. She's wrong, by the way. And I hope she realizes it."

17

"It's a wasted hope."

"You don't know that. But even if she doesn't ever change how she sees you, remember: as far as east is from west—that's what the Bible says. You're not carrying your past around anymore. It happened. But you can't wear it around anymore, letting it weigh you down. East from West, man."

"It doesn't feel that way," Jackson said. "I can still see every person I used and hurt. It's still all right here with me, all the time."

An alarm blared in the background. "I've got to go. Look, sometimes we don't feel the truth. We have to actively choose to believe it. Are you at home?"

"Yeah."

"Go hit the bag, Jax."

Five minutes later Jackson had stripped down to a T-shirt with his hands taped, ready to go to war on his memories and feelings. Jackson warmed up with a few jabs, feeling the tension leave his body as he hopped lightly from foot to foot. The first couple of hard swings sent pain shooting up his hands and through his arms, but after a few minutes, he felt nothing but the power of his hands connecting with the heavy bag. Just over the dunes, the ocean roared, an echo of his emotions.

As his fists connected with the bag again and again, Jackson let his mind move freely. This was a good way to start to let go, just allowing his thoughts to roam. They always roamed back to the same place. Or, rather—person.

His mind wound back to the moment that woke up the feelings that had been sleeping inside him for years. Twenty of them, give or take.

From the back of the church, Jackson had watched Jenna walk in through one of the doors up front. Jenna had tugged on a simple pearl necklace she wore over her black dress, as though she didn't want to be wearing it. Her hair was pulled back and, as she faced the front and sat next to her sister, he found himself admiring the elegant line of her neck.

This is a funeral. You shouldn't be thinking about how beautiful her neck is. Where is her husband?

He knew now that she and her husband had separated. Word always got out on the Island, even about people like Jenna who had left. Surprisingly, he didn't know details. Just that they weren't together.

At the funeral, Jackson had been furious with the absent-husband. Someone should have been there for her. Rachel sat next to Jenna, but also had her husband and three girls with them. Jenna was completely alone. Jackson had ached with the desire to wrap her in his arms, tuck her head beneath his chin, and be her comfort. It gutted him to see this and to know that even if he wanted to comfort her, she wouldn't have let him. Instead of even speaking to her, Jackson slipped away without Jenna even knowing he was there. She probably had no idea that her mother was in Jackson's Sunday School class. She might have laughed if her mother had told her.

Jackson poured his bitterness, his anger, his shame, his regret into his fists. Again and again he hit the bag. Now that he was warm, he focused his thoughts, taking them away from Jenna and the worries of today. Lately he had tried something new: timing his punches with the words from Bible verses that helped calm him.

I-*punch*-can-*punch*-do-*punch*-all-*punch*-things-*punch*-through-*punch*-him-*punch*-who-*punch*-gives-*punch*-me-*punch*-strength.

That was one of his favorites, Philippians 4:13. Beau once explained how this verse was usually misunderstood.

"People think it means that you can accomplish your

goals or do what you set your mind to," Beau had said during one of their Bible and Breakfasts. "But if you read the verses right before, Paul is saying that he's learned the secret of getting through all situations: being content no matter what happens. When he says he can do all things, he means, he can be content in any circumstance."

Those words stayed with Jackson: he could be content no matter the circumstance. Even if that circumstance was Jenna still hating his guts.

The muscles in his arms twitched. His hands were numb, his T-shirt soaked with sweat. Jackson knew he should stop if he wanted to be able to use his arms tomorrow. He worked out most days, but it was always a harder workout when he was angry. He had never been fat, but he also had never been athletic. Now he had chiselled arms and a six pack, a bonus from working through his feelings with his fists.

Not that it mattered. Jenna clearly cared more about a person's heart, and she thought his wasn't worth caring about. He rested his forehead on the bag for a moment, closing his eyes and hearing only the cry of gulls and the pounding of surf. His thoughts had cooled, but they still hovered around her.

Was she staying long?

Was she staying permanently?

What could he do to get a fresh start with her?

His phone buzzed from where it sat on the wooden picnic table nearby. Jackson groaned before he had even finished reading the message from his daughter, Megan.

Megan: hey "dad." Kim is shipping me 2u this weekend for babysitting duty yay

. . .

20

He watched the phone as the little dots indicated that she was typing a message. Jackson had only found out he had a daughter a few months before. Megan was twelve and barely tolerated him, though from what he had seen, she tolerated her mother, Kim, even less. That felt like a small win, even though he had no idea how to start parenting a pre-teen from scratch.

When Kim, whom he hadn't talked to in twelve years, called to tell him about Megan, he was at first terrified, then thrilled. He had sort of given up on the idea of having kids, along with the idea of getting married. At thirty-eight and single, realistically, time was winding down. But any joy he felt at the idea of being a parent was stripped away when Megan started spending one weekend a month with him. The only things they had in common was a mutual disdain for Kim and a love of sushi. Megan spent every waking hour on her cell phone or tablet. He continued to try but felt like most of his efforts to connect with her failed.

Megan: she said if UR busy too bad
Megan: and not to tell you that she said that
Megan: oops

He probably shouldn't foster her dislike for Kim, though to be fair, Kim was as completely self-absorbed now as she had been back when they had dated. But Jackson struggled with calling Megan on any of her behavior. Telling her to be respectful to Kim would take away one of the two flimsy things they had in common. He wasn't ready yet.

Jackson: Sounds good. Anything special you want to do while you're here?
Megan: ignore each other per the usual?
Jackson: I might be too busy ignoring other people to ignore you too.
Megan: hahaha just stock up on frozen pizzas & im good
Jackson: Can I bribe you with sushi?
Megan: maybe. what are you bribing me to do in exchange for sushi
Jackson: One activity outside the house. Your choice.
Megan: i'll think about it. CU Fri

Jackson stripped off his shirt, leaving only his board shorts on. It was still too cold in March to swim without a wetsuit, but the shower under the house had hot water. He stepped inside the wooden shower enclosure, relishing in the feel of the hot water on his skin in the cool air.

Megan's texts seemed slightly warmer, even if she still played it cool in person. She was joking with him, which was a good start. Maybe if he could thaw Megan out, there was hope for Jenna after all.

CHAPTER THREE

RACHEL CALLED as Jenna was waiting for the coffee to finish brewing. She was a little concerned about the outcome. She had remembered to buy coffee, but not filters. She was using a paper towel and hoping for the best. It did not bode well. If anyone was to blame, it was Jackson Wells.

After seeing him, Jenna had forgotten the rest of her list and arrived home with half the things she needed and the start of a stress headache. Less than twenty-four hours home and she had already run into the most infuriating man— other than her ex-husband—she'd ever known. Actually, Jackson was more infuriating than Mark, which was a hard feat. Her ex inspired less fury and more a crushing sort of pain. With Jackson, it was pure rage.

The fact that he was even more attractive than the last time she had seen him only made her more furious. "Pretty is as pretty does," her mother used to say when they were growing up. Jenna wished that the phrase worked literally. If it did, Jackson would be an ugly man. But of course, life wasn't fair. Jerks could still be overwhelmingly hot.

"How is it? Overwhelmed? Getting lots done?" Rachel always spoke hurriedly if they talked during the day. Her oldest daughter, Ava, was in third grade, but the twins were only three. The sound of Casey and Olivia playing or screaming was a constant soundtrack in the background to their phone calls. "GET OFF THE TABLE, OLIVIA!"

Jenna put it on speakerphone, so she wouldn't have to have Rachel shouting directly in her ear.

"Are you kidding? I haven't even started. Is there a blog post somewhere with a checklist on how to clean out your childhood home? Maybe we should just burn it down. Also, did you know that Bohn's still has that stupid rule about not buying wine before noon?"

There was a pause and Jenna realized her mistake. "Why are you trying to buy wine before noon, Jens? STOP HITTING YOUR SISTER, CASEY. Are you okay? How much are you drinking?"

"Simmer down, sister. Not that much. I don't even get drunk. Just a glass a night." Or two. Sometimes three. Jenna flinched.

Maybe wine *had* become too much of a crutch lately. She hadn't grown up drinking. Her mom never did, hence the need to buy the corkscrew at Bohn's. She hadn't lied about getting drunk, though—she never did. It was more about having something to look forward to at the end of the day. Something that took the edge off. When you lose your marriage and your mom in the same year, you should get a reward for surviving, right? Maybe not being able to buy wine was a good thing. It might be time to think about a different kind of reward. Or to just accept the fact that life was rough and getting through the day was a basic expectation, not an accomplishment. She sighed.

She used to turn to God. Prayer, church, her Bible study.

But Jenna had let all that fade away over the past year. She liked to pretend that it just kind of happened: miss a week of church and then another, forget to open her Bible for a few days. If she was being honest with herself, though, she felt angry with God. Abandoned. She didn't slide away so much as walk away, one step at a time. Now he felt so far.

Rachel interrupted her thoughts. "You know I'm going to keep asking you about this. You've had to deal with more than anyone should this past year. I don't want to see you spiraling into some kind of place where I have to stage an intervention."

"I'm fine. And will continue to be, if for no other reason than to avoid an intervention."

"Good. Speaking of wine, you should ask Bohn's for wine boxes. I left some in the house last time I was there, but there aren't nearly enough. That's where you start packing. Free boxes from Bohn's. Jackson will give you some. Oh, and Jackson's company can help with sales! Wells Development. They have a residential real estate arm. You can ask him when you ask for boxes. See? I helped."

Hearing Jackson's name made her stomach sour. This was one of the reasons she had been so eager to move Off Island and not return. Sandover was too small a town. She couldn't avoid even the things—or people—she most wanted to, and it seemed like little changed. Other than all the development on the island.

Because of its location—just north of the popular Outer Banks—and the single toll bridge, Sandover had remained somewhat unknown for years. Until *Southern Living* ran a feature on it about fifteen years ago, calling it an "undiscovered gem." Now the old, historic beach cottages were all-too-quickly being replaced by beach mansions like the one she'd seen the other night by the beach access. The one with the creeper who waved at her the night before.

Jenna had her real estate license but didn't want to sell the house herself. She wasn't objective enough. In her emotional state, she might really lose it hearing people talk about the pink tile in the bathroom—even if it was hideous— or the worn carpets and dark wood paneling. The word she feared most was *teardown*. Their neighborhood was a mile from the beach, but backed up to the wildlife refuge, with the Sound just on the other side. Realistically, it might be worth more for the property than the 1970s-style home.

"Let's not talk about Jackson Wells. Please. I already saw him this morning. Before I had coffee, even. It was horrible. Did you know that he still works—"

"NO SNACKS. WE ARE HAVING NO SNACKS. NONE. I SAID OFF THE—" The sound of wailing came from the phone. Double wailing. "Jenna, I've got to go. Sorry. I'll try to call again tonight. Or at nap time. But either way, I'll be there this weekend. Party time! Give Jackson a break, though. He's really—OLIVIA, NO!"

Rachel hung up before Jenna could respond. Jackson was really *what*? She stared at the phone. How could Rachel defend Jackson? She was the one who suffered through the fallout from the rumors he had probably started. If anyone should still be mad, it was Rachel.

No, Jenna was not going to give him a break or ask him for boxes or for help selling the house. In fact, Jenna should start shopping at Harris Teeter just to avoid his smug smile and those amazing eyes.

Amazing? Ugh.

She could not think about the fact that he was attractive. It was all on the outside. Like a poison dart frog. She didn't know why she was thinking about frogs, but it was the perfect comparison to Jackson. Beautiful on the outside, drawing you in, but toxic.

Why couldn't she stop thinking about Jackson? For as much as she hated him, he consumed her mind. She knew what that usually meant, at least in movies or romance novels. Even in Shakespeare. If the lady doth protest too much ... but no. She did not harbor secret feelings for Jackson. He simply infuriated her and happened to be attractive. That's it.

Jenna opened the junk drawer. She needed paper and pen to make a to-do list. As she had hoped, Rachel hadn't cleaned this out. Something about its contents shook loose her emotions. She stared down at rubber bands, paperclips, cherry lip balm, fingernail clippers, takeout menus, a black plastic comb, keys to something, stamps, pencils with no points, and a spool of thread. Her mother didn't even sew.

She clutched the sides of the drawer, her breathing fast and shallow. This was a drawer of the living. This drawer—it was the real stuff. It was the slap in the face to remind her that her mother was gone.

When she felt like she could move again, Jenna plucked out a piece of amazingly blank paper from the middle of a stack of Chinese takeout menus and closed the drawer. She sat down at the kitchen table with her coffee—which was surprisingly passable. She wrote down an order that made sense to her: dining room and the formal living room first, since they were used less and had fewer items. Then the TV room, bathroom, and her old bedroom.

Her mother's door was shut. Jenna knew she couldn't open it without Rachel there. Both because she didn't think she could handle it alone and because it felt like something they should do together.

Rachel had already emptied out her own bedroom, just as

she had with the kitchen. When Jenna looked into Rachel's room that morning, it looked bare and lacked all Rachel's vibrant personality. It hurt to look at it. For the first time Jenna really realized what it meant to sell their childhood home.

Before she arrived, Jenna had considered what it might be like to move back in permanently. At the moment she was basically floating through life. Though the divorce had been finalized just before her mother's stroke, she and Mark had been over for years. Well, if breaking your wedding vows by having affairs counted toward a marriage ending, then technically, their marriage had been over from the start. Too bad she hadn't gotten the memo until she went to see her OB and found out that she had contracted an STD.

Nothing could have prepared Jenna for sitting in a crinkly paper gown with no panties on as her doctor explained that she had Chlamydia. Which meant that Mark had Chlamydia, which also meant that Mark had been unfaithful. She had waited until their wedding night—they both had, she thought. And there she was, humiliated and heartbroken, finding out from her OB that her marriage was a sham.

The conversation with Mark after the doctor visit had been as shocking as the diagnosis. "What happened to the man I married? Where's *that* guy?" she had half sobbed, half shouted.

"I'm sorry, Bug," Mark had said, using his pet name for her. She had always hated it anyway. "This is me. I'm just not hiding it anymore."

He moved out by the morning, taking very little. Apparently, he already had an apartment where he was doing all the affair-ing. Jenna had thought he was on business trips or working late. Such a cliché. She had felt so utterly foolish in the truest sense of the word.

For the past year she had lived in their condo, every day seeing the plates they picked out for their registry and the couch they bought together. The only things Mark took from the house were some clothes and a few personal things. He must have already furnished the apartment. Jenna wanted to leave but didn't know where to go. It took her six months to even call a lawyer about a divorce. Not that she'd had any hope of wanting to reconcile, but Jenna simply hadn't been ready. She didn't even want anything from him. Not the condo, not anything they'd purchased together, not her ring, not one thing. After they sold the condo, she lived in an Extended Stay for a few months until she felt ready to come back to Sandover and deal with the house.

Now everything she owned was in the car sitting in the driveway. She owned less now than she had when she graduated college, which seemed shameful somehow. Even then she had an overstuffed arm chair she had purchased at a thrift store her sophomore year. Mark had insisted they get rid of it after they got married. He was too fancy for thrift store finds. That should have been a warning sign.

Could she move in here? Take over the master bedroom, paint, and redecorate?

The house felt too much like her childhood and Jenna felt childish in it. As though the moment she stepped over the threshold, she had reverted to her teenaged self. In a way Jenna wished that she could go back, to have her whole life stretching open before her again. Only, she would take the wisdom she had now and use it to keep her out of relationships with guys like Mark. Steve should have been a lesson enough in high school.

The thought of Steve reminded her of something else she had left in the car: a Fiddle-Leaf Fig plant she had brought down to give to Steve's parents, who still lived in the house next door. The plant rode shotgun on her drive and she had named him Fred the Fig. She had talked to him on the drive.

"Terrible traffic, eh Fred?"

"This is my favorite song, Fred."

"Come here often, Fred?"

He had looked a little worse for wear that morning when she'd gone to Bohn's. She should have gotten him out the night before. It was too cold for Fred in the car. Now he looked even worse, but maybe Ethel could bring Fred back. "Sorry Fred," she said as she crossed the lawn, carrying the big pot.

Gifting a house plant to your high school ex's parents should have been a weird thing to do. But before she and Steve had started dating, they were best friends. His parents, Ethel and Bob, had been like her second parents. For years, even after the big break-up, Jenna always made time to stop over for coffee. She realized suddenly that she may have had more of these talks with Ethel perhaps than her mom. She and her mother had been close, but there was an ease with Ethel, perhaps because she didn't have to do all the work of raising Jenna, so their relationship lacked the normal mother-daughter conflict. Regret, sharp and sudden, flared in her chest.

Now it was too late. These words were like a repeated line in the song of her life, flashing through her mind whenever she had a realization of a new layer to her loss. She tried to swallow down the thoughts. She and her mother had an okay relationship. Even if she never worked up the nerve to tell her that she and Mark were over. She died not knowing.

Did that mean she knew now? If she knew, did she care? Jenna had read a lot about heaven in the Bible, but some things just weren't clear. It made her desperately sad to think about heaven, which made no sense. Her mother would be there and be happy. Not there and feeling sad at the state of her eldest daughter's life. That, by definition, would not be heaven.

Ethel answered the door after Jenna's third knock, wearing a pair of khaki pants, a red cardigan, and pearls. It had been her uniform for as long as Jenna could remember. Different colored cardigans, but always khakis or a skirt.

"Hey, Mrs. Taylor," Jenna said. In her head, she was always Ethel. In real life, manners dictated that she was Mrs. Taylor.

Ethel grabbed her in a fierce hug. Jenna did her best not to drop Fred the Fig, who was pressed between them.

"So good to see one of my daughters back home," Ethel said. "Come in, come in! Bob! Jenna's here!"

"How's my girl?" Bob said. He did not get up from his recliner, which she suspected he slept in at night as well.

Jenna took his hand, warm and dry, and gave it a squeeze. "Hi, Mr. Taylor."

He seemed to have grown heavier since Jenna had seen him a few months before. He wasn't moving well then, leaning on the metal arms of a walker, the kind with tennis balls on two of the legs. It now sat next to his recliner and a small side table filled with a mix of cough drops and candy wrappers, a glass of water, and the television remote.

"Tell your mother that I let the police know about those kids that were parking down at the cul-de-sac. Shouldn't be a problem anymore, I bet."

Jenna swallowed and gently pulled her hand away. "I'll tell her."

Ethel met her eyes, then motioned her to the formal living room. "Sit. I'll bring the coffee."

As Jenna sat down in one of the matching upholstered chairs, she noticed a framed photograph on the end table.

She picked it up, feeling all the moisture from her mouth dry up as though it had been sucked away somehow. It was a picture of Steve and Anna.

It should get easier to see them together after all these years. It wasn't jealousy, exactly. At least, Jenna didn't want to be with Steve. She had dodged a bullet—another cheater. But just as her anger with Jackson lingered, so did her feelings of betrayal. They had been best friends, then together for a few years, talking about marriage and long-term life plans. Before Anna.

She looked almost unchanged from high school, when she had stolen Steve away. Stylish haircut, but same high cheeks, big brown eyes, and a wide white smile. This was a woman who got a man and kept him. She didn't worry about getting Chlamydia from her husband. In another picture on the table, Jenna saw their two little girls, who looked like mini-Annas.

She had always wanted children. She and Mark got married in their late twenties and had the same argument about having kids again and again. She wanted them. He didn't. Now it made so much more sense. And made her feel even more like she had wasted so many important years of her life in a colossal way. Her eggs might be stale by now. What was the likelihood she could meet a man she could trust, fall in love, get married, and get pregnant in the tiny window she had left? It was probably a dream best to give up on. Let the Annas and Steves of the world repopulate with beautiful babies.

"Here we go," Ethel said, setting down china cups with saucers.

Jenna replaced the photograph. Ethel didn't mention it. That was their unspoken rule to keep this relationship working: Don't talk about Steve. "Thank you."

Ethel never remembered that Jenna didn't take sugar, but she never complained. She took a few sips, trying to gather her thoughts. Normally the talk came easily, but today Jenna didn't know where to start. She didn't want to talk about her mother or her failed marriage and they couldn't talk about Steve. Not that she wanted to.

"Well, they finally put in radar," Ethel said, landing on an utterly safe topic. Jenna smiled. She realized when she moved away that most people called it a speed trap, not radar. Must be an On Island thing. "Cops are sitting out there most days of the week, giving out tickets like candy."

Jenna relaxed into the chair, cradling the coffee cup in her hands. "It's about time. Have they gotten Mr. Andrews yet?"

Mr. Andrews lived a few houses down and drove an old boat of a car. He did not acknowledge driving laws. He consistently blew through the stop sign at the end of their street, barreling out onto the busier road that went out to the causeway. For years they had waited to hear the inevitable sound of a crash. So far, God—or luck—had been on his side.

"They finally put him in a home." Ethel's lips turned down.

This news somehow made Jenna feel deflated. "Really? I thought he'd live there forever."

"We did too. New couple lives there now. Only one child. Redid the kitchen and added onto the back. Can you imagine? Needing more space than that with just one child?" She shook her head and made a tsk sound.

"I guess we should all just be glad he didn't kill anyone. I was sure he'd go down in a blaze of fiery glory."

"He'd probably prefer that to where he is now," Ethel said. "Those greedy children of his. They just wanted to sell the house."

"The market's still hot I take it?"

"Oh, yes," Ethel said. "With all these Off Islanders buying up the land, razing homes that have been here for years, and putting up their oversized homes. It's disgusting. Our boys are always asking us when we're moving out. They try to be coy, but I'm no dummy. Have you decided what you're going to do?"

That was awfully close to talking about Steve. Jenna's stomach tightened. Was he really trying to push his parents out of their home? Bob had dementia, but not to a degree that he was harmful to himself or others. At least, not that she knew of. It was a lot for Ethel to deal with on her own. Maybe Steve and Jeff had their best interests in mind. Ethel sipped her coffee, looking at Jenna over the rim of the china cup.

"I just don't know."

"How are things with Mark? I couldn't help but notice your ring was gone. Temporary or for good? Your mother hadn't said anything."

Jenna rubbed her ring finger, which still felt naked with nothing on it. "I hadn't told her yet. It's over. For good," Jenna said. "And it definitely is good."

"I'm glad. I never did like him." Ethel slapped a hand over her mouth and giggled. "Sorry."

Jenna laughed so hard that she had to set down her coffee on the table, so it wouldn't spill. "You could have warned me beforehand. Saved me some years."

Ethel smiled, her lips still sporting the coral color she always wore. "Would you really have listened?"

"Nope."

"Sometimes you just have to learn for yourself. Even if it's the hard way."

Though Ethel never treated Jenna differently after the breakup, she had to wonder how Steve's mother felt about it, and about her. Moms took their kids' sides. Always. But for years, she and Ethel sat in these same chairs and talked as though nothing had changed between them. Was it because Ethel knew it wasn't Jenna's choice to break up? If she had been the one to dump Steve, would things be different?

Had enough years passed that they could break the rule and talk about Steve? She did wonder how he was doing. As much as he hurt her, dumping her for the prettier, more popular, much more perfect Anna, Jenna still had a sense of nostalgia. Well, mixed in with the feeling of betrayal. That's what happens when you fall in love with your best friend. You might lose them, but you keep the first memories you had of them, before things went bad.

"So, how...are the boys?"

Ethel set down her cup and threw her hands in the air. "You know: boys. Never call, never come by. They're busy with their families, but still. I hardly see my grandchildren. How are things over at the house?"

It took Jenna a moment to recover from the comment about grandchildren. She couldn't imagine why Steve and his older brother Jeff wouldn't be more involved with their parents. It seemed so cruel, though Ethel passed it off like they were just forgetful. She wanted to say something more about this, but Ethel's subject change was clear code: Stick to the plan. Keep to the rules. No talk of Steve.

"It's really ... tough. I'm going to take one room at a time, starting with the things that matter the least. But the smallest things sometimes, they get me."

Ethel patted her knee. "I'm so very sorry. I know I've said that. But I'll keep saying it. Are you doing okay? Not with the house, but with her?"

Jenna swallowed and blinked back her tears. She couldn't speak, a sob hitching in her throat, so she shrugged instead.

Ethel looked out the front picture window and Jenna was thankful for the privacy this look away gave her. She wiped her eyes and swallowed. "I don't know what I can do but let me know if I can help. Anything at all. Okay?"

"Thank you. It's really nice to know that you're here." Jenna squeezed Ethel's shoulder and stood. "I need to head back."

As they walked out, Jenna ducked into the TV room to say goodbye to Bob.

"Hello there, Jenna!" he boomed. "Stocks are on the rise!"

"Good to see you again, Mr. Taylor."

"Don't let me catch you breaking curfew again," he said, pointing a stern finger at her. "I'll have to have a conversation with your father."

"Yes, dear," Ethel said, giving Jenna a nudge toward the door. "She'll work on that. Thank you."

On the porch, Ethel grabbed her in a hug that felt tight and desperate. Jenna's eyes grew hot with tears. She missed her mother. Jenna gave Ethel another squeeze, then pulled back and wiped her eyes. Ethel and her mother had been close friends, maybe best friends. It was too easy to think about what loss meant to you and forget how much it impacted other people.

"Thank you," Jenna said, touching Ethel on the arm. "For watching over the house, for just...everything."

Ethel's eyes brimmed, and she pressed her lips together tightly. Jenna walked away before Ethel could see her own tears, back to her mother's house where more memories waited to weigh her down.

CHAPTER FOUR

"Is it weird that your love interest used to be my babysit-ter?" Beau grinned at Jackson.

Jimmy started laughing so hard that the other patrons in the diner glanced over at their table. They usually attracted a lot of attention anyway: two firemen and a cop in uniform. And everyone knew Jackson. As much as he'd prefer to slide under the radar, he couldn't do that when he owned half the island and kept the favorite local grocery store in business. He had just finished telling the guys about his disastrous run-in with Jenna. They already knew about her as the one Jackson let get away.

Jackson pointed his fork at Beau, who was still smiling. Even Cash, normally the most serious and reserved of the group, was chuckling. "It would only be weird if she had been *my* babysitter. But now I feel very aware of my age, so thanks for that. My age and my maturity, I should say. Does this make me your babysitter?"

"You couldn't handle us." Jimmy wiped tears from his eyes with a napkin.

"Clearly." Jackson took another bite of eggs as the waitress came back to refill their coffee.

"Everything okay over here, boys?" Eileen winked at Cash · as she brushed back her graying brown hair. He sat up straighter and looked down at the table as his neck grew red. He tugged on the neck of his uniform. Out of the four guys at the table, it was hilarious that Eileen chose the least friendly one to flirt with.

"Speaking of older women …" Jimmy said, wiggling his eyebrows as Eileen walked back to the counter. Cash glared and Jimmy held up his hands. "For real, though. My first love was older. She was my big sister's best friend. Talk about torture. For years she practically lived at my house. But she always saw me like a little brother. That's actually why I'm here. I moved away from Richmond because I couldn't stand to see her all the time."

"First love? That implies there has been a second. Does that mean you love Amber?" Beau asked.

Jimmy made a face. "Dude. It's been a few weeks. She's a great girl but we're just dating."

"And you're still in love with Emily." Jackson nudged his shoulder further into Jimmy's. "I recognize the signs."

Jimmy swivelled as much as he could in the seat to look at Jackson. The four of them hardly fit into this booth. None of them were small guys. "I'm not saying I'm still in love with her. But I will say that if she walked through that door right now and said she was interested, I'd jump. Never going to happen, though. She made it very clear how she felt the last time I saw her. If we're all going to talk about our feelings, when are you finally going to get up the nerve to ask Mercer out?"

Beau shrugged. "The time isn't right."

"You've been saying that for months," Jackson said. "I'm

pretty sure all the girl does is work at my store and go home. When will the time be right?"

Cash took a sip of coffee and looked between Jimmy and Jackson. "Isn't this Bible and Breakfast? This is starting to sound like a middle school girls' sleepover. Enough about your pathetic love lives."

Jackson rolled his eyes, ready to snap back, but Beau spoke up first, in a much nicer tone of voice than he would have used. "Fellowship is part of these breakfasts. That includes sharing what's going on with us. Right now, Jackson's dealing with a woman he has feelings for, but also the feelings associated with his past. If we can't talk about that here, when can we?"

Cash nodded as he pulled out his wallet and threw down a ten-dollar bill. "You're right. Sorry. I've got to get going anyway."

Beau stood from the booth to let Cash out. Without another word, Cash strode across the diner. Eileen called out a goodbye, but he simply raised a hand as he pushed through the doors.

"Is he ever going to get less prickly? I mean, come on." Jimmy shook his head as Beau settled back in the booth.

"Give him a break," Beau said. "The three of us have been friends for a few years now. He's new to us and still holding a lot of things close to the vest. I hope he'll open up, but even if he does, he's just a more serious guy."

"With constant PMS." Jimmy kept going even though Beau opened his mouth, probably to defend Cash again. "Anyway, back to you, Jax. What can we do to help facilitate project Win-Jenna-Over?"

"Keep your voice down, first of all. I know you didn't grow up here, but you know how much of a small town this

39

is. Bunch of gossips. And they all know her. That said, I don't think it's a project. More like a dead end."

"You had one bad run-in with her."

"Two. She practically sprinted away when I waved to her the other night from my house."

"Maybe she didn't recognize you," Beau said. "I mean, it was dark, right?"

"Maybe. Either way, she's not thrilled to see me. I'm not going to go out of my way to seek her out. She may not even be here long. I think that avoidance is my best option."

"You wanted to apologize to her, though, right? About her sister?" Beau had a way of poking right into his business in a way that didn't feel intrusive. He didn't let things go, but had a way of pushing gently. More than once, Jackson had the thought that Beau could be a pastor as well as he could be a firefighter.

"I don't know that she would believe or accept an apology."

"Maybe not, but that's on her. Her sister did. That should give you hope. Anyway, we've got to get to the station too. Don't give up. You don't know if she's here to stay or if she'll forgive you. But you'll always regret it if you don't try."

Jackson stood to let Jimmy out. The three of them dropped cash on the table. They always overpaid, and Jackson usually left an extra ten-dollar tip on top of that.

Jimmy slapped Jackson on the back as they walked out to the parking lot. The fire station's red SUV was parked next to his Jeep. "You do what you feel like you need to do. But if I had the chance to try again with Emily, even after everything that went down, I'd do it. That's the thing about love: sometimes it makes you foolish. But if you aren't willing to put yourself out there, maybe it's not love."

Jackson was still thinking about those words as he went

home for a run on the beach. Exercise after eating wasn't the best idea, but he felt like punishing himself today. The cool air battled with the heat from the morning sun. Another few months and running would be unbearable in the sun. For now, it was the push he needed, other than the eggs and toast sloshing around with the coffee in his belly.

A mile from his house, Jackson slowed to a walk. He moved to the shoreline, where the sand sank a little under his bare feet and the occasional wave rolled over him, sending icy chills up his legs. Everything about the beach felt like home to Jackson. Did Jenna miss this when she left Sandover?

He could see her as she stood the other night on the crosswalk, looking out over the ocean. Maybe it called to her the same way it did to him. He couldn't understand how anyone left Sandover.

Actually—he could. Often, he wished that he could escape the scrutiny of the On Islanders and the feeling of living inside of a glass bubble, or one of those snow globes they sold at the tacky tourist beach shops. That he got. But moving away from the powerful sounds of the ocean and the smell of salt on the air? The thought made him feel claustrophobic. Spending four years at Davidson College a few hours inland had him itching to get back home. He never planned to leave again.

Did Jenna feel the same pull? He recognized something in the way she stood there the other night, staring at the moonlight on the waves. After college, though, she had rarely come home, not even for their ten-year reunion. He knew she had gotten married by then, but still kept watching the door, hoping to see her walk through. Now that he knew she was on Sandover, he'd be looking for her everywhere. He had avoided Bohn's that morning, just in case she came back in, and had found himself turning every time the diner doors had opened while he was with the guys. Even now, the woman up ahead on the beach looking for shells reminded him of Jenna.

Jackson sighed. Beau was right. Until he apologized, he would be looking for her everywhere. Maybe that wouldn't change after he said his piece, but he could hope.

As he neared the woman, he slowed. She didn't remind him of Jenna; it *was* Jenna.

Her head was bent as she studied the line of shells left on the beach after the high tide moved out. Every few feet she bent to examine a shell. Some she dropped back on the sand and some went into a small plastic grocery sack with the Bohn's logo on it. She had on dark jeans that were wet at the bottom, despite being rolled up almost to her knees. Jackson smiled. She had probably put her feet in and gotten hit with a rogue wave.

His heart felt wild in his chest. He wanted so badly to have things be different between them. Not just forgiveness, but something far beyond that. Jackson longed to be able to walk up to her and throw a casual arm around her waist. He wanted to spin her into his arms, to hear her laughter and feel the brush of her hair on his face as he kissed her. He wanted her to look at him with something other than anger, distrust, and dislike.

Jenna chose that moment to turn. She froze, seeing Jackson.

"Hey, Jenna." He closed the distance between them before she could do something like turn and walk away.

"Jackson. You seem to be everywhere these days."

Her gaze dropped to Jackson's bare chest and then snapped back up. He hadn't worn a shirt for his run. Maybe it was shallow, but at this point with her, his physical appearance was about the only thing he had going for him. Her cheeks flushed and she was looking anywhere but his torso.

He grinned, feeling a small victory. "Small island. You know how it is, right?"

"I do, actually. That's one reason I left."

Her voice was curt, but Jackson still had Beau and Jimmy's words knocking around in his head. Maybe it was foolish to push, but where had his pride ever gotten him? She still stood talking to him, when she could have already walked away.

"You miss it, though. The beach at least, if not the people." He smiled and was rewarded with a smile that actually looked genuine.

"I do miss the beach. The people ..." She met his gaze, eyes looking a little softer. She smiled again. "The jury is still out. *Some* of them I'm glad to see."

And some, like Jackson, she wasn't. Her meaning was obvious as she looked down at the scattered shells. Still—her voice had a hint of teasing to it. And she hadn't stormed off yet. Progress.

"Mind if I walk with you?"

She snorted, eyes still on the sand. "You really want to look for shells with me, Jackson?"

"If you can stand my company. Why don't you tell me what you're looking for?"

She was quiet for a moment, then bent to pick up a few shells. He stepped closer when she stood and held out her palm. Her eyes flicked briefly to his and Jackson saw a vulnerability that made his heart swell.

"These are Augers and Shark Eyes. I called them unicorn horns and snail shells as a kid."

Jackson could see that. The first was longer and twisted just like a horn. The second was a smooth, swirled shell with

43

a dark dot in the center. "Did a snail actually live in here?" He touched the second shell, sucking in a breath as his fingers brushed her palm.

She stiffened slightly but didn't move away.

"Yep. Moon Snails. They actually feed on other mollusks —and sometimes each other—so when you see a tiny hole like this one—" She pointed to a hole smaller than the dot of a pencil. "—that's where another snail or mollusk drilled in and ate it."

"That's a little harsh. Mollusk cannibalism, huh?"

She did not smile. "You know nature—red in tooth and claw. People aren't so different. Maybe not always as literal. But in other ways."

Ah, so we're not talking about shells anymore.

Jenna crouched down again and Jackson tried to steady his breathing. He had known that Jenna was angry with him, or still thought of him in a negative light. But until hearing the pain in her voice, he hadn't understood how he had *hurt* her. She stood, another shell in her hand, this one spiky and white. Jackson swallowed as her shoulder brushed his.

"This one is my favorite." Her voice was quiet, and Jackson wished that he could see her eyes, but she had her chin down.

"What's it called?"

"It's called a Lettered Olive. Another predatory mollusk. They spend a lot of time burrowed down in the sand, hunting food, so the shell isn't as rough or worn as some of the others." Jenna dropped the shiny gray shell in a bag.

"Is this something you do often? I mean, when you're here On Island."

She knelt in the sand, turning over shells and tiny pieces of driftwood. He almost repeated the question, thinking she hadn't heard him. But then she spoke, her voice hardly more than a whisper.

"It was something I did with my mom. Almost every weekend growing up. She taught me all the names and told me about each one."

Jackson felt a shudder of grief. He could hear the way loss coated her words. Jenna's mother had reminded him so much of Jenna. Well, how she had been back when they were in high school: full of easy laughter, smart, kind, and vivacious with a sharp wit. Jenna's mother had the same kind of unabashed laugh that Jenna did—or that he remembered. Jackson had yet to hear Jenna laugh. Jenna even had her mother's dark blue eyes. He had always loved those eyes, the color of the sea on a stormy dusk.

Jenna now seemed so much heavier, with sharper edges. He got the sense that it was protection or self-preservation, not meanness. He knew her marriage ended somewhat recently. Then had lost her mother and had to come back home—it would be a lot for anyone. It made him want to push harder to get past the walls she put up. She was hurting and Jackson wanted nothing more than to soothe the ache. Even if she never wanted more from him than friendship, he could at least offer that.

He wanted to crouch down beside her and put a comforting hand on her back. But he could see the tension in her from where he stood. She had opened up slightly, but if Jackson pushed, she would run. He could sense it. She still may not know that he had spent time with her mother the past few years. It felt wrong to tell her now. Like he would be discounting her grief somehow by acting like he had any right to share in it. The words he wanted to say died before they reached his lips.

45

He cleared his throat. "How do you decide which to keep and which to throw back?"

Jenna stood and met his eyes. He couldn't read her expression as she studied his face. "Can I ask you something? Why do you care? I mean, what are you doing here, standing with me on the beach, asking about seashells? Shouldn't you be bagging groceries? Or ruining someone's reputation?"

Even though her words stung, she gave him an easy opening. Jackson ran a hand along his chin, realizing he probably needed to shave again. *Focus.*

"I had this all planned out. For a long time, actually. It's much harder than I ever thought it would be to apologize to you. Which is odd, since I apologized to Rachel. That felt much easier somehow."

"Wait—you apologized to Rachel? And she forgave you? Is this your roundabout way of apologizing to me now? Because it wasn't much of an apology."

Jackson knew this would be hard, but Jenna seemed determined to make it as difficult as possible. "I did. She did. And I haven't gotten to the apology yet. I'm working up to it. Clearly, this isn't something I'm particularly good at."

"Surprising, considering you've had a lot to apologize for over the years. At least when I knew you. Probably more later." Jenna's eyes blazed.

She knew just where to aim her verbal attacks. Jackson knew that he deserved it. Though it was surprising. Jenna hadn't ever been cruel. He'd never heard her say an unkind word. Except to him, this week. He knew that he had messed up with Rachel, but had underestimated how much Jenna still took issue over it. Unless he had done something else that he didn't remember? Entirely possible, he thought with

46

shame. He spent most weekends in high school drinking. A lot of his memories were fuzzy.

Though it was a risk, Jackson touched Jenna's shoulder. She stiffened, but did not pull away. "Look, Jenna—an apology can't make it right. I can't fix what happened with Rachel or any of the other stupid things I did back in high school. For what it's worth, I am sorry. Truly. I didn't mean to hurt her or hurt you. If I could do it all over again, I wouldn't make the same choices. About that or a lot of other things. I'm sorry."

Jackson had thought through this scenario in his head many times as he went over the apology again and again. His real-life version hadn't turned out terrible, though it wasn't particularly great. It was honest, and he hoped that she could see that in his face and hear it in his voice.

He licked his lips. "I hoped that maybe we could start again."

Jenna pulled away. "Start what again? We were hardly friends back then. You did something awful to my sister, now you've apologized. Good. I hope you feel better."

Turning away, Jenna stormed down the beach. He watched her go, standing there among the empty shells, thinking that maybe the mollusks' way of eating each other was more civilized than the ways people hurt each other. Only when she disappeared over the crosswalk did Jackson realize that Jenna had left her shoes behind. He carried them to his house and left them just inside the back door next to his own. Looking at them together, he could almost imagine that Jenna didn't hate his guts and that she belonged right here, beside him.

CHAPTER FIVE

JENNA SAT in the Harris Teeter parking lot for ten minutes, unable to make herself get out of the car. She had sworn that she wouldn't go back to Bohn's to avoid Jackson. And doubled down on that commitment after seeing him at the beach a few days ago. But Harris Teeter was too new, too Off Island, too touristy. A *chain*. She had shopped at one weekly in Raleigh, but it felt wrong on Sandover. Even after years away from home, she couldn't shake the sense of island loyalty.

She needed food and boxes. The last few days she had spent packing the dining and family rooms, making Goodwill runs whenever she had enough to load her trunk or back seat. She filled boxes with fake plants, ceramic animals, books, vases. A few nicer things went to Classy & Trashy, a consignment store a few miles down the beach. She couldn't bear to dump her mother's good China at a thrift store, though neither she nor Rachel wanted to keep it. Anything Jenna had an emotional attachment to or thought Rachel might want, she put in a separate box in her bedroom.

Rachel was driving in tomorrow, which meant that she needed to pull it together. Jenna hadn't taken a shower or left the house in three days. Her only meals had gone straight from the freezer to the microwave to her mouth. She went to bed late and slept in until almost noon most days. The sting of the hot shower this morning had pulled her out of the slump she hadn't realized that she had been in. Jenna felt hungry, *really* hungry, for the first time in days. The fridge was empty and the trash full.

When she finally drove away from Harris Teeter, Jenna told herself that it was because she wanted to support On Island business. But it wasn't only that feeling that had her pulling up in front of Bohn's. If she was being really honest with herself, she wanted to see Jackson.

Well, she did *and* didn't want to see him. She sat in the Bohn's parking lot almost as long as she had in Harris Teeter's. Jenna had spent a lot of time over the past few days going over the conversation with Jackson at the beach. He had been surprisingly sweet. A word she never would have thought she'd use to describe him. He listened to her talk for too long about shells. He genuinely seemed interested—or faked it well. She also couldn't complain about the way his sculpted body glistened with sweat, though she had done her best not to ogle him. What kind of workouts did the man do to get in such shape? He could have graced the cover of magazines or calendars.

And then he had apologized, honestly and humbly. This set her off somehow, snapping her walls back into place. Just like that, her anger with him bubbled right back up to the surface. After he apologized for something he had done to her *sister*, yet Jenna insulted him—again—and left him standing alone on the beach. Not her finest moment. She had even left her shoes, but was too prideful to go back. She could buy another pair.

She owed Jackson an apology. But she couldn't find the words to compose one when she still didn't understand why she had carried around the emotional weight of this for so long. He said that Rachel had forgiven him—why couldn't she? She felt foolish and immature and as she finally forced herself out of the car and into Bohn's, she couldn't decide if she wanted to see Jackson or avoid him more. No, despite everything, the way her eyes darted around the store and the butterflies took flight within her stomach revealed what she really wanted more.

When Jenna hadn't seen him after passing through most of the store, disappointment washed over her. She had filled the cart with food for the weekend and wandered through aisles she didn't need to go down, just to spend more time in the store. Now she just needed to ask for boxes. Jenna found a woman who looked like she was in her early twenties, standing with a nametag that read Mercer, taking notes on a clipboard in the produce section.

"Excuse me. I'm packing up for a move. Do you happen to have any boxes I could have?"

Mercer tucked a strand of her wavy brown hair behind her ear. It was a pretty color, bringing out the blue in her eyes. She was strikingly pretty. Jenna felt a wave of irrational jealousy roll over her. Did Jackson think she was pretty? Ugh. That was the last thing Jenna needed to think about.

"Is it okay if the boxes are already broken down? We have some, I think, but they're flattened already."

"I don't mind putting them back together. Honestly, I'll take whatever I can get."

Mercer had a soft voice and an even softer smile. "I'll go grab some. Can I meet you by the registers in five minutes?"

"Sounds great." Jenna wandered back up the candy aisle as Mercer disappeared to the back. Rachel still loved Twizzlers, so she dropped a big pack in the cart along with a package of Red Vines for herself. The Twizzler/Red Vine debate had been raging in their household since childhood. Her father had loved Twizzlers and her mom had preferred Red Vines.

Jenna stopped and rocked back on her heels, resting her forehead on her hands, still clutching the cart. It had been so long since she really thought about her father, who had died when she was in college. With her eyes closed, she could see his warm brown eyes and his beard, flecked with gray. But she couldn't remember the sound of his voice. He was fading from her memory.

Would it be the same with her mom? The idea of her mother slipping away from her had Jenna almost panting, feeling her stomach cramp as her fingers cramped around the handle of the cart.

"Back so soon?"

It was the worst possible time to hear Jackson's voice. She couldn't hide, and probably couldn't even mask the emotions overwhelming her. She took a few deep breaths before straightening and locking eyes with him. He wore a look of concern so sincere that Jenna's chest tightened, threatening to pull all her emotions back to the surface. She looked down at her hands, hoping he couldn't see the way her lip trembled.

She shouldn't care what he thought. But letting Jackson see her in this state felt way too vulnerable. When her breath steadied, she looked back up, half-expecting him to be gone. But he stood at the end of her cart, hands in his pockets, waiting, still looking concerned.

"Are you okay, Jenna?"

Today he didn't have on a Bohn's apron, but wore a dark suit with a light blue button-down shirt. The sight made her stomach flip almost as much as the sight of him shirtless and sweaty on the beach. She hated to admit her growing attraction to this man, but it was welcome compared to the grief that almost brought her to her knees right there in the candy aisle.

"Sure. You know how it is: shopping." Jenna gestured to her full cart, trying to keep her voice light. "I ran out of food and am trying to load up. Rachel's coming tomorrow."

His eyebrows lifted. Jenna wanted to kick herself for the reminder of her sister, which brought to mind his apology and her freak-out on the beach. She definitely didn't want to talk about that right now. The fact that he seemed concerned about her, not angry with her for being an immature brat only made Jenna feel worse about everything. She wished that he would walk away so she didn't run the risk of completely falling apart in front of him.

Then again, a part of her wished he would close the distance between them and hold her. The thought made her brain short-circuit. It was much easier when her feelings for him weren't confused but were clearly in the negative column. She needed to shut this down, fast. She took a breath and went to her default: sharp, barbed words.

"You're looking a little dressed-up for a bag boy."

His mouth twitched, and he looked past her. It hurt Jenna to say the words. She had felt sick every time after she had been harsh with him. But insulting him felt like her only armor to steel herself against him. Especially now that he had shown her nothing but kindness since she had come back.

"There you are. I've got your boxes." Jenna turned to see Mercer pushing a cart full of flattened boxes.

"Oh, great! Thanks! I was just about to check out. See you around, Jackson."

Jenna did a quick U-turn with her cart, heading away from Jackson as fast as she could. Mercer shot a look between them but followed Jenna to the registers. Jackson did not. Per the usual with her messed-up emotional state, Jenna felt relieved and also disappointed.

"In a hurry?" Mercer asked.

"Yep." Jenna didn't want to make small talk and Mercer seemed okay with silence, hovering near the end of the aisle with her cart of boxes while Jenna checked out.

She was just taking her receipt when Jackson appeared at the end of the aisle. "I can take care of this, Mercer. Jenna and I are old friends."

Mercer nodded and walked away. Jackson put a paper grocery sack on top of the boxes in the cart Mercer left behind and waited for Jenna to join him with her cart.

"That's really not necessary," Jenna said.

"Let me help you out to the car. We pride ourselves at customer service here at Bohn's."

Jackson gave her a wide smile that only made Jenna feel worse. Why did he continue to be kind when she was doing her best to push him away? Jenna didn't speak again as she led the way to her car. Jackson put the boxes flat in the trunk and helped her arrange the plastic bags of groceries in the back seat. He seemed comfortable working in silence, though Jenna felt anything but comfortable. Guilty, yes. Nervous, yes. Strangely happy? Also yes.

"This is for you." Jackson handed her a paper grocery sack. Seeing her face, he laughed. "It's not poison. You left your shoes the other day at the beach. I brought them up here in case you stopped by."

"Oh. Thank you. It's heavy. What else is in the bag?"

"I added a few extra things. Think of it as a care package."

Jenna flushed, and she stood next to her car, awkwardly holding the bag. She immediately wanted to dig into it and see what kinds of things Jackson Wells would put in a care package for her. It probably had safe choices like ice cream or chips—snack foods anyone would like. Jackson put his hands in his pockets, looking pleased with himself. She set the bag in the passenger seat. Jenna tried not to let his crooked smile affect her in any way. *Must resist that roguish charm.*

"What do I owe you?"

"Nothing. It's a gift."

"Thank you." Her voice came out softer than she had meant it to. His kindness overwhelmed her. "Well, I guess I better go."

"Great to see you again, Jenna." She was about to shut the door when he grasped the edge of it, holding it open. "I know that we haven't been friends. But if you need anything, I'm here. Literally, here at Bohn's, as you've discovered. But here for *you*."

Jenna's mouth went dry. Jackson's honey-brown eyes held her captive, stealing the thoughts right from her head. The fading evening light made his cheekbones look more defined, his jaw stronger. He looked like the kind of person she could confide in, the kind of man who could take care of her. For the first time, she realized that she was seeing him as he was now, not colored with the bad memories she had of him.

She wanted to be strong. Strong enough that she could handle the events of the last year without completely falling apart. Strong enough that she could rein in the flurry of emotions set free in her when Jackson stood close. After everything she had been through with Mark, she couldn't afford to trust another man. The only two guys she had ever loved had cheated on her, leaving her heartbroken. And

Jackson Wells was a bigger player than either of them. Or had been.

Who was he now? Could she trust in the image he was selling now, or was it just that—an image that he was selling? She couldn't afford to find out. There wasn't enough of her heart left to risk.

"I ... I need to go." Clenching her jaw, Jenna pulled the door hard enough that Jackson was forced to let go. Jenna pulled away, but couldn't help looking in the rearview mirror. He stood where she'd left him, hands in pockets, watching her drive away. The sight made her want to turn the car around and take him up on his offer. She didn't know what she needed or what exactly he was offering, but she wanted to say yes. Badly.

She really should have gone to Harris Teeter.

CHAPTER SIX

JACKSON STOOD WATCHING Jenna drive away, wishing he could chase her down and remove the note he'd put in the gift bag. It was enough that he had picked out special things for her. Why had he written her a note?

She had practically run him over to get out of there after he offered her friendship. The note took it a step past that. It didn't outwardly state his feelings, but it was pretty obvious. In general, Jackson was being pretty obvious about his feelings. And Jenna—well, she was being clear about hers too. It didn't just hurt that she wasn't interested. When she looked at him, it was like she saw who he used to be, and it brought memories and regrets rushing to the front of Jackson's mind. He had spent more time than ever this week under the deck with the punching bag.

After talking to Beau and Jimmy at breakfast, he decided to risk it, to put himself out there. He probably should have listened to Cash instead. He seemed to have a good handle on the fact that love ended in disappointment.

Why the note? He was really kicking himself over that. So

far, Jenna could have just written him off as a guy trying to make amends. The note took it firmly beyond that. It was also cowardly, hinting that he wanted more. That was the kind of thing he should have asked for in person.

But just maybe he was starting to wear her down. She hadn't said anything rude when he walked her out to the car. In fact, she had seemed grateful and for the first time, her tone had been kind. Then again, maybe he just caught her in an emotional moment. When he walked up to her in the candy aisle, she was obviously trying to hide her tears. Though he hadn't lost either of his parents, he knew that grief was like that—it could just sneak up on you. After his grandpa died, he once saw his mother crying in the kitchen, holding a box of matches to her cheek. Jackson had only been eleven, so he simply backed out of the room before she noticed him. He never found out if the matches were his grandpa's or if it was some memory that the box triggered.

Something had triggered Jenna and the sight of the raw emotion on her face had made Jackson want to sweep her into his arms. He couldn't protect her from the pain or take it away, but he could let her know that she wasn't alone. If she would only let him.

He did his usual evening walk-through of the store, hoping the routine would help distract him from thoughts of Jenna. Jackson paused in the canned goods aisle, looking at the shelves. Mercer had been here. Every can lined up perfectly on the shelf, labels turned outward just the right way. He wished there was something left for him to fix. He desperately needed something he could control right now. A problem to solve. Somewhere that he was needed.

But moving from aisle to aisle, everything looked perfect. Cereal boxes lined up perfectly flush at the end of the shelf. Even the designated clearance area had been straightened.

There wasn't so much as an empty cart or a spilled box on the floor. Things looked perfect, but this was also a sign that not enough people were shopping at Bohn's.

It had been a slow and steady decline over the past ten years since he started running the store. Bohn's had been a family store for years, but the original Bohn, Charlie, had died. His sons didn't want to run the place. They had moved Off Island, places with actual cities and had corporate jobs, probably, or just lived off their inheritance and the money from the sale to Wells Development.

Jackson's father purchased it for him as a gift and an investment. Or, a gift with the understanding that it was an investment. Alex Wells was investing in Jackson's future as much as he was in the financials, and he wanted a positive return. Not that he needed it.

When his father gave him Bohn's, he set protections in place, keeping everything in Alex's name, stipulation that certain managing staff stayed on, requiring weekly meetings. He probably expected Jackson to run the business into the ground. And he might have, had Jackson not run himself into the ground first.

His rock bottom wasn't any one particular event. Neither was his conversion a dramatic, born-again kind of moment, though the impact on his life was a complete change. Jackson had simply woken up one morning, still smelling like the night before, and walked through the doors of Hope Church. He thought the music was weird and made mental notes of everything he disagreed with in the sermons.

But something drew him back. He went over his objections and questions with Beau and Jimmy, sometimes over breakfast, sometimes over drinks or dinner. That was the beginning of Bible and Breakfast. After a few months,

Jackson realized with some amazement that he wasn't disagreeing anymore, just discussing.

As these changes took place, so did Jackson's interest in the store, and his ability to run it as a business. At first, he had been half-hearted. He simply kept things going, doing the bare minimum not to mess it up. Now he ramped up his care and concern. Bohn's was his and he wanted to make it amazing. For his father and for himself.

His dad had slowly removed the safeguards, little by little trusting his son more, before finally turning it over fully to him, along with the rest of Wells Development when he retired. Bohn's was sinking, but it wasn't because of Jackson, more because the growing tourist economy preferred chain stores like Harris Teeter. They were familiar. If people were going to spend extra money, they wanted to spend it on a dinner out or gifts. Not at the grocery store. They simply couldn't compete with chain prices, no matter how much Jackson poured into Bohn's.

Jackson came around the last aisle to the produce department and stopped, sucking in his breath with surprise.

A new wooden cart sat front and center before the main sections of fruit and vegetables. *Shop Bohn's Local!* had been painted on the side of the cart in professional hand-lettering that was a nod to the look of the produce stands that used to populate the roads on the way to Sandover. Mercer had worked quickly.

A sign stood next to the cart and Jackson walked closer to read it. The top showed a photograph of one of the fruit stands Jackson remembered, mostly because of the owners, an older black couple with wide smiles. His mother had made him drive Off Island to that particular stand for watermelon once. He could still remember how sweet it was, the feel of juice dripping down his chin.

Below the photo was a little blurb. Jackson began to read.

Farm-Stand Produce Now Right at Your Doorstep!

When you shop Bohn's Local, you are supporting the rich history and culture of coastal North Carolina. You don't have to leave the Island anymore to buy farm-fresh produce. The produce stand is coming right to you! All fruits and vegetables served in season and sourced from local farms. Keep our rich culture and family-owned produce stands alive when you shop Bohn's Local!

He didn't realize that he'd been holding his breath until he finished reading. It was genius. The display held bright green asparagus standing on end, mounds of broccoli, and shiny red and gold apples, all in baskets made from thin strips of curved wood. He remembered them from the fruit stand. It really was like the stands had been brought right into the store.

"Not a lot of fruit in season right now." Mercer's voice startled him. He hadn't heard her come to stand beside him. "But the asparagus looks amazing, don't you think? And we have apples. Next month we should be getting some strawberries. That will add some color. Is it … too much?"

He smiled and turned back to the cart, running a hand along the wood edge. "It's perfect. Everything about this: the display, the signs, the new 'Bohn's Local' idea."

"I've got the first Farmer's Market set up for two Saturdays from now."

"You work fast. I wonder if we could work this into the store. Picture it: Bohn's Local throughout the store with locally sourced specialty items. Honey, home goods, fresh pies, paintings—anything we could put under the umbrella of being On Island or nearby."

"Like a whole new line?"

"Exactly. On Islanders are our biggest customer base, not tourists. Let's give them more On Island things to consume. Whatever you want, however you want to do it. I trust your judgment and your eye for setting things up."

"We'll need a logo designed."

Jackson smiled. "Beau could do it. Do you have his number?"

He enjoyed watching Mercer's face, which flashed with a few different emotions before she moved a neutral expression. "I don't."

"I'll pass yours on and have him call you."

"You don't think you should handle it? I mean, I don't know about design ..."

"I trust you. I trust Beau. Great work, Mercer."

"Thanks. I better get started on the details. I'll need to rearrange shelf space." Mercer disappeared, heading toward the back of the store.

If Jackson wasn't going to get the girl, at least he could help Beau get his. Though maybe he should mind his own business. Whether it was Bohn's slow demise or his inability to win over Jenna, everything he touched lately seemed to be doomed to fail.

CHAPTER SEVEN

BEFORE HEADING home from Bohn's, Jenna made a pit stop for a latte at McDonald's. The only local island coffee shop closed at four o'clock, as though that's when they thought people should stop drinking coffee. Since college, coffee at night had been her calming ritual. She had worked at a coffee shop on campus the last three years. Drinking coffee for a seven-hour shift four days a week essentially broke caffeine's ability to affect her. At least, it didn't send her heart beating like crazy or keep her awake. Often the very last thing she did every day was drink two cups of coffee.

McDonald's coffee was surprisingly good, less bitter and cheaper than most coffee shops. But if you didn't remind them and tell them 100 times not to add anything they always put in liquid sweetener or, inexplicably, hazelnut syrup. She had forgotten that reminder today and got syrup, sickly sweet. Even though her latte tasted like a cupcake, it did the trick, easing the tension building in her shoulders since she saw Jackson. She felt like she was losing a battle with herself, a battle being waged over her heart. One she couldn't afford to lose.

It threw her the way Jackson just continued to be kind even when she was rude. Going out of his way to talk to her when she clearly didn't want him to. Giving her gift bags of who knows what. Was he trying to redeem himself from the past? Or, maybe, was he trying to win her over? That thought sent her heart racing.

As Jenna turned onto Dunesway Road, she realized she was speeding, and heard the echo of her mother's voice: *Now, normally you don't want to be driving forty miles an hour in a twenty-five-mile-an-hour zone.*

Jenna had been almost sixteen, learning to drive in her mother's silver minivan. Most of her friends' mothers were terrible to learn to drive with—always screaming or jamming on invisible brakes. Her mom had been completely calm, a perfect teacher.

And then Jenna was crying. Again. Tears that she had held in while standing in the candy aisle of Bohn's and tears for this current memory of learning to drive. She could hardly see through the tears as she pulled into the dark driveway and she sat there, engine running, blasting heat at her toes. She didn't want to lose the memories or have them fade the way they had with her dad. But it was so hard to have her grief knock her over like a rogue wave whenever a thought like this hit her.

It didn't seem fair. Many people her age still had grandparents. Most had their parents. Mark's parents had divorced and remarried, so he had almost an excess of family. Jenna had only Rachel and her girls. Her parents had been older when they had kids, but they were still so young to be gone. Her life was so thin. She felt unmoored, floating loose without people or a place to anchor her.

Jenna pressed her head into the steering wheel and sobbed, thinking of her three nieces, probably the closest she would ever come to having kids. She thought of the divorce papers that she had signed with her lawyer not so long ago. A divorce her mother never even knew about.

After a few minutes Jenna was sweating under her jacket. March was unpredictable and the temperature had dipped into the forties over the past day. Jenna realized that the radio station was blaring, playing song after song that all sounded remarkably like Taylor Swift wannabes. She shut off the car. The moment the car's headlights shut off, there was a tap on the window next to her.

Jenna screamed and dropped her keys.

A familiar face grinned at her. She knew those white teeth even in the dark. Steve. Her heart fluttered with a confusing cocktail of emotions. Almost as confusing as the feelings she had around Jackson. But where her walls had started to crumble around Jackson, just the sight of Steve made her want to reinforce the walls with steel and maybe a moat.

"It's just me," Steve said, voice muffled through the window. He held up a bottle of wine. "I come bearing gifts. You coming out or what?"

Jenna threw back her head and laughed, knowing that it was not a good sign of emotional health to move so quickly from sobbing to laughter. She opened the door and he hopped out of the way.

"Hey, now. Watch where you swing that thing."

"Steve." Jenna felt awkward as she stood. She had instinctively been going in for a hug, but now questioned that move. She put her hands into the pockets of her jacket instead.

Studying him, she couldn't help but think of the boy she had spent hours playing with in the woods and riding bikes to the beach. They had been friends first, after all. Even after what he did, so many of her good childhood memories involved the guy who had been the boy next door. Rachel always said that she had a soft spot for him, and that she didn't see him the way everyone else did. She should have been angry with him or at least as upset as she had felt with Jackson when she ran into him for the first time this week. But she didn't feel angry, just resigned and emotionally spent.

"Well, don't just stand there," he said. "It's as cold as you were to me senior year of high school." He had that way of trying to disarm her with humor and a crooked grin. She could get on board with light humor. Much easier than going deep.

"Wow, really? That's where you want to start? Also, you totally deserved an arctic winter. But do we really want to rehash the whole you-dumping-me-for-Anna thing?"

Steve rubbed a hand over the back of his neck. When he did, Jenna realized that he wasn't wearing his wedding ring. *What did that mean?* He gave her a lopsided grin. "Truce? At least for the night. I did bring a peace offering, after all."

"I thought you said the wine was a gift. Now it's a peace offering?"

"Can it be a little bit of both?"

"Only if you make yourself useful and help me bring in the groceries."

Their pattern of witty banter returned so easily. Carrying groceries in was a nice distraction and allowed Jenna to center herself. This was Steve. Her first best friend, first boyfriend, first heartbreak. They were different people now. When all the groceries were inside, they stood across the kitchen from each other like it was the most normal thing in the world.

Except Jenna felt an odd sense of warning, like she needed to keep that whole kitchen between them. Steve may have been her best friend at one time, but he no longer felt *safe*. The bag Jackson sent with her shoes sat behind Steve on the counter. She wished he would go. She was dying to see what kinds of things Jackson had thought to put in the bag. But not in front of Steve.

"It's good to see you, Jenns."

It bothered her that he used her nickname. Only Rachel still called her Jenns. "What brings you here? It's not every night I have a creeper waiting outside my car for me."

"Creeper, huh? That's what I've been reduced to? It just happened to be your lucky night. I was visiting my mom. I procured this bottle from her kitchen when I saw your car. Would you like a glass?"

"I don't have glasses. Just red plastic cups." Jenna handed Steve the corkscrew she had bought at Bohn's, pushing the thought of Jackson from her mind. Did she want a glass? She hadn't had any wine since she arrived and couldn't buy it at Bohn's. Now that she thought about it, she didn't miss it. Which felt like progress. Drinking with Steve seemed like a definite backward step.

Steve grinned. "Red cups. Just like the old days."

"Maybe for you. I didn't drink in high school, remember?"

That had been one of the points of contention between them back then. Steve had gone to church the same way that Jenna did, but any faith he had was confined to Sunday mornings. Not that he was a bad guy, just maybe a stereotypical one. For Jenna it had always been more. Faith colored her decisions. Which meant, among other things, no drinking until she was twenty-one, something Steve constantly pushed her on. Just like her stance on waiting for marriage to have sex.

Anna had no problem going to parties and drinking whatever was on tap from a plastic cup. She also had no problem stealing boyfriends. Probably not having sex either.

"One for you?"

Jenna held up her McDonald's cup. "I'm good. I've got coffee."

Steve made a face. "Doesn't that keep you up all night?"

"Nope."

She watched Steve tip back his wine, eyes crinkling up at the sides as he caught her staring. It wasn't fair that guys like Jackson and Steve somehow managed to look just as good now as they did in high school. Better, even. The two of them could almost have been brothers with their thick, dark hair and brown eyes. They also shared a mutual animosity. She wondered if that had settled down over the years, especially with them both staying On Island.

Something was different about Steve's eyes, but she couldn't quite pinpoint what it was yet. He now sported a tiny white scar the length of his eyebrow and just above it. She could have asked him a million questions and probably should have started with what happened to him and Anna that led to him not wearing his ring, but she zeroed in on the scar.

"How'd you get that?"

"This?" He traced over it with a fingertip. His nails were clipped short and his hands looked rough and calloused. "I run charters now. Mostly day trips, fishing for tourists. Sometimes sunset cruises. You know, romantic dates for couples." He wiggled his eyebrows and Jenna felt herself start to blush. "It was just one of those timing things. The boat pitched as I was getting something out of the cooler. Busted it on the boat. Five stitches. Sexy, right?"

It was. She wished that she didn't think so. But thinking that did nothing to ease the niggling sense of worry in the back of her mind about him. Jenna gave him a fierce stare. "The question is: how does *Anna* feel about it?"

Steve sighed and took another drink of wine. He drank in long swallows, like it was water. "I'm not sure how Anna feels about anything anymore." When he was done, he set the cup on the counter and waved his ring-less left hand at her.

So, they weren't together. There was still a tan line from where it had been. Recent breakup, maybe? Especially since his mother still had a framed picture of them in her house.

"You've changed," Steve said.

Let's hope so. Steve's words had Jenna feeling suddenly self-conscious. She looked down at her shoes. Converse, just like she wore in middle school. They kept coming back in style and she never stopped liking them, so bought a new pair a few months ago. These were turquoise, not bright pink like the ones she had when she was thirteen.

"I'm not sure how you can tell that after five minutes, but okay. I'll take it as a compliment."

"Nothing needed fixing. But I don't mind Jenna 2.0 either."

He smiled, and Jenna felt a rush of memories moving like a slideshow playing on high speed through her mind, warming her. She saw that same smile when they were exploring the wildlife refuge behind their houses and came across a baby rabbit. She saw his eyes crinkle up when they carved their initials into the beech tree out back. He had smiled that way before he brushed her hair back from her face and kissed her.

She saw that same smile, directed toward Anna as they walked down the hallway together, holding hands.

That image sobered her, stealing the warmth that had started to form in her chest as she'd thought about the good times. Maybe he and Anna weren't together now. But that didn't erase what he had done to Jenna or all the history in-between. She had given Jackson such a hard time about something he had done to her sister. Why was it so much easier to want to let Steve get a pass for how he had hurt her? And why did she suddenly wish it was Jackson, not Steve, across the kitchen from her?

Steve turned to the counter behind him to pour more wine and noticed the bag from Jackson. "You forgot to unload one. What's this?" He pulled out her sandals.

"It's nothing."

Jenna tossed them toward the back door leading out to the deck. Steve continued to pull things out of the bag: a bottle of wine, a crusty loaf of bread, a half-wheel of Brie, a bar of expensive dark chocolate with sea salt. Wow. Jackson had really gone all out. The realization sent guilt flooding through her, along with a feeling of appreciation. Now she owed him an apology and a thank-you.

"Jackson Wells?" His voice dripped with disdain. He held a note in his hand and began to read it out loud in a mocking voice. "Dear Jenna, I wanted to say again how sorry I am—"

Jenna snatched the note from him, seeing Jackson's name embossed at the top. "Hey. Stop."

His eyes looked heated now and his fingers gripped the counter behind him. "Why is Jackson Wells writing you notes? You're not dating him, are you? I knew he was fast, but ... "

Hot anger burned in her throat. "No. Not that it's your business. I just left my shoes—it's a long story. But nothing is happening between me and Jackson Wells. Trust me." Except that didn't exactly feel true now that she'd said the words.

He stared hard at her face, like he could read the truth there. Why did she feel like she had betrayed Jackson somehow?

"You know I hate that guy."

She rolled her eyes. "What are we, still sixteen? As far as I remember, the feeling was mutual. I never knew why, though."

She remembered the time Steve came to school sporting a black eye that supposedly came from Jackson. It was senior year, so she and Steve weren't together, and soon after the rumors about Rachel. She never got the full story, but always wondered what brought them to blows. They had always seemed to hate each other from a distance.

"No one particular reason. That guy was—and is—a jerk. You should stay away from him. Far away."

"I just ran into him at Bohn's. Not a big deal."

Also, not your business who I hang out with. For whatever reason, Jenna had no problem speaking her mind to Jackson, but here with Steve, she kept holding back. Why was that? Not for the first time, guilt for all the rude things she'd said to Jackson washed over her.

"Then why is he writing you notes and giving you back your shoes? You should shop at Harris Teeter. I do. Just to avoid running into his pompous, lying face."

"Wow. Seriously, what happened with the two of you? Was it because you got in a fight that one time? Are you still holding onto stuff that happened in high school?"

"Are you?" His question felt pointed and invasive and like it was about something wholly different than their current conversation. He stared at her with hooded eyes, an intense expression on her face.

"No. I've moved on."

Steve took another long drink of wine. When he set down the cup, his expression had changed. The edge was gone and the familiar smile was back. "Are you going to sell the house?"

"Probably. I can keep it if I want, but I don't know if I could live here."

"Will you stay On Island?"

"Another question I can't answer. Yet. I thought I'd get through packing things up first and see how I feel. I'm kind of ... between things right now. What I mean is that I can stay or I can go. I'm not really tied to a place."

Because my husband was a cheater and my marriage is over and I have nowhere to live and no job. Steve had once known her so well. Could he still read the things in her face that she left unspoken? She hoped not.

"You know, our initials are still out on the tree out there. If you sell the house, the new owners will get that as a little bonus." He grinned.

Jenna took a sip of coffee. "I'll put that in the listing as a selling point."

"You should. It really brings up the value of the place. The neighbors aren't so bad either. Maybe you should hold onto it. Good memories." He watched her over the lip of the cup as he took another drink.

"Some were. Some ... not so much.'

Steve set down his cup. His smile disappeared, and his eyes burned. "Jenna, there's something I need to say to you. I should have said it a long time ago."

Not another confession about the past. Or an apology. Jenna felt suddenly like she had been thrust into A Christmas

Carol. Except there was only the Ghost of Christmas past, haunting her present and keeping her from the future.

Jenna's phone began to ring on the counter, startling them both as it buzzed against a cutting board. It was Rachel. "I've got to take this."

She didn't actually, but needed Steve out of her house before he said whatever he was going to say. Jackson's apology was all she could take for the moment. And despite her mixed feelings towards Jackson, Steve didn't give her mixed feelings. They were all sour, getting more so by the minute. She wanted him to leave. He may have been her oldest friend and her first love, but their history needed to stay firmly in the past.

"I'll show myself out." Steve brushed her shoulder with his hand as he walked back by, then leaned in, his whisper sending a shiver down her back. At one time, it would have been pleasant. Tonight, though, it felt like some kind of warning. She clutched the still-ringing phone in her hand. "Keep the wine. I'll be back. Probably when you least expect it. Good to see you, Jenns."

Again with her nickname. Jenna held the phone up to her ear, though she had no intention of answering it and Steve had already gone, the sound of the front door closing behind him giving her a sense of relief. She closed her eyes, taking deep breaths.

Jenna realized that she had crumpled Jackson's note in her shaking hand. She crossed the room and smoothed it out on the counter next to the Brie and the other things Steve had pulled out of the bag.

Dear Jenna,

I wanted to say again how sorry I am about Rachel. I was

a jerk in high school and for a long time after. It's hard for me to think about the guy I used to be. If you gave me a chance now, I think you'd see that I'm someone quite different. I'm trying. Here are a few things I thought you might enjoy.

-Jax

PS- I don't think I said it before, but I'm so sorry about your mom. She was an amazing woman and she reminded me so much of you.

Jenna read the note. Then she read it again. One more time, with fat tears obscuring her vision.

She didn't know what part to focus on. If she gave him a chance to ... what? Be a friend? Something more? He was trying ... to do what? Be a better man? A different man? Jenna's mother was an amazing woman ... and Jenna reminded him of her? That one brought on the tears. And then he had signed it Jax. A nickname. Not one she'd ever heard anyone use for him in high school. He had always been Jackson. Or Jackson Wells—the kind of guy where people almost always used both of his names.

She was thankful that she had pulled the note away from Steve before he read the whole thing. This wasn't a casual note from a guy she happened to run into. She didn't know exactly what this was, but it felt more like an invitation or an open door.

Her stomach growling reminded her that she still hadn't eaten. Jenna opened the package of Brie and spread it over a slice of the crusty bread. Delicious and perfect. *Thank you, Jackson.* If she'd had his number, she would have been tempted to text him.

She had expected that it would be difficult to come back,

both in terms of packing up the house and running into old acquaintances. But Jenna had been completely unprepared for the emotional upheaval that Jackson Wells was causing. Add Steve's visit to the mix and her life had become something of an afternoon soap opera. Or maybe it had just reverted to high school drama.

Which was exactly the reason why she needed to get everything done in the house: so that she could put it on the market and get Off Island as soon as humanly possible. She didn't want to live stuck in a loop of the past. It was time to move on. But when she woke up, still clutching Jackson's note in her hand, Jenna realized that this might be even harder than she had thought.

CHAPTER EIGHT

"RACH!"

For what felt like the fiftieth time in the past few days, Jenna was crying as she ran out onto the front porch. Rachel darted through the rain, holding her purse over her head like it would do something to block the deluge. Her light brown hair was soaked by the time she reached Jenna. They embraced on the edge of the porch, ignoring the rain until thunder crashed and made them jump. Rachel screamed. Jenna was laughing as they ran into the house.

Rachel hugged her once more. "So good to see you. It's been too long."

"It's been like a month. But you're right. We need to do a better job of seeing each other. I need to come to Burlington more. It's easier than you trying to cart the girls around."

"Whatever. I can do it. We've got a DVD player in the car. I can drive wherever. I just need to know where that wherever is. Or, you could always move to Burlington." Rachel waved a hand and Jenna noticed the flash of a ring on her right hand.

Jenna grabbed Rachel's hand and looked at the ring, a big blue gemstone. "Holy bling, Batman. Is that a sapphire?"

Rachel pulled away self-consciously. "Brady's having a good year. It's nothing."

Jenna scoffed. "It's okay to be happy and married and have money, Rach. Don't make it weird. That ring is *gorgeous*."

It had been hard to have a younger sister like Rachel. Jenna wasn't jealous, exactly, but it hadn't always been easy to watch the way Rachel sailed through boyfriends and college and marriage and kids. Her life seemed like a direct contrast, revealing what Jenna lacked. Not that Jenna was a total wallflower or that it was all easy for Rachel—Jenna got a front-row seat to her sister's heartbreaks and the struggles. But somehow Rachel always floated back up to the top. She was buoyant, while Jenna kept sinking.

Thinking about it like that was depressing. Jenna learned years ago that she needed to be happy for her sister and celebrate with her. That way jealousy and bitterness didn't rise up to choke her.

Rachel held her hand out, looking down appreciatively. "Okay, fine. It is gorgeous, isn't it? I love it more than you should love a thing. Brady is amazing."

"He is a great guy. I love that he's babysitting the girls so you could come."

Rachel rolled her eyes. "Don't call it babysitting. They're his kids. He's being a dad. A solo dad. But yeah, he's great. A lot of my mom friends have husbands that don't do anything with their kids. Like, anything. I simply don't get that." Rachel stopped, her eyes wide. She grabbed Jenna's arm. "Hang on—shh! Shh!"

Jenna froze, hearing only the distant rumbling of thunder as the storm receded. "What?"

Rachel threw her head back and laughed. "Nothing! That's just it! That's the sound of no children whatsoever calling 'Mommy Mommy Mommy!' You know I love them. I do. But I needed the break. I want to enjoy every second of this." She made a face.

"Totally understand." Jenna forced out a laugh. She did know that Rachel loved her kids. Through their phone calls and time together, Jenna also knew that they were exhausting. Rachel had the right to complain about being exhausted or to enjoy time away. Still, it stung a tiny bit thinking about the fact that Jenna might never have kids of her own.

"Okay, so packing up Mom's stuff isn't the best. But we can make the best of it together. Right? Sister bonding! You've done a great job so far. It's practically empty."

"Hardly. It seems like I do one thing and then five more things pop up that I need to do. I feel like I'm playing whack-a-mole, but with stuff. How was the drive?"

Rachel rolled her eyes. "Remind me never to drive out on a Friday. It's not even tourist season and the line at the toll booth was ridiculous. Did I hear they're getting rid of that thing?"

"You know how it is. I heard they're voting on it. But City Council is never going to pass something getting rid of the toll booth. The thing is an institution. And it's really the last thing standing between Sandover becoming like the rest of the Outer Banks—just enough inconvenience to keep some people away."

"They need to pick. Either Sandover is going to become a tourist destination or not. No more of this halfway business."

"It's more than halfway. I mean, other than the fact that we have more of a year-round population of On Islanders,

79

we've become a vacation spot. It will help us get more for the house, apparently."

"Does that mean you've called a real estate agent?"

"I did, but I hated her. She knew the neighborhood and told me over the phone without even seeing the house that it was probably a teardown. Worth a lot for the property and the fact that it backs up to the refuge, but the house wouldn't stay."

"It probably is, though, right? You said that yourself."

"Yeah." Jenna shrugged. "It's different somehow when someone else says it."

"Do you want to stay? You know we don't have to sell. Or do you want to be the agent? I know you said you didn't want to represent it, but you could. It's whatever you want."

Rachel's voice was intentionally even. This was not their first discussion over the past few months about the fate of the house. Mostly they went in circles about it, ending with Rachel telling Jenna she had to decide.

"I can't stay. And if I can't handle an agent talking about it, no way could I show it and listen to people's feedback. Yuck."

"Leave it to me, then. I'll call in the morning. I want to go to the beach in the afternoon. The storm is apparently bringing back the warm weather, thankfully. I brought my bathing suit. I need the sand and sun."

"Even if it warms up, it's not going to be hot enough to swim."

"I just want a little tan. I don't need to get in the water. I'm pasty like Casper. You can join me. You look like a vampire."

"I'll take vampire over ghost. They're usually hotter."

"Have you been watching *The Vampire Diaries* again?

Because we've been over this: you're too old for the Salvatore Brothers."

Jenna scoffed. "Not a chance. They were pre-Civil War, remember? They're at least like a hundred years older than me."

"Yeah, but they *look* like they're in their twenties. Which makes you a cougar."

Jenna made a gagging sound and clutched her throat. "Call me a vampire, but please don't ever call me a cougar again."

Rachel pursed her lips and looked at Jenna seriously. She had a tendency to switch from silly to serious on a dime, giving Jenna whiplash. "Are you doing okay?"

"Sure. I'm just feeling a little lost, you know?" There were too many choices now. Jenna felt like she was in a long hallway full of open doors that all looked equally uninviting. She longed to be a kid again, when all the decisions fit into the easy boxes of whatever you were supposed to do: breakfast, school, homework, play time, dinner, bedtime, repeat. High school, college, job, marriage, kids. That's when it all fell apart.

"I'm really sorry, sis. About Mark and just everything. I hate that it happened to you. You deserve so much better than what you got. It plain sucks. That's an understatement, but I don't have any better words for it."

"Yeah, well. My life certainly went a different direction than what I planned."

"Like if you had married Steve?" Rachel's face scrunched up like she smelled something rotten.

Rachel had never made a secret of the fact that she hated Steve. What would she say if she knew he had been in this very house the night before? It felt sneaky not to tell Rachel, but she didn't want to have a conversation about Steve. Not now. Maybe not at all. The same way she didn't want to talk about the way she kept running into Jackson. Or how her resolve to hate him melted a little more every time.

"Would that have been so horrible if I married Steve? I mean, it couldn't have been worse than Mark, right?" Why was she defending him? She had defended Jackson to Steve and now was defending Steve to Rachel. Her life really had reverted to high school.

Rachel made a gagging noise. "Jenna, you had blinders on from the start with that guy. I heard that he cheated on Anna, so he never changed. We need to find you a nice guy and ..."

So that's what happened to Steve's marriage. Her stomach twisted. Jenna stopped listening to whatever Rachel was saying. It shouldn't be surprising. After all, he had gotten together with Anna while he was still with Jenna. Once a cheater, always a cheater. Why had he come last night, really?

"I'm not interested in dating anyone. Like, ever. I think I'm done. Singleness is a gift, right? I think the Bible says that somewhere."

Rachel looked sad, but didn't say anything. Then she shook her head and clapped her hands. "Let's get going. I feel restless. Where should we start?"

"I haven't even started on the bedrooms. Just some of the bigger things in the living areas," she said. "I haven't been able to go in there."

Rachel nodded. That was the thing about having a sister. You didn't have to say everything out loud. "We'll do mom's room tonight. Together. Or ... maybe tomorrow."

"Tomorrow. I'd prefer never, but if I have to do it, I'm glad it's with you."

"Aw, you've turned into a sentimental woman in your old age."

"Shut up. You're two years behind me. Menopause is right around the corner. Now, pick a room, any room. Dealer's choice."

Jenna may have been older, but it was Rachel who made quick decisions and saw them through. She barreled into situations like she was born to do it. No hesitation. Jenna once read a book on birth order and personality. According to it, Rachel was the firstborn and Jenna was the second. If Rachel was there, she took charge, no questions asked. Some people might have been bothered, but for Jenna, it was a relief to fall back into these patterns.

"I'll take the family room for 500, Alex."

"And the answer is: Daily Double!"

They both laughed, and Jenna felt an ease slip over her that she had been missing since she arrived on Sandover. As they began pulling things off the shelves in the family room, Jenna thought about what it would be like to move to Burlington. Rachel said that real estate was booming there. She could see her nieces more. If she wasn't going to have her own kids, she could just be the best aunt ever.

The thought of living here in her mother's house felt wrong, but so did the idea of moving away. Sandover was full of ghosts, but something about it called to her. Was it just the pull of the ocean? To her history and childhood memories? Or was she drawn to a particular man with honey-brown eyes who refused to give up on her?

Jenna sat in the café at Bohn's, low in her chair so that she was almost out of view from the rest of the store. She told Rachel that she wanted to call another real estate agent, but the truth was that she was hiding from Jackson. It felt embarrassingly desperate to be here again, but Rachel had insisted. She practically screeched when Jenna suggested going to Harris Teeter.

"Are you broken? We don't shop at the Tweeter. At least not On Island. The house is filled with junk food. I want something healthy, like salad. And ice cream. Don't judge."

She couldn't explain to Rachel why she didn't want to go back to Bohn's without explaining the pattern she and Jackson were in: he does something nice, I insult him. And repeat. She needed to thank him for returning her shoes, for the gift bag, for the note.

Especially for the note, which she had reread multiple times the night before and that morning. What did it say about her that it was the closest thing to a love letter she had received in her adult life? Something else Steve and Mark shared was that apparently neither was a romantic.

Where do you go after a note like that? Jenna's desperation was exactly why she needed to hide here in case Jackson was working. She had to admit that the café was a great space. It had been added in the last five years or so. There was a gas-burning fireplace with a stone face and nicer tables than you'd typically see in a grocery store. It had a row of glass counters with pre-prepared foods and a menu of food-to-order. Everything from grilled panini sandwiches to Asian stir-fry. The smell of garlic hung in the air.

The woman on the phone—Kelly?—had asked Jenna another question about the house. "I'm sorry—could you repeat that?"

"Of course. You sounded unsure and I just wanted to make sure that you had really decided on selling. Is this something you want to do?"

Jenna knew what she was going to say, but it took effort

to get the words out. They felt so final. "Yes. I'm going to sell."

"Great. Can you stop by the office for paperwork tomorrow? Or I'll come to you. That might be better so I can walk around and get a feel for the place."

At least she didn't mention "teardown." Jenna's phone beeped and she held it away from her ear. She was at 3% battery life. She must have forgotten to charge it the night before. "Kelly, can you hang on a sec? My phone is about to die."

There was a charger in Rachel's car, but Jenna didn't have the keys. She looked around for Rachel, but she must have been lost in the freezer section still. A preteen girl who looked a few years older than her niece Ava sat a few tables away with her phone plugged into a pink charger.

Jenna walked over to the table. The girl looked up at her with a bored expression, then back down at her phone.

"Hi. Sorry to bother you," Jenna said. "Can I borrow your charger really fast? My phone is dead and I'm in the middle of an important call."

The girl continued scrolling through some video app. "I'm not supposed to talk to strangers."

Jenna almost snorted. "Look, five minutes. Probably less. I'll sit right there where you can see me. I'm not some weirdo, promise."

"That remains to be seen." The girl sighed and pulled the charger out of the wall socket. Before Jenna knew what was happening, the girl lifted a phone snapped a photo of her. "If you steal my charger, now I have a picture of you I can show the police."

Jenna stared at the girl for a moment before heading back to her table and plugging everything in. She was, as Jenna's mother would have said, a piece of work. Where her mother would have meant it in a disapproving way, Jenna liked her gumption.

Gumption? Ugh, now I'm officially an old lady.

When she had been that age, she would never have spoken to an adult like that. Much of the time she felt like she was still young, not a few years shy of forty. Until she actually talked to younger people, when she felt decidedly *old*. Like right now.

"Sorry," Jenna said to Kelly. "I had to plug in my phone."

She half-listened to Kelly talking about paperwork and staging and a walk-through. She knew the drill, but for whatever reason had not mentioned that she had her real estate license. As Kelly droned on, Jenna watched the girl a few tables away. Would Ava have that same attitude in a year or two? Doubtful. Ava was that quiet and perfect first child—good grades, polite manners, sweet, cute.

The girl at the table was recording a video of herself talking. Jenna was so glad cell phones didn't exist when she was young. The stupid things she would have publicly shared with the world ...

"Tomorrow at three sound okay?"

"That should be fine. I'm sure my sister would like to talk with you as well."

"Good. I'll see you then."

Kelly hung up without so much as a goodbye. The woman was all business, which was fine. Jenna didn't want to make small talk about it.

She let the phone charge for a minute or two, getting up to 20% before walking it back to the girl at the table. "Thanks," she said.

The girl nodded, but didn't say anything. "What?" she asked, when Jenna didn't leave.

"Nothing. You just ... I have a niece about your age."

"Now you're just being creepy. I'm twelve and it's totally legal to sit in a café by yourself. It's not legal to harass minors. My dad owns this place. He'll be happy to kick you out if I ask."

Jenna shook her head, but smiled. *This girl!*

"Thanks again for the charger. You can get back to your selfies and social media now."

The girl's head snapped up and Jenna smirked. She obviously hadn't expected a smart remark back.

Instead of looking mad, the girl narrowed her eyes for a moment and then nodded like Jenna had made it into some kind of club. Jenna felt an odd sort of pleasure that she had crossed over this invisible barrier to approval. It shouldn't matter if some random pre-teen thought she was cool. But it did. She glanced down at the girl's phone. It was open to some kind of video-editing app.

"What are you working on?" The question popped out before she could think about whether or not it was a good idea. It probably wasn't.

But the girl narrowed her eyes and then said, "I create mini-documentaries."

"Wow. Like, all on your phone? The video, editing, all that?"

"Surprising fact: phones aren't just for calling people. Yeah, everything's on here that I need. I can film clips, then splice them together, put music over it, effects. This is a paid app, but still was pretty powerful for the price."

"Where can I watch them? I mean, are they published on YouTube or something?"

"You want to watch them?"

Jenna shrugged. "I don't think I've ever seen a mini-documentary. It sounds interesting. And, no offense, but you're young. I'd like to see what you can do. I have a feeling I'd be impressed."

Before the girl could answer, Rachel called out her name. "Jenna!" Rachel waved from near the exit. She had a cart full of paper grocery sacks.

"Well, better go. Thanks again and best of luck with the videos," Jenna said to the girl, who had already gotten back to her project. Turning to Rachel, she eyed the cart. "That's a lot of salad. What else have you got in there?"

Just before Jenna reached Rachel, Jackson appeared. Jenna stopped in place, a few feet away. Rachel smiled up at him like they were old friends. He put his arm around her and gave a quick squeeze. So casual, so easy. Why could Rachel do that, while Jenna made everything awkward or terrible?

Should she thank him for the gift bag? Tell him how much the note meant to her? Jenna's heart felt wild and erratic and she knew her cheeks were flushed. If she said anything now, that would mean explaining to Rachel. Which she definitely didn't want to do.

Jenna forced herself to close the distance between them. "Hey, there. I see you caught up with the Bohn's Employee of the Month."

The moment the words left her mouth, she wanted to take them back. Rachel turned, giving her a shocked look. Jenna flinched. She didn't want to look at Jackson, but finally did. He wouldn't meet her eyes.

"Good to see you again, Rachel." His voice was clipped. He brushed past them both.

Jenna had an urge to chase after him, but of course she didn't. She stood there, feeling small and mean. Rachel smacked her on the arm. "What is *wrong* with you?" Jenna shrugged and Rachel made a sound of disgust. "I didn't get to finish telling you on the phone the other day. He apologized to me last year. I really think he's changed. You can stop defending my honor, if that's even what this is about."

"What else would it be about?"

"I have no idea, honestly. Jealousy comes to mind."

"Jealousy? Of what? Of whom?"

Rachel sighed. "I don't know. I kind of got the impression after Steve that maybe you liked Jackson. Even though he was a jerk back then. I sort of thought part of the reason you were so mad about the rumors about me and Jackson was because you liked him. By the way, you know he didn't start the rumors, right?"

Jenna was too shocked to even touch the rest of Rachel's words, so she zeroed in on that one thing. "He didn't? Who did?"

"Steve, of all people. How have we not talked about this? I swear I told you this."

"You most definitely did not tell me any of this."

Rachel rolled her eyes. "You had to know that. Remember the big fight they got in and Steve came to school with a black eye?"

"That was about you?"

"Yep. So maybe you should go apologize to Jackson for what you just said. He's still right there."

If only Rachel knew how much Jenna had to apologize for and how many times she had been rude to him that week. Jenna glanced over and realized that he was talking to the sassy girl in the café. He had his hands in his pockets while the girl was still messing with her phone. Something dawned on Jenna, but slowly. The thought made her stomach drop.

Jenna's forehead began to sweat. "Uh, quick question. Jackson—does he work here?"

Rachel gave her a look. "He owns the store. That and half

the island. He's like a billionaire now. Don't tell me you didn't know that."

"I did not know that. I'm not sure how, but I missed that rather significant piece of gossip."

The girl at the table looked to be giving Jackson the same verbal lashing she had given Jenna. His shoulders slumped.

Jenna tried to wrap her mind around all of this. Jackson Wells had beaten up Steve because he had started the rumors about Rachel. He owned Bohn's and apparently was a billionaire, a concept she could hardly fathom. He had a daughter with a sassy attitude. And he had tried—and maybe now given up on—starting fresh with Jenna.

She grabbed the cart from Rachel and started pushing it for the door like a mad woman.

"Where's the fire?"

"I just want to get out of here."

Rachel fell in step beside her, studying her face. "You're being totally weird. You have been ever since I mentioned coming here. Oh my gosh—it is Jackson, isn't it? Do you *like* him?"

Jenna rolled her eyes. "I do not *like* him."

"He's single, you know. Handsome. Wealthy. And he knew Mom. They were in the same Sunday School class. She told me how much she enjoyed getting to know him."

Jenna's throat constricted. Of *course* he was in their mother's Sunday School class in addition to everything else. He had gone from being a class-A jerk to Mr. Perfect. Which made Jenna the jerk. A big one.

As they were loading groceries into Rachel's car, Jackson and his daughter walked out to the parking lot. He put his hand on her shoulder. She shrugged out of his touch and continued to walk a few feet behind him, staring down at her phone.

"And he has a daughter?"

"Yep. That must be Megan. I've heard about her but haven't met her. Looks like a surly little thing."

"Surly is one word for her. I met her just now in the café."

"It's a messed-up situation. He doesn't have primary custody and barely gets to see her. He didn't even know about her until like a year ago. The mom sounds like a real prize." Rachel's voice dripped with disgust.

"Let's back up here. When did you become the resident Jackson Wells expert?"

"That time he apologized—he actually took all of us out to eat. I was visiting Mom with Brady and the girls. Jackson took us all to lunch. It was quite an event. You know the twins don't sit still for more than five seconds. I never would have imagined it, but he's a really great guy. Why are you asking so many questions about Jackson? You *do* like him." Rachel squealed.

"No. He just—I'm just ..." Jenna sighed. "Can we go, please?"

"Oh! I've got one more thing to go in the plus-column for you dating Jackson."

"I'm not dating Jackson." Jenna slammed her car door.

"He has a massive house. Right on the beach. I know how much you love the beach."

Jenna's throat felt suddenly dry. She had a feeling that she knew exactly which house. The one right by the beach access where someone—she would bet money on Jackson—had waved to her the first night here. "Is it by our old beach access?"

"I'm not that much of a stalker. Ooh—Jenna and Jackson! So cute. Your names both start with J. It's meant to be."

Jenna made a choking sound. "What are we, twelve?"

"Methinks the lady doth protest too much. Seriously. I don't know what's stopping you."

Jenna wanted to strangle her sister. What was stopping her? Just a lifetime of failed relationships, the fact that she was still neck-deep in grief, homeless, and jobless. And the fact that Jackson probably hated her now. Today he finally seemed to take the not-so-subtle hints she'd been dropping. It was the first time he had been cool toward her. She must have pushed him just too far. The regret she felt was instant and deep.

As Rachel pulled out of her parking space, the clouds were rolled away, revealing a gorgeous sky. Jenna watched Jackson open the door of a Jeep for Megan. She climbed in without looking at him, still lost in her phone. Jenna may have been imagining it, but it looked like his shoulders sagged as he closed the door. She only realized when Rachel pulled out onto the causeway that her own shoulders had slumped as well, an echo of his emotion.

Jenna had completely screwed things up with him, assuming the worst and judging him on his past. No wonder he had finally been snippy today. She must have hit the end of his patience with her. Probably better for them both, but she couldn't deny the disappointment that flooded her as they drove away.

CHAPTER NINE

"Isn't that your lady friend?"

Megan's voice startled Jackson. He looked up from his laptop and over the railing of the third-floor balcony. He was doing his best to spend quality time with his daughter, which somehow ended up looking like sitting together while on different electronic devices. It was at least something. She hadn't shut herself in her room. He'd take it.

"Lady friend?" He glanced at her, but she didn't look up from her phone. Down on the beach he saw a man walking a dog and a few people walking. None he recognized.

"Girlfriend. Woman. Love interest? Whatever your generation calls them."

Jackson huffed and shut his laptop. He hadn't been getting any work done, looking over the numbers for Bohn's. It was depressing, and he didn't mind stopping. "I don't have any of those things. If I did, though, I'd call her my bae."

Megan dropped her phone. It clattered on the wooden deck. "You did not just say 'bae.' I thought we talked about this. Using terms that teens use doesn't make you cool. It just makes it seem like you're trying too hard. Where did you even hear the word 'bae'?"

Jackson burst out laughing at her horrified expression. The one sure way he had found to connect with Megan was humor, especially the self-deprecating kind. He liked to think that he was thawing her out. "I heard it in a song. The last time I was out at the club, getting crunk."

Now she groaned, but he could see the smile threatening to emerge. "I feel like I need to tutor you on how to talk. That term is like, way out of date. At the same time, I don't want to encourage this behavior."

"Thanks?"

"Anyway, isn't that your lady friend down on the beach? Not to be confused with your *bae*. Since you are never using that word again."

Jackson stood and leaned over the balcony, looking out over the beach below. The sun had emerged earlier, helping to warm up the cool weather. It was a great day. He should probably take advantage of the weather and get out his surfboard. Before this visit, he had bought Megan her own wet suit and board, but hadn't told her yet. After his week of having Jenna shoot him down, he didn't think he could handle one more rejection.

Speaking of Jenna ... Megan was right. She and Rachel were coming back toward the beach access under his house, carrying beach towels. Rachel had on a beach coverup, while Jenna wore black athletic pants and a T-shirt. He loved the way the ocean wind blew her hair around her shoulders.

Right as he was thinking that, Rachel spotted him. She waved and said something to Jenna, whose head jerked up to look at Jackson. He lifted a hand and realized that Megan was waving them up toward the house, an invitation. Rachel gave a thumbs up and grabbed Jenna's arm, half dragging her away from the crosswalk and down below his house. Nerves jumped in Jackson's chest. They were coming up.

"You're welcome." Megan walked back into the house, buried in her phone again.

Jackson felt like he was having a minor heart attack as he ran down the three flights to the door. This couldn't be good. Jenna had made her feelings about him abundantly clear. He had put himself out there in person and then in the note. He had taken the risk like Beau and Jimmy suggested and Jenna shot him down. It was done. So, why was his heart like a sledgehammer pounding away in his chest?

He swung open the door before they could knock, trying to take on his nerves with the direct approach. "Hey! Come on in."

Rachel walked right in, eyes huge. "Wow. This is...just wow."

"Thanks," Jackson said. He felt equal parts proud and self-conscious about the house. Jenna hesitated outside the door.

"I don't bite," he said lightly.

When her eyes met his, Jackson felt a shudder move through him. Jenna gave him a small smile and stepped inside.

Rachel had no problem walking right in and poking around. Jenna trailed her through the first floor while Jackson hung behind them, hands in his pockets. Was it too much?

It felt like the most important project of his life, working with the builders on this house. Most of the work he did with Wells Development was focused on purchasing properties and planning future development, not design or architecture. Jackson's real joy, though, had been in the plans for this house. Working on the layout and the design elements felt like hope, like he was writing out plans for his future. It was a commitment to being a new man, leaving the old behind.

That all felt silly now, watching Rachel and Jenna. It was just a house. Too big, too ostentatious, too new. The weathered outside he had chosen looked more like the classic Sandover beach cottages, but it was too big. Especially considering Jackson lived alone, other than the few weekends he got to see Megan.

Rachel asked a million questions about flooring and the kinds of windows and the art on the walls. Jenna kept whatever she was thinking behind her eyes. Did she love it? Did she think it was too much?

Probably. It was a five-bedroom, four-bath house and he lived alone. Only when Megan was here did a secondary bedroom see any use. And then she spent much of her weekend locked in it as she was now. They could all hear music blasting from behind a closed door.

"You've got a hot tub out here!" Rachel said, flinging open the doors to the first-floor balcony. "And balconies on every floor. Love it."

"With this view, I had to. You're welcome any time. The hot tub during winter is particularly fun."

"Tempting," Rachel said, dipping her hand in the water. "Jenns, feel this."

Jenna walked past Jackson and put a hand in the water. "Nice."

Nice? What was with her? Jackson almost missed the sharp-tongued Jenna who had lashed out at him multiple times.

Rachel went back inside and was halfway up the stairs to the next level. Jenna lingered on the balcony and Jackson waited. Their eyes met again as she turned to go back inside. He wanted to look away, but held her gaze until she looked down. There was an energy between them that made his heart do a full-on somersault. Wordlessly, she moved past him up the stairs. Jackson made a conscious effort not to stare at her legs and backside as he followed her up. He wasn't going to be that guy. Even if she had great legs.

Rachel and Jenna moved on more quickly from the second floor—which was more bedrooms and another balcony. Music came from behind Megan's closed door.

The real star was the top level. Jackson loved how the light hit you before you got to the top of the last flight of stairs. The top level was almost all windows. It felt like you were ascending out of shadows into the light. The blue-gray paint he had chosen for the walls was a perfect extension of the sky and sea views all around.

Having the master and main living area on the top floor was the opposite of most classic floor plans, where the kitchen, living areas, and master bedroom would be on the first floor. But with the sweeping views on the ocean front, it made much more sense to have the main living areas and his bedroom on the third floor.

"This is a lot of stairs," Rachel said, breathing heavily. "But the views! Wow. Totally worth it."

Jackson stood near the kitchen, leaning against the granite-topped island as they took in the room with its high ceilings, simple furniture, and incredible sweeping view of the ocean. Rachel threw open the glass doors and went out to the main balcony. Jenna paused at the half staircase tucked away just off the living room, leading up to what Jackson called the

Tower Room. At the top of a half staircase, the small square seating area had windows on four sides, making it seem almost like a castle turret. If he wasn't on one of the balconies, Jackson spent his time up in the Tower Room. It was where he had his morning devotionals. His Bible and journal were still up there, probably open on the table ...

Jackson's mouth suddenly felt dry. Jenna was going up. He followed as quickly as he could without chasing her. He definitely didn't want Jenna reading his feelings laid bare in the private journal of mixed thoughts and prayers.

He reached the top of the six steps up and grabbed the open journal from the couch and tucked it and his bible under the other book he had up here: *Field Guide to the Birds*. Jenna turned a slow circle, a panoramic view of the island. The table also held a pair of reading glasses and binoculars.

"You found my favorite room in the house," Jackson said. "I call it the tower room."

Jenna turned, an unfamiliar look on her face. Jackson realized that it was awe. He felt the swell of pride. "It's...amazing. Truly. These views. I don't think I've ever seen the whole island, end to end." These were the first words she had spoken since she entered the house. Her voice was softer than he had heard it this week. Jackson felt a thrill of pleasure.

"Does it make you want to stay?"

She looked away, down the beach. "I don't know what I want."

Jackson could work with that. Not knowing, whether she was talking about staying at Sandover or something more, gave him hope. Hope that she might stay, hope that she might see Jackson in a different way.

She picked up *The Field Guide to Birds*, one eyebrow raised. "Yours?"

He smiled. "Busted. You like shells; I like birds. The reading glasses are mine too. And the binoculars." He held up the binoculars to his face, then switched to the reading glasses, the binoculars, the reading glasses. "Far away, close up. Far away, close up."

She giggled and he felt a rush of joy at the sound. Maybe his plan of attack to warm Megan up with humor would work for Jenna too.

"I'm getting motion sickness just watching you."

"Yeah, that was a poor choice." Jackson set them down on the table. "Luckily, when I'm watching your house, I just need the binoculars, not the glasses."

"What?" Her eyes went wide before she whipped her head around to look toward the wildlife preserve near her neighborhood. There was no way to see her house from here. Jackson covered his mouth to stifle his laughter. She turned back and pushed his shoulder. "Shut up."

"You believed me for a second there. Which makes me feel like maybe I'm giving off too much of a creepy stalker vibe."

"I only like non-creepy stalking. When you get to the point of using binoculars, it's gone too far."

Jackson smiled. This felt like Jenna. The way he always saw her with other people. Never him. Lightness and humor —that's how he remembered her.

She stared at him, assessing. He felt a warmth rising in his cheeks at her gaze. She looked like she was about to say something. He waited. Sometimes people needed a little bit of time. He'd learned that with Mercer. Listening really was an active thing—making a conscious choice not to fill the silence with words, allowing room for people to say what they really needed to say. In this moment, he could hear his heart beating in his chest like a kick-drum.

"Hey, Jackson—"

She was interrupted by Megan's voice, calling up the tower room staircase.

"When's this super fun old-people party breaking up? Aren't we doing sushi, J?" Turning to Jenna, Megan stage-whispered: "He likes to eat mid-afternoon so we can get the happy hour prices. He may be rich, but he's cheap."

Jackson felt immediately and intensely embarrassed. Megan had a way of doing that. She liked throwing adults off-balance by her casual and often disrespectful way of talking to them, especially with Jackson. He didn't mind as much when it was just the two of them, but what would Jenna think about his brash, outspoken daughter? Did she even know he had a daughter before today? Now that he had warmed her up, would Megan be a deal-breaker?

"Hey, that's just smart. I appreciate a good deal," Jenna said. Jackson shot her a surprised but grateful smile.

Jackson started down to the main floor. Jenna followed him. "Megan, have you met Jenna and Rachel? We were all *friends* in high school." He emphasized the word "friends." The last thing he needed was her making a comment about his interest in Jenna, which Megan obviously had noticed.

"We've met," Jenna said as Rachel came in from the balcony.

"Wow. High school, huh? I bet you've got some great and embarrassing stories."

"Oh yeah," Jenna said. Jackson's eyes went wide. "You wouldn't believe half of them. Like that one time Jackson streaked—"

Megan's hands flew to her ears. "La la la la la! I can't hear you!"

Streaked? He had never streaked anything—that's one road he'd never gone down. Jackson met Jenna's smug face.

She totally read that situation right and shut Megan down. Color him impressed. When Jenna winked at him, Jackson almost fell over.

Rachel rolled her eyes and thrust out her hand. "You must be Megan. I'm Rachel. It's good to meet you."

Megan shook her hand limply, with an exaggerated effort. "Cool. So, dinner, J? Tick tock. Feel free to invite your *friends* to daddy-daughter bonding time."

"We've got dinner plans later," Rachel said.

"Another time, maybe." Jenna looked right at Jackson. Was that an invitation?

"We'll leave in a few minutes, Megan. Want to meet me downstairs?"

"Yep. Good to meet you and all those polite things I'm supposed to say."

Rachel snorted as Megan stomped down the stairs. "Is this what I have to look forward to in a few years?"

"Doubtful," Jackson said. "I've seen you with your kids and you're amazing. I have no idea what I'm doing. And Megan's mom…" He made a face. There was nothing nice he could say about Kim.

"Hey, is this an elevator?" Jenna asked. She pulled on the locked door leading to the elevator, then ran her hand over the button on the wall next to it.

"It is." One part of the design that the builder had insisted on was an elevator. Apparently, this was standard for houses three stories or more, especially where the living areas were up top.

"You may not think you'll ever sell this place," the builder had said. "But you might. And for these three-story homes, people expect these now. Think of lugging groceries up three flights of stairs."

Reluctantly, Jackson had agreed to a small (and slow)

elevator, which he almost never used. Jenna pulled at the door, which looked like an ordinary wooden door with the elevator button next to it in the wall.

"It really helps with bringing up groceries," Jackson said. "And I'm also planning ahead for my retirement. These knees won't last forever."

"Can we ride in it?" Jenna asked. She looked excited suddenly, happier than Jackson had seen her.

Spending a few minutes in a small space with Jenna? "Absolutely." He pushed the button to call the elevator. The sound of the machinery whirred to life almost as noisily as his heart beating in his ears.

Rachel frowned. "I didn't think you liked small spaces."

"I don't. But it's an elevator! In a house! It's just three floors. I'll be fine."

Jenna bounced on her toes, her face bright with excitement. It was a beautiful look on her. Jackson turned back to stare at the elevator door, hoping his feelings weren't totally obvious.

"I'll take the stairs, thanks. Jackson, thanks for showing us around. Your place is incredible! You're sure you can handle that, Jenns?"

Jenna rolled her eyes. "Race you to the bottom!"

Jackson turned to Jenna as Rachel started down the stairs. "She'll win. In about ten minutes, this thing will have made its way up from the bottom floor. In another ten minutes after that, we'll make it down."

"So, what you're telling me is that this thing is a glorified dumb waiter."

Jackson grinned. "Precisely."

"Cool." Jenna pulled at the door again. "Why is it locked?"

"That stays locked until the elevator arrives. There's a magnet that unlocks only when the elevator stops in front of the door. Keeps people from falling down the shaft. You know. Safety first." The elevator reached their floor with a thump. There was no ding, but a metal clack. "See? Magnet." Jackson opened the door and pulled aside an accordion-like partition to reveal the tiny space inside. "Ta da! Welcome to the dumb waiter."

"It's adorable! Not as small as I thought it would be." Jenna followed Jackson inside.

It was small enough that Jackson could smell the sunscreen on Jenna's skin, something fruity and tropical. Her hair brushed against his bicep as she moved next to him. "Shut the outer door, then pull that sliding door shut, and we'll be in business."

Jenna pulled both the doors closed behind her and the elevator hummed loudly to life again. She grinned over at him, still looking like she was on an amusement park ride. "Wow, loud."

"Loud and slow. This is only like the third time I've ridden in this thing."

"I'm sure for rental homes this would be a great feature. People carrying in all their coolers and groceries up to the top floor."

"Kids taking joy rides is more like it. My elevator guy said that kids are always breaking these in the rental houses."

"I bet. Are we even on the second floor yet?"

Jackson realized too late what was about to happen as Jenna stretched her hand toward the sliding partition door. Time slowed. Jackson knew before she did it that Jenna was going to pull it open. He reached to stop her, but he was a step too far away.

"Don't—"

She pulled open the door. The elevator lurched to a stop.

Jenna pitched forward and Jackson grabbed her arm to steady her. They stared at each other, eyes wide. As aware as he was of the stuck elevator, he was more aware of his hand on her arm.

"Did I just break your elevator? Are we stuck? Tell me we aren't stuck. Please, Jackson."

Her voice was hardly more than a whisper, already edged with desperation. He could already see sweat beading on her forehead. He hadn't noticed that it was hot in here, but it really was. Hotter now that they weren't moving. Or was he imagining that? All these things seemed tiny compared to the way it felt when his name fell from her lips in a plea.

He had expected her to pull away from his grip on her arm, but if anything, she leaned closer to him. He loosened his grip and slid his hand around to her back. "I've got you. I'm right here." Jenna nodded, and Jackson began tracing circles on her back with a flat palm. "Stay with me and just breathe, okay?"

"Okay."

"I'm sure it's fine." Jackson was completely unsure of this. He examined the panel of buttons on the wall. "Close the door again."

Jenna stepped away slightly and his hand fell from her back. She slammed the accordion door closed and Jackson waited a few seconds, then pushed the button for the first floor. Nothing. Jenna shuddered and leaned into him. Having her stand so close to him was something he wanted to welcome, but he could feel her starting to shake from terror. He needed to get her out of here before she totally lost it.

He wrapped an arm around her shoulders, pulling her in

more closely, then studied the panel on the wall. It had a button for each floor, a yellow button that said Reset, and a switch that said On/Off. He had honestly only used this half a dozen times and tried to think about what the man who installed it had said about these. Or maybe he hadn't said anything at all. Because people typically don't open elevator doors while it's in motion. Later, when she wasn't shaking and afraid, Jackson hoped he could tease her and they could laugh about this.

"Let's try this bad boy," he said, and flicked the On/Off switch. Two times, three. Nothing. He pushed the yellow Reset button quickly, then held it down for a few seconds. No response. He pushed the button for the first floor. The elevator did not move and the motor stayed quiet. "I don't actually know why these buttons are here, as none of them actually seem to do anything."

"I am so sorry," Jenna said. Her voice was now edged with panic, her words tumbling out like she couldn't control them. "I don't know what I was thinking—I wasn't thinking. I just wondered where we were and then I was opening the door. I've done nothing but mess up your life since I came back this week. I don't know how you're still talking to me after everything. I'll pay to fix it. Whatever it takes. Just—I need to get out of here."

Her breathing was rapid and shallow. He felt the fear coming off her in waves. Jackson had never experienced a panic attack, but if he had to guess, that's what this felt like. He needed to help her calm down.

With a gentle tug, Jackson pulled her to his chest, wrapping his arms around her shoulders. Her head tucked neatly underneath his chin and she sighed against his chest.

"Hey," he said softly. "I know I'm the last person you probably want to be stuck in here with. But I'm right here and I've got you. We're safe and we will get out of here, okay?"

She nodded against him and her arms linked around his back. If only this were happening in some other moment, one where she really wanted to be near him rather than being forced into closeness because of the situation.

"Jackson? You're not the last person I'd want to be stuck with."

With her cheek pressed into his chest, could she feel the way his heart sped up? "Oh?"

"More like the second to last."

Jackson groaned and then a laugh rumbled through him. He knew she could feel that because she began giggling and the vibrations thrummed against his torso. "I guess I'll take it."

"Jenna? Jackson? Are you guys okay?" Rachel's voice drifted up to them. It sounded like she was down on the first floor, but it was hard to tell.

"I'm going to let you go for just a second. But I'm still here." Jackson lifted his arms from around her shoulders, but Jenna made a small sound and clung to him. He chuckled. "Okay, that works too."

He shuffled to the doors with her hanging onto him and pulled open the sliding door again. Above their heads, Jackson could just touch the bottom of the outer door with his fingertips and see a crack of light underneath it. If the outer door were open, he might be able to lift Jenna up enough so that she could wiggle out. But the magnet locks wouldn't open unless the elevator was stopped at the floor itself. They were well and truly stuck.

"Rachel? The elevator got stuck. I think up in the kitchen I've got the number for the elevator guy in a drawer. Can you go call him?"

"You're stuck?!" Rachel's voice was more of a screech. Jenna's fingers curled into his back. Her fingernails were going to leave marks, even through his shirt. Jackson heard Rachel's feet pounding on the stairs next to the elevator shaft. Then her voice came through more clearly. She must have stopped on the second floor. "Jenns, are you okay?"

"We're fine," Jackson said. "Just give him a call and let him know that we're between floors and the thing won't reset."

"I'm on it. Hang in there, Jenns." Again he heard footsteps on the stairs as Rachel ran up to the top level.

Jackson put one hand on Jenna's shoulders and tipped her chin up with the other. She still clung to his waist to the point it was painful.

"Hey, Monroe. You're going to be okay. We'll be out of here soon. Rachel will get the elevator guy. He lives close and can get us out of here no problem. But I need you to retract your talons. I think that you're about to do some permanent damage on my back."

Jenna's eyes went wide. She loosened her grip on his back, but didn't let go of him. "I'm sorry! I didn't even realize I was doing that. You called me Monroe."

"I did?" Jackson hadn't even realized. "I guess I did. Is that okay?"

Jenna smiled. It wasn't quite at full strength, but she had definitely calmed down. "Does this mean we're regressing? We've gone from first-name to last-name basis." She made a face. "I don't think I can call you Wells."

"My friends call me Jax."

He wanted to pull the words back in as soon as he said them. They held too much pressure. Jenna didn't want to be friends. The only reason they were currently inches apart was because they were stuck in the elevator and she was scared.

EMMA ST. CLAIR

He had no doubt that she would bolt as soon as they got the thing moving again.

Jenna opened her mouth to answer. Before a sound escaped her lips, the elevator light went out and they were plunged into darkness.

CHAPTER TEN

JENNA SCREAMED in the darkness and Jackson's hands pulled her close. She felt his lips on her hair as he murmured comforting words, words she couldn't hear because she was still screaming. His hand cupped the back of her head and this grounded her enough to close her mouth, her scream becoming more of a dull whimper against Jackson's chest.

"Hey, I've got you. Just a little bit of darkness. We're still fine, Monroe. Look—can you see the light from up there? That's the second floor right there. It's going to be okay."

Jackson's words shouldn't have calmed her so much, but she didn't question the effect they had on her, or how she was basically clinging to his body. Or the fact that she got a thrill every time he called her by her last name. They could deal with what all that meant later. Or not.

After the humiliation of how she had attached herself to him in this tiny, hot space, she might run from his house and not look back. Especially considering this whole thing was her own, stupid fault. Who opens the door of an elevator while it's moving?

No matter what happened after they got off the elevator, right now Jackson was the only thing standing between her and sheer panic. She wasn't going to question it. Instead, she pulled even closer to him, despite the fact that she could feel sweat dampening her shirt. Her eyes sought out the tiny sliver of light from the floor above. After a moment or two, her eyes adjusted. It was still almost pitch-black, but with the little light from under the door above their heads, she could just see the slope of Jackson's shoulders and his head.

Jackson moved one of his hands from her shoulders and brushed it lightly over her lower back. "You okay, Monroe? Talk to me."

"I think so." It hurt a little to speak after the screaming. She really liked the feeling of his hands on her back. Not that she would say that to him. And she liked how he called her by her last name. No one had ever called her that. It felt right.

As much as the darkness had startled her, she felt more comfortable with all the touching now that she didn't have to face the intensity of Jackson's face. It also kept her mind off the size of the elevator. It was more than small. It was tiny. Did the darkness make it feel like it was getting smaller?

It wasn't getting smaller, was it?

Her breathing hitched and she felt the panic welling up again.

Breathe.

"Jackson? Can you talk to me? About anything. I don't even care. I need something else to focus on so I don't lose it."

"Sure," he said. "So, I've never been stuck in an elevator before. Have you?"

She groaned and pressed her forehead into his chest. "Not about elevators. Anything but elevators. Something else."

"Sorry. Any favorite topics?"

"Bears. Gardening. Politics. Celebrity gossip. Books. I don't care. I just need a distraction."

"Bears, politics—hm. Not sure I can speak to either of those. Don't keep up with celebrity gossip and haven't read a book in a while. Other than the Bible and *The Field Guide to Birds*." He was quiet for a minute and Jenna almost groaned again. "How about a confession?"

That got her mind off the elevator. "You're not a murderer, are you?"

"Interesting that your mind went there first. We might need to have a conversation later about the way you see me. No, I am not a murderer." He cleared his throat. "You ready?"

"Jackson, *just keep talking.*"

"Sorry—I'm pretty bad at this. Drumroll please! Here's my confession: I had the biggest crush on you in high school. Like, embarrassingly huge."

Jenna was already sweating and hot in the small, almost airless space, but heat still rose to her face. Something fluttered in her stomach. She was suddenly very aware of every place that they were touching and the soothing way his hand moved over her lower back. It still felt comforting, but also now seemed to wake up every nerve ending in her body.

"You did not. You dated like half the school, but never showed any interest in me."

"It's true. Cross my heart. I had this picture of you I cut out of the school paper and I kept it in a book on my bedside table for years. It's probably still in the book, packed in a box somewhere."

If the lights were on, he would see the blush that she could feel on her cheeks. She was having trouble wrapping her head around this. "Wow, I was not expecting that. I

111

mean, again—you never even flirted with me or asked me out. We hardly talked in high school. *Did* we ever talk?"

"I asked you about English homework once. And you didn't know because I was so smooth, obviously. Like a ninja. Or a kid with absolutely zero game."

Jenna snorted, thinking of the long list of girls Jackson *did* date. "Oh, you had plenty of game. Game was not your problem."

For a moment, Jenna had reverted right back to the snappy remarks she had been tossing at Jackson all week. She mentally chastised herself. This was the guy currently holding her close in a sweltering, dark elevator. He had given her plenty of reasons this week to let go of her anger. She was about to apologize when he spoke again.

"Ouch. You're right, though. I did date a lot of people. But I didn't like any of them the way I liked you. I really did like you and it made me afraid to ask you out. I wasn't used to that."

That sounded like such an excuse. Then again, it wasn't like people were mature in high school. This reasoning sounded like the next evolution of a boy pulling a girl's braids on the playground when he liked her.

"What book did you keep the picture in?"

He did not answer right away as though surprised or embarrassed by the question. Hopefully it wasn't the kind of book he might be embarrassed about. That would take all of this in a totally different direction. "You don't have to tell me," she said quickly.

"*War and Peace*," he said after a long pause. She could hear a smile in his voice.

"You're joking. You read *War and Peace* back in high school?"

"Nope. It was just my cover to hide your picture. Very effective."

She giggled. When he laughed along with her, the vibrations warmed her chest. It reminded her of a purring cat. Tension started to slip from her shoulders. When she wasn't fighting against Jackson—or was it fighting her feelings for Jackson?—he had a calming effect on her. She felt safe, even here.

"That was definitely not the confession I was expecting. I mean, not that I expected a confession at all. I didn't think you knew who I was back then. Except for the whole trying to date my sister thing. Wait—if you liked me, why did you try to date Rachel?"

Jackson groaned. "If I could go back and kick some sense into myself, I would. Don't hate me. I thought maybe if I dated Rachel, you'd notice me."

"You were using my sister to get to me?"

Though she and Rachel looked similar, something in her sister's bubbly personality had always made her outshine Jenna. It shouldn't have been flattering that Jackson tried to use Rachel to get to Jenna. That was messed up. And yet, it made some small part of her happy. He had wanted *her*.

The idea that Jackson had liked her made Jenna's heart start racing, but not like it had when the elevator stopped or when the lights went out. This was a pleasant rush of emotion that made the corners of her mouth tug up.

"I know. That makes me a terrible person. And it didn't even work, obviously. Just left you with years of pent-up anger toward me."

"I wasn't mad that you tried to date her, but about the rumors. Which, until a few days ago, I thought you started."

Jackson groaned. "We have your buddy Steve to thank for that. Though I should have done more to stop them than punching him. Sure did feel satisfying, though. What did you see in that guy? That was something I never understood."

Jenna realized that she was clutching his back again. She loosened her fingers, searching for an answer. When she thought back to Steve, there were warring emotions. She could see the boy who'd been missing a front tooth and was always up for an adventure. She thought of her first kiss, Steve's lips on hers while they sat in the dunes, sea oats brushing against her shoulders as they waved in the breeze. Then there was the Steve who had showed up at her house this week, the one with something dark in his eyes and a new scar on his face. And of course, the Steve who didn't even see her in the hallways because his arm was around Anna.

"He was my friend," Jenna said. The words sounded defensive. Was she defending Steve? Should she? She didn't know how else to wrap up all their history, which she still felt conflicted about.

Jackson made a noise in the back of his throat. Just like with his laugh, she could feel the sound in her body. It gave her a thrill, being so close that his sounds moved against her.

"He never deserved you." Jackson's voice sounded tight, like it was wrapped around a passion that he barely contained. For reasons she couldn't quite explain, Jenna felt hot tears in her eyes. She didn't disagree with Jackson, but it also made her angry to hear him say it.

It reminded her of Mark and the pain of finding text messages from another woman on his phone. Not that she had been looking. Nope, she'd been clueless up until that moment. Jenna had been trying to update something on his calendar while he was in the shower. He had even given her the passcode to do it. She wondered later if he had wanted her to find out. A text came through while she was adding in a dentist appointment. The contact name was Andrew. But the words and then the image that came through were definitely not an Andrew.

"And you think you did deserve me?" she whispered.

Jenna sniffed, wishing that she could suck back the tears that were threatening to fall. Jackson tensed up. The words cut her to say, but it was like she couldn't help herself. The heaviness of the moment started to crush her and she lashed out. Not that it made this right.

His hand on her back stilled. She hadn't realized that he was still making circles over her shirt until he stopped. A single tear squeezed out and ran down her cheek. She didn't want to move her hands from where they clutched his shirt to wipe it away.

"I know that I didn't," Jackson whispered. "Still don't."

His words turned something over in her heart. As though his acknowledgment of not being good enough somehow assured her that, in fact, he *was*.

"Jenns?" A shadow moved in front of the light as Rachel called down. It sounded like she had put her mouth to the crack under the door.

"I'm here." Not that she could have been anywhere else.

"I got the guy on the phone. He's Off Island today so he recommended I call the fire department. They're on the way."

"Perfect," Jackson muttered. One of his hands left her back and she could see the movement in the dark as he ran a hand through his hair.

"I hate to bring this up now," Rachel said. "But the meeting with the realtor is right now. I almost forgot. Should I call and cancel?"

"I totally forgot too. Just go," Jenna said. "I don't need to be there. I just want to get it over with. I'm sure it will be a while before they finish getting us out."

"Okay! I can come back and pick you up after."

"I can drive her home," Jackson called out. "Is Megan okay?"

"She's fine," Rachel said. "Hungry and still, um, saucy, but fine. She said she'll let the firemen in. Call me when you get out. I want to know that you're okay."

"Okay," Jenna said. She was suddenly aware of the heat again. The temperature felt like it was still rising. There was no circulation in the space. Her shirt was damp and her forehead slick. Jackson's body heat on hers was almost unbearable, but she couldn't pull away. Or didn't want to.

Guilt felt just as cloying as the heat in the small space. It had been too easy to turn her hurt outward to him yet again. And why? She hadn't been rude to Steve even once the other night in her kitchen. He cheated on her. He had started the rumor about Rachel. Yet she let him inside her house and had a perfectly normal conversation with him.

Jackson brought out the very worst in her, cruel words she didn't even know that she had the capacity to say.

Rachel had gone. Megan was quietly waiting somewhere in the house for the fire department. She and Jackson still clung to each other, but the air felt charged with tension. Jenna knew she owed Jackson multiple apologies. She couldn't keep lashing out at him. It wasn't fair. And she didn't really mean the things she said.

"I'm sorry." The words sounded so cliché. She wished that she had better ones or that he could feel the weight of how deeply she felt them.

"It's okay. I was a jerk back then." He paused and there was pain in his voice when he spoke again. "I don't know if I'm any better now. Though I'd like to be."

Slowly, Jenna lifted a hand from Jackson's back toward where she knew his face was. She hesitated only for a moment and then touched his cheek with her fingertips. He drew in a breath. She traced her fingers over his jaw and cupped his face, feeling the rough scratch of stubble on her palm.

"Jackson, no—I really am sorry. Not about what I just said, but *all* the things I've said. I've been treating you horribly since I've been back. I have never spoken to someone the way I've spoken to you this week. You totally didn't—and don't—deserve it. I've been the jerk and I'm sorry."

He leaned slightly into her hand, bending closer toward her so when he spoke, she felt his breath on her cheek. "You mean like how you thought I was a bag boy at Bohn's? Because that was actually pretty funny, I have to say. Your opinion of me could not be much lower, could it?" She could hear the smile in his voice through the dark.

"Oh, it could have been lower. Still can, so you better watch it. But seriously, even if you were a cashier or something, I shouldn't have been a jerk about it. I don't know what's gotten into me. You just seem to bring out some kind of reaction in me. I don't know what it is about you. I'm working on it."

He was so close it felt like his cheek almost brushed hers. She closed her eyes, listening to the rush of her heartbeat in her ears.

"I bring out a reaction in you, huh?" His voice was teasing and light, just like the breath she felt over her lips.

Was he going to kiss her?

Now that she had the thought, Jenna's mind and her mouth were drawn to the idea of his lips.

"You do. Not always a bad reaction."

"No?"

Her breath caught. Jenna felt a rush and elation she

hadn't felt since she was a teenager. There was teasing still in his voice, but also a hint and a promise of something. The heat she was feeling now had less to do with the cramped, airless space and more to do with the attraction that was very clearly moving between them.

Could it be this easy? To go from thinking she hated Jackson to letting him kiss her? She wanted him to, more than she had wanted anything in a long time. This was the first time in as long as she could remember that Jenna wanted anything. Not just physical touch or romance, but even the spark of desire. The longing to live. Too long she had been going through the motions of a life that felt empty.

Cloaked in the darkness of the elevator, Jenna felt brave. She leaned the slightest bit closer to him and felt his arms tighten around her. She trailed her hand from his face down to his shoulder, feeling the muscles tense and bunch beneath her fingers.

The light scrape of his stubble on her cheek made her gasp. When Jackson chuckled, his lips brushed the skin near her mouth. Jenna froze completely, the shock of his skin against hers startling her into the inability to respond.

"I did everything wrong before." Jackson's words moved against her skin as his lips dragged over her cheek. Her body almost vibrated with the anticipation. If he moved his mouth slightly to the left …

"I want to do things right this time. I would like to kiss you, but I want to know that's what you want too." His breath on her cheek made Jenna shiver. "Though I'm honestly afraid of what might come out of your mouth, based on your track record."

Jenna giggled, more from nerves than humor. "I can't say that I blame you."

When Jenna spoke, her lips moved against the sandpapery

stubble on his cheek. Why hadn't she just said yes? *Yes, please kiss me.* He was asking for permission. Jenna wanted him to kiss her more than she remembered wanting anything in the last few years.

But her nerves flared in equal strength to her desire. What was she thinking? Did he really want a relationship? Did she? Hadn't she just been insulting him? Could her feelings really change that fast? Her heart was galloping and her brain was misfiring, her thoughts scattered, bouncing everywhere.

She couldn't seem to summon the bravery she had felt only moments ago to say that one word. Three letters. Yes. That's all, but Jenna couldn't manage to choke out the word as the silence grew more awkward between them. If she couldn't say it, she could show him instead. Jenna inched closer and pressed a soft kiss to his jaw.

That was the permission he needed. His mouth found hers in the dark, strong and firm and full of passion. Jenna sighed against his lips and moved with him. She poured out her apologies into the kiss, as well as the feelings for him that she had denied, both then and now. In answer she felt Jackson make his own apologies and promises. It was both fervent and tender, carrying with it what felt like years of passion. Jackson's lips drew her to follow as they slid over her mouth.

It was the best kiss of her life. She had never felt such adoration and love in a kiss before. But that wasn't right—Jackson couldn't love her. The thought almost shocked her out of the moment, but she sank right back into the bliss of the moment as his kisses turned featherlight and teasing.

Maybe not love—not yet. But an intensity brewed where their skin met. This felt like something sure and trustworthy. Something much bigger and more significant than a crush or some stolen moment. Jackson's kisses felt like he was making declarations and vows. A surge of hope filled her as she knit her fingers into his hair, tugging gently until he made a small moan and pulled away.

"Do you hear that?" he whispered, resting his forehead against hers.

Did he mean her heart? It had never been so loud as it was in her ears. But could he really hear it? Maybe he meant her breathing, which sounded embarrassingly like she had just been sprinting.

But then she heard the keening cry of a siren, growing louder. "Oh no."

"Oh yes. That would be the fire department."

"This is going to be really embarrassing, isn't it?"

"Considering that I'm good friends with most of the guys, yes. And, given the way Sandover gossip spreads like wildfire, even more so. Have you ever been in the Island paper? I have, and it's delightful."

"Stop it. This isn't news."

Jackson laughed. "You've been Off Island too long. This is huge news. Huge. Everyone will know about this by the end of today."

Jenna knew that he meant getting stuck in the elevator, not the kiss. But she suddenly felt an overwhelming sense of fear. Had kissing Jackson been a terrible idea? What did it mean? What would happen when they got out and didn't have the darkness to hide behind?

Jackson ran a hand down her cheek and Jenna was suddenly aware of how slick her skin was with sweat. He must think she was disgusting.

She stepped back slightly as the sirens came to a stop. Everything—the heat, the kiss, the thoughts now racing through her head—overwhelmed her. Nausea rose in her stomach and her teeth were inexplicably chattering even as she realized that the heat had become almost unbearable. Her face was completely slick with sweat and her shirt stuck to her back in an unflattering way.

Jackson noticed and ran his hands up and down her arms. They too were sweaty and she pulled away from him, feeling suddenly embarrassed.

"Hey, are you okay? Are your teeth chattering? You can't be cold."

"I think I'm just … emotional. Or something. I don't feel very good. But at least I forgot for a bit that I was scared. You did a good job with distraction."

There was a pause. In it, Jenna was suddenly aware of male voices and footsteps on the stairs inside the house.

"Did you think this was just about distracting you?" Jackson asked.

Jenna reached up, feeling for his face and touched it lightly with her fingertips. It was too hot to cup his face between her palms. She swallowed and tried to channel the bravery that came from being in the dark. For once, she wanted to say the right words to Jackson. "You misunderstood me. I wasn't trying to cheapen it. That was the most treasured I have felt in I don't know how many years. Maybe forever."

He kissed her forehead. "I'm sorry. Not for the kiss, but for my brief moment of panic just now when I thought maybe *you* thought I was taking advantage of you in the moment or something."

"What? No! Maybe we need to have more conversations and say the real things we're feeling. We don't seem to be very good at that. At least, I'm not."

"I'm all for more conversations. Lots of them. And more … distractions."

"But maybe when we aren't so sweaty? I feel disgusting. And light-headed."

Jenna sensed Jackson leaning toward her when there was a rattle and a clacking sound at the door. Light flooded the elevator. Jenna jumped away from Jackson, her back hitting the wall. She looked toward the opening as a grinning face appeared.

"Well, if it isn't my best friend and my old babysitter. This sounds like the beginning of a joke. Yikes—that heat is no joke. How are you two doing in there?"

"Beau?" Jenna had been friends with Beau's older sister, Hope. She remembered him as a mischievous blond boy who was always kicking around a soccer ball. He had been about ten years younger: a surprise baby for Hope's parents when she was almost in middle school. Same smile and the blond hair, but older. And he looked massively built, even from the little she could see of him.

"You remember me? That's good. I'm glad I made a lasting impression."

"I remember you as being trouble."

"Looks like the tables have turned, doesn't it?"

Jackson laughed. "Beau. I've always dreamed about the day when you'd need to rescue me. How about you get us out of here? I think we're about to melt and Jenna isn't a fan of small spaces."

"Will do. You should be thankful that we had a magnet key for this door," Beau said. "Otherwise I would have been axing my way through it."

"Thank you for not destroying my house, man."

The teasing dropped out of Beau's tone. "Okay, Jenna. We're going to get you out of here first. You guys are at a tough spot, though. The elevator won't start again, so that's a bust. It's a pretty narrow opening and I can't just pull you out from here because of the angle. Jackson? Do you think you could hoist Jenna up here?"

"No," Jenna said, just as Jackson said, "Yes."

She narrowed her eyes at Jackson. "No way."

The thought of him having to pick her up felt too intimate. She had admired his wide chest and massive biceps on the beach the other day, but what if she was too heavy? Nothing would be more humiliating.

Beau's head filled the opening again. "Jenna. This is my job, okay? I'm going to get you out the easiest and safest way possible. This is the best way. Jackson's strong. You're small. It's completely fine. We're going to try it and if it doesn't work, we'll move to other options. I'm going to take your hands and Jackson is going to lift you by the hips. Together we are going to get you safely out. Don't make my job any harder. Let's get you out of there."

Jenna hesitated and then took Beau's hands. She could feel the strength in them before he even started to lift.

"I'm going to grab your hips now," Jackson said from behind her. "Don't freak out or kick me, okay?"

She nodded and then his arms were around her hips, lifting her as though she didn't weigh anything at all. Jackson guided her up as Beau gently pulled her, his hands wrapped around her wrists and forearms. She ducked her head and wriggled through the opening.

Jackson's hands fell away from her hips, but she felt them help push from her thighs, then calves. She gave a final push with her feet against his chest to make it all the way out of the elevator. Beau released her arms and Jenna crumpled against the wall, sweating and shaking.

Beau kneeled in front of her, grinning. "Hey, there. You trusted us. Thank you. It's really good to see you! How are you feeling?"

"Hot. Shaky."

"Hey, Jimmy," he called. "Let's get Jenna some water, okay? You just sit tight for a few minutes while we get Jackson out. Okay?"

He patted her leg and stood. It was hard to reconcile the little boy she babysat with this man—wide shoulders and thick muscles straining his navy T-shirt under the suspenders and bright yellow fireman pants.

Jimmy, who could have been Beau's brother with his strong build, blond hair, and friendly grin, knelt in front of her and handed her a bottle of water. Jenna drank it down in long swallows and then closed her eyes, listening as they worked to get Jackson out.

"Give me a minute and I'll check you out," Jimmy said. "You're in good hands, okay?"

Jenna nodded.

It was a little more difficult to get Jackson out, given that he was bigger than Jenna and didn't have someone to help push him out. The angle made it impossible for Beau and Jimmy to pull him straight out.

"Can you brace yourself on something? Is there a railing or anything to push off of?" Beau asked.

"No," Jackson said. "Wait—maybe if I try to wedge my feet against the control panel. Hang on."

Jackson's hands appeared on the ledge, then his face. Beau and Jimmy were quick to grab him around the upper arms. There was a cracking sound and Jackson jolted back down an inch or so and groaned.

"The door I had my foot on broke off," Jackson grunted. "I think I've cut my leg."

"We'll see in just a minute," Beau said. "We've got you now, man. Hang on."

With lots of grunting and a version of what looked not

unlike a game of Twister, Beau and Jimmy managed to help wrangle Jackson through the opening. All three lay in a pile on the floor after, breathing heavily. One of them, maybe Jackson, started to laugh and soon all three of them were laughing. Jenna smiled, in spite of how badly she felt.

"Mind telling me how that even happened?" Beau asked. "We get calls for kids getting these things stuck all the time. Never adults. Was this your plan? Because you know that you can just ask a girl out. You don't have to get her stuck in an elevator with you to make a move."

Beau winked and Jenna was glad her face was already flushed so they didn't see her blush.

"No comment," Jackson said.

"It was my fault," Jenna said. "I opened the door while it was moving."

Beau shook his head, tsk-tsk-ing. "Jenna. Didn't think you'd grow up to be a troublemaker. Jackson, let's get a look at that leg. Oh, my. That's some blood."

"How about we get out of this hallway," Jimmy suggested.

"Yes—let's go upstairs and sit down. Jimmy, you give my boy Jackson some support there."

"I'm fine," Jackson said.

"Sure you are, tough guy. I'm more worried about you getting blood on your fancy carpet. I've got Jenna. Tom, can you put some caution tape up over these elevator doorways. Make it official until you can get the repairman over here."

Beau helped Jenna stand on unsteady legs and practically carried her up the stairs, his arm around her waist. At the top of the stairs, Jenna realized that Megan stood nearby, filming the whole thing on her phone. Oh no. Was this going to go in one of her mini documentaries?

Normally Jenna would care more, but a wave of nausea passed over her. Black dots danced in front of her eyes, but cleared as Beau sat her down at the dining table, Jackson just across from her with his bloody leg propped up.

"Are you okay?" Jenna asked.

"It's nothing," he said. "A scratch."

"A scratch that cut right through your shorts," Jimmy said. He had the first aid kit and rolled up Jackson's pant leg, revealing a long, thin cut down the front of his leg.

"That's not nothing," Beau said. "Doesn't look like it needs stitches, but we'll see once Jimmy cleans you up. Jenna, you look pale. I'm going to get you some more water, okay?"

Jenna nodded and closed her eyes, hearing all the conversations around her as though they were happening in another room. She felt exhausted, like she might fall asleep right here at the table. Beau nudged her with a cold bottle of water.

"Drink," he said. She took a few sips then closed her eyes again.

Beau and Jimmy and Jackson were talking about something related to church and Wednesday nights. "All finished," someone—Jimmy?—said. Behind that sound she could hear Megan's voice asking questions, one of the other guys answering. The roar of the ocean grew louder in her ears, as though it was rising up and up and up toward them on the third story.

"I feel…" she started to say, but couldn't find the strength to finish.

That's when everything went black.

When Jenna opened her eyes, it took her a moment to place the smiling blond man hovering over her. He could have been Beau's brother: bulky muscles, wide grin, and hair that looked like it belonged in a surfing catalogue. Jimmy. That was his name. He had just said something and looked like he was waiting for a response, but she didn't have one.

"Hello." That seemed like a reasonable thing to start with. Her mouth felt dry, almost like her gums were pulling away from her teeth.

Suddenly it all rushed back: the memory of pulling the elevator door, her terror as the lights went out, Jackson's arms around her. When the memory of the kiss hit her, she gasped.

Jimmy's smiled disappeared into concern. "Are you okay? Jenna?"

She felt her skin flush. "I'm fine. Sorry."

From her position lying on the couch, she couldn't see anything but Jimmy's face and the ceiling. Was Jackson nearby? How did he feel about everything that just happened? Her gut clenched with worry. What if stepping outside the elevator flipped a switch, like what happened only existed in there? She blinked quickly, hoping to keep in the sudden tears that threatened.

Jimmy shifted over and Jackson's smiling face moved over her. The couch shifted as he sat next to her and took her hand, kissing her fingertips. Instantly her body released the worry that had tightened around her heart.

"I've got Megan until tomorrow, but would love to take you out in the evening. An official out-of-the-elevator first date. If you'll have me."

A date? A date!

"Yes." Jenna's smile was so wide that it hurt and when it released the tears she had been trying to stuff down, Jackson didn't look bothered at all, but simply brushed them away with his thumbs, smiling right back at her.

CHAPTER ELEVEN

"YOU KNOW that I'm the first person who wants your undying happiness, Jenns. But if you keep smiling like that through this whole dinner, I might lose my appetite."

"Smiling like what?" Jenna blinked innocently at Rachel, then laughed as her sister rolled her eyes and snapped open the thick, leather menu.

"Like you're in love." As Jenna choked on her water, Rachel kept going as though she hadn't just said that. "This place has changed a lot. What do you order now?"

"I'm sorry. Hit rewind. I am not in love with Jackson Wells."

"Yet. Not in love with him *yet*. Or ready to admit it anyway. Seriously, though, let's stick to the pressing matter at hand right now: tell me about this food."

Jenna gave Rachel a death glare, then sighed and picked up her menu. For now, she would let the comment rest. She didn't—couldn't—love Jackson. She had literally just gone from hating him to clinging to him and sharing a passionate kiss. And then agreeing to a date. Sure, there were feelings. But love?

"The last time I ate here was probably about the last time you did. It's been years. As long as the hushpuppies are still good, I don't really care."

She and Rachel were at JC's for dinner, the oldest seafood restaurant On Island. Rachel had insisted on seafood from near the actual sea, so here they were. When they were kids, coming with their parents, the restaurant had been full of scarred wooden tables, paper menus with grease spots, and the best hushpuppies in the world. Now it had dim lighting and linen tablecloths. The waiters and waitresses wore black slacks and pressed white shirts. Jenna felt underdressed in her jeans and button-down blouse.

"You and your hushpuppies," Rachel said with a groan.

"Look—you can get good seafood places in cities not on the water. Fresh shipping and all that. But you cannot get good hushpuppies everywhere. It's a fact. Forgive me for liking a side dish more than the main course."

"How do you mess up hushpuppies? It's fried cornmeal."

"Fried cornmeal and a whole lot of magic. Oh, trust me. You can mess them up."

"Okay, weirdo. Can you believe this is the same space as where we came as kids?" Rachel shook her head, looking around the dining room.

"We should see if either of our names are written on the bathroom wall," Jenna said.

"Stop. Neither of our names were ever on the bathroom wall anywhere. We weren't bad enough."

"Maybe we should write them there then. I think I've got a Sharpie in my purse."

Rachel laughed. "This place is fancy enough that you'd

probably get arrested now if you tried it. It's strange. The whole island has morphed into a very different place."

"It has. I don't like it. I mean, it still feels like it used to, but then not."

"Does it bother you that Jackson's company is responsible for a lot of the development?"

Clearly Jackson was going to remain the hot topic for the evening. She had already rehashed the kiss in the elevator multiple times. It filled her with giddy, girlish thrills when she had talked with Rachel about it. She'd much rather talk about his mad kissing skills than Wells Development.

Jenna made a face. "The reality is that the island is going to change. I'd rather have someone like Jackson who grew up here behind it than someone Off Island. A place like Sandover can't stay secret forever. The Outer Banks still retain some of the old with the new. We'll survive."

"It feels less like home every time I come back. And now—"

When Rachel broke off, Jenna knew exactly why. Her own throat had closed up as well, thinking of their mother. Of home. And the house that was and was not home, that was and would soon not be theirs anymore. Their eyes met across the table, both fiery with emotion. Naturally, the waiter chose that moment to return.

As they placed their orders, Jenna thought about the afternoon of packing up. The real estate agent had been gone by the time Jackson dropped her off. Rachel had avoided sharing what Kelly had said or what they discussed. Jenna knew it was coming, but had been content to let it go so far. She had other things on her mind. She and Rachel had finally cracked open the vault that was their mother's room and started going through her things together.

As they were packing up her mother's closet, Jenna came

across that yellow sweater she had always hated. Just the sight of that ugly yellow sweater had set her crying, clinging to the scratchy acrylic material among all the empty hangers. That started Rachel crying too, and they both sat weeping in the floor of their mother's closet until the crying turned to laughter about how much they both hated that sweater. And then they fought over who got to keep it. Finally, they decided it deserved joint custody. Rachel would start with it, then mail it to Jenna in a few months—a new tradition.

"Okay, sister. You've been tight-lipped about the meeting today with Kelly. Time to share how that went and why you put off telling me."

Rachel started fidgeting with her napkin and then moved on to play with the sugar packets, lining them up by color on the table. It was bad then. The house wouldn't sell? Or needed thousands in repairs? She needed to stop thinking of all the things it could be while she waited for Rachel to answer.

"We talked about the market and made a list of what needs to be done. She was impressed with how much we've —you've—done."

"And?"

"And we agreed to put the house on the market Saturday."

Jenna swallowed hard, her throat suddenly bone-dry. She took a sip of water, which had slices of cucumber and lemon. Normally, Jenna might like that touch, but today it made the water taste like plastic. She didn't want to have a fight with Rachel in their limited time together, so the pause gave her time to measure her words. It didn't really work.

"*We* agreed?" She scoffed. "Let's try you agreed. To seven days from now—*that* Saturday? You agreed to put the house on the market in one week. Even though you are leaving tomorrow and aren't coming back to do anything else. You're just dropping this in my lap and going?"

Jenna's voice rose with every word until she realized that she was close to shouting. Rachel looked apologetic, but it was the kind of apology where she wasn't sorry for what she had done, but sorry that Jenna was upset about it.

The waiter appeared with Jenna's Caesar salad and a cup of lobster bisque for Rachel. He had the worst timing.

"I'm sorry," Rachel said when the waiter had disappeared. She put her hand across the table, but Jenna moved out of reach. "I knew it would be challenging, but I thought it might be a good thing to rip the Band-Aid off."

"It's not your Band-Aid."

Rachel looked hurt, but also angry. "It's both of ours. We're in this together."

"We are in this grief together, yes. But as far as the house? We're only in it together this weekend. When you leave tomorrow, you're leaving me in it. Alone. To do whatever all needs to be done on the list you made without me, on the timeline you decided without me. And you just expect me to jump because you say so."

"I can't be here, Jenns. I have a life to get back to."

Jenna dropped her fork and it clattered against her salad plate. She was halfway to the bathroom before rational thought broke through. Her hurt and anger burned so deep that it seared her numb. When she reached the ladies' room, she gripped the countertop and stared at herself in the mirror. Her cheeks were flushed, her blue eyes darker than usual, a stormy sea.

They fought so rarely that Jenna didn't know how to do it. Rachel decided things. Jenna agreed. That's how it went, and she was mostly happy with it, or at least content to not have the weight of decisions fall on her shoulders. This was too much. The "I have a life" comment cut too deeply. The truth in the words made it hit harder and hurt more.

Rachel had all the things Jenna thought she would: the great husband, the kids, and the shared faith that kept them all together. Jenna had an ex-husband, which felt worse to her than never having a husband at all, no house, no job, no roots. Her faith had been shaken and her future felt like looking into fog.

But Rachel was right—these things made Jenna the only one of them who really could take on the project of their mom's house. She had even agreed to it. Jenna knew this, but that didn't dim her strong feelings about it. Right or not, Rachel should have asked. And she shouldn't have said what she did. It was a low blow.

Though it was justified, Jenna's anger felt ugly, the same way that it had when she said so many cutting things to Jackson over the last week. She didn't want to be this person. Was it grief? Had it made her ugly and angry?

Jenna sighed out a breath and washed her hands, even though she didn't need to. The cool water soothed her and the scent of the lavender soap made her feel fresh and lighter. Rachel would apologize. Jenna could let it go. And she could gather her strength together and get the house ready.

When she came back out to the table, there was a plate full of hushpuppies sitting in the center of the table that she hadn't ordered. Clearly, a peace offering. Rachel's eyes were full of apology.

"Two things," Rachel said, chewing. "First of all, I'm sorry that I made the decision without asking you. We can totally call Kelly and shift the dates." Jenna nodded, waiting. Rachel swallowed. "And second, you were completely right about the hushpuppies. They should be their own food group. How am I just figuring this out?"

"I've tried to tell you for years."

"I should have listened."

"You should have." Jenna took one of the hushpuppies from the plate. It was still warm and just the right color brown. Sometimes they got over-fried, leaving them too-brown and burnt-tasting. When she took a bite, the inside was still soft, almost doughy. The flavor of herbs and onion in the mild cornmeal exploded over her tongue. She moaned.

"Yep. They can change the décor all they want as long as they keep this recipe. Still the best On Island."

Rachel took a sip of water. "The other thing I'm sorry for is that comment. I honestly didn't mean it how it came out. It was a horrible thing to say and an apology isn't enough. Neither is a basket of hushpuppies."

"Actually, I think the hushpuppies made it all good."

"Are we okay?" Rachel asked.

Before answering, Jenna reached across the table and touched her sister's hand. "Yes. Don't bother calling Kelly to change the dates. I'll finish things up this week. It will be a good challenge for me. Though you now owe me, big time."

"Totally. One giant favor, owed to you. Done. Are you sure, though? I know this means rushing, but you can also make the closing date later if you need to. Kelly made a list of things she thought you could do before Saturday so they could have an open house. We can go over it if you want."

"I'll be fine. Remember I sell homes for a living? I know what to do and how to stage a house for sale. Let's just enjoy dinner and not worry one bit about plans and packing and sad things. Okay?"

The waiter, finally timing this well, arrived with the main courses. The table was crowded with plates since Jenna had barely touched her salad and the plate of hushpuppies was definitely staying. She was relieved for a few minutes without conversation as they ate in companionable silence.

Seven days. This felt like another loss somehow, even though Jenna had known it was coming. Putting it on the market felt like a definitive ending. Not just to the house, but to her marriage and her mother's life. To life as she knew it. It was an ending without a beginning on the other side. At least, without a beginning Jenna knew about. She wouldn't need to move out right away. It might not sell quickly. But if it did, that didn't necessarily mean a quick closing date. She still had time to figure out the rest of her life. Or, at least, the next step.

To figure that out, she needed to know more firmly what was happening with Jackson Wells. They would have dinner tomorrow. She was already as nervous as she was excited to see him. Today had been such a 180-degree switch. At least for her. Jackson had been nothing but kind to her since she came back, so the flip had been all her.

Had he simply been waiting? Hoping? Did he really want her, specifically, or just someone? What had happened to him that he was so different now from who he had been? So many questions that she hoped to get answered. No matter what the answers were, though, she also did want more of the not-talking and just kissing. The thought made her smile around her food.

After a few minutes, Rachel set her fork down and groaned. "I don't want to go home tomorrow. Back to having every conversation interrupted by little people—even though I've missed them like crazy—and back to a diet that can't include fried shrimp. I have the perfect solution! Let's both move back into mom's house together."

"I'm sure Brady won't mind at all."

"He would veto this plan, even though he is a saint.

Maybe he and I should move back On Island, though. I mean, if you stay. It would be kind of amazing to raise kids here. I don't know about his law practice though and how much work there'd be here."

"On Islanders need lawyers too. But I don't know if I'll stay anyway. I've thought about moving to Burlington."

"Really? That would be amazing. I would love having you close by. The girls would freak. But Jackson. I mean, what's happening there?"

"I don't know. Today in the elevator, it was like Jackson unleashed. Telling me openly how he felt, kissing me. What if it was just in the moment?"

"Didn't he ask you to dinner after you got out?"

Jenna bit her lip. "He did."

"Maybe the situation simply allowed him to be bolder. It doesn't sound fake and you didn't feel like it was. Do you think something serious could happen between you?"

Jenna couldn't remember the last time she smiled so much in one day. "Ask me tomorrow night. Or later in the week. I honestly don't know. This whole thing is such a shock to me. I mean, even if things progress, could I stay for him? Should I? I've had enough of my life revolving around men and making bad decisions because of them."

"This was where you grew up. If you do stay, it wouldn't just be for him. It's different. For what it's worth, I think he's a great guy. My teenage self would be shocked to hear me say this, but we aren't kids anymore. There's a humility and a kindness to him that I think is rare. And if we're being shallow—"

"Which we're not." Jenna pointed her fork at Rachel.

"Which we're not, obviously, because we're better than that. But if we were—he does own our favorite grocery store and has a killer house on the beach."

"But we aren't being shallow."

"Never. We aren't those women. Deep and wide, deep and wide."

Jenna snorted. "Did you quote a classic Christian song to describe us?"

"Deep and wide are very general terms. But yes, I most certainly did. Problem with that?"

"None at all."

"Good. One last thing on Jackson. I wouldn't be a good sister if I didn't tell you to be careful."

Once again, Jenna felt whiplash from Rachel's words. "You just said all this good stuff about him! Now you're telling me to watch out. What happened to him being awesome and mega-rich and blah blah blah?"

Rachel toyed with her fork and Jenna's stomach sank. She had already been through a range of emotions today between the elevator, the packing, and this dinner. What little control she had left was hanging by a thread.

"I do like Jackson. The thought of you with a great guy makes me happy. I just want you to be careful. I'm worried about you. You've been hurt worse than anyone should be and haven't been loved the way you deserved. Not ever. I worry that it's too soon for you to trust someone else. Jackson isn't the guy we knew back then. But that doesn't mean he can't break your heart."

Jenna's stomach fell. Worry began to gnaw at her and she grimaced. "I wasn't thinking about having my heart broken, but now I am. Thanks for that."

"Aw, sis. You know I'm just trying to look out for you."

"Yeah, well. I'm the big sister, so that's supposed to be my job for you. And I'd like to stop talking about big deep issues and finish these hushpuppies instead." She gave Rachel a smile that she hoped conveyed a lightness and a confidence she definitely didn't feel. "The sad thing about hushpuppies is that, like most fried food, they don't reheat well. So, we need to eat them now. Your shrimp can go home in a box. These can't. Eat up."

"Yes, big sister. Whatever you say."

Jenna tried to push away her worries and all the heavy things that hung over her to simply relish in her favorite food with her sister. But just under the surface, all those things sat, gathering and growing in the dark, like they were just waiting to rise to the surface. Rachel was probably right—this was too soon to get into a relationship. No matter how great of a guy Jackson had become or how quickly he had begun to invade her heart.

CHAPTER TWELVE

THE TASTE of sushi had grown on Jackson slowly, but the way it provided easy conversation made him an instant fan. Turns out that Megan could talk sushi for hours. Her mother, Kim, was just the kind of woman to raise her daughter in pretentious sushi restaurants. But for this one thing, Jackson was glad.

Most of the time, Megan spoke to him in annoyed sounds: huffs, grunts, eye rolls. Okay, eye rolls didn't make noise. She still did all these things across the table from him at Tsujiki, but she loved sushi so much that her reactions were all tempered. They became affectionate somehow. Like they moved from: "you're so annoying, I hate you" to: "you're so annoying; it's adorable." She seemed to like Jackson's questions. And, for this little window of time, she wasn't just staring at a screen of some kind.

"Tempura ... do I like tempura?"

"Yes. Tempura is that fried batter. You know, the little crispy crunchies that come on top of the Spicy Crunchy

Yellowtail? There are also some rolls that are put in tempura batter and fried, so they're warm not cold. Like the Dynamite Roll."

"I like crunchies. Warm sushi? Pass. Eel sauce—do I like that?"

"You aren't a fan."

"Good to know."

"You do realize that you could write this down. Or put it in a notes app on your phone or something." She sighed and he smiled.

"I should really do that." He wouldn't.

Megan rolled her eyes. "I want to try something new—are you in? Let's try the Spider roll. It has soft shell crab fried inside it. The presentation is fun."

"Fried anything is always okay with me. And crab, yes. You got me all excited about the crunchies, so I want the Spicy Crunchy Yellowtail. You pick the rest. New or old, I don't care. I do want vegetables tempura if you'd like to split."

"Are these dinners the only time you eat vegetables?"

He grinned. "Maybe."

Megan dipped her head to write down their selections on the paper sushi menu, but Jackson caught her smile before she did. Just like sushi softened her annoyance with him, it tempered his frustrations over her bossy, precocious attitude. How was she twelve and talking to him—an adult, her father —the way she did? But over sushi, he appreciated her taking charge.

Not for the first time, Jackson wondered who Megan would be if he had been in her life since the beginning. Probably not much different, considering that he had been a mess for a long time. If Kim had told him that she was pregnant, maybe he would have walked through the doors of the church sooner, at least from desperation.

It felt inevitable that he had ended up there, like it hadn't even been a choice, as though God had been sitting there, looking at his watch, waiting for Jackson to arrive. Maybe that was a blasphemous mental picture, but Jackson didn't particularly care. He liked the idea that God had just been waiting on him to wise up.

Maybe Kim would have told Jackson and then he would have married her. He wasn't so much of a jerk that he wouldn't have at least offered. Even if they really couldn't stand each other. She put up with him now, the little they texted about Megan's schedule, because of the money. He knew that. And it was one of the only times that he was glad that he had money. It meant that he could have a relationship with Megan.

He did wish that it had started earlier. That she hadn't been so fully-formed when she met him. Obviously, Kim had filled her head with a lot of ideas about him, probably some of them true. He deserved a lot of the terrible things people said about him, just as he had endured Jenna's insults. Then her harsh words changed into something very different.

"Are you still smiling about your new girlfriend?"

"You mean my bae?"

Megan grunted. "Getting trapped in an elevator is a cliché, you know. We aren't actually living in a Hallmark movie, so the likelihood of you guys ending up together is slim in real life."

"Thanks for that reality check, I guess."

"I always appreciate people speaking the truth to me. I'll do that for you. It's a sign of affection."

Jackson stared at Megan. She had never said anything that remotely hinted at the fact that she liked him. He probably should have kept things light, but he couldn't. "You have affection for me?"

Cue the eyeroll. "Of course, J. We're blood. Even if you wish we weren't."

She said that last part in little more than a mumble as she picked up her phone. Jackson ripped it from her hand and then dropped it, taking her hand in his own. She gazed up at him in shock.

"I would never—have never—wished you weren't mine. Not one time. Is Kim telling you this? Or have I given you any even a tiny indication that I wasn't glad to have you in my life?"

He had never seen the look on her face, mouth hanging open. "I—" She closed her mouth and looked down at her hand in his.

"If I have not shown you that I am so happy to have you in my life, then I am so sorry. I will start to fix that right now. It was an amazing day when Kim called to tell me about you. I wish she had done it years earlier. I hate that I've missed most of your life so far, but I don't want to miss the rest of it. That is my commitment to you. I want to be here, be involved. However you'll have me. I'll let you choose. But it will never be because of me that we aren't close. I will do all that I can."

Was it too much? Had he pushed too hard? Maybe he was still feeling overwhelmed with the rush of feelings that came out of the afternoon with Jenna. He held his breath, waiting for Megan to make a wisecrack and go back to eye rolling.

"Jenna," she said suddenly. Not what he'd been expecting.

He blinked. "What about Jenna?" He loved the way her name felt on his lips. Not as good as the way her lips had felt on his, but still good.

"She's cool. I like her and I hope that it works out with you guys."

For the second time that night, Jackson felt shocked. Thankfully the waitress arrived with a giant plate full of sushi. He needed a moment to adjust his face and temper his reaction. The one parenting lesson he'd learned quickly was that keeping your composure was a necessity. Shock and hot reactions to things had the effect of blood in the water. Megan wanted to shave half her head? That's fine. She thought socialism and communism had a lot of valid points? Okay.

Half the time she said things, he felt like it was just to get a reaction. If he had freaked out about the idea of head-shaving, she would have done it, and then told Kim it was his fault. If he had explained the effects of communism and socialism on various countries, she probably would have joined some kind of communist school club. Or started one. Would schools even allow it? Probably.

By the time the waitress moved away, he had schooled his face into something more relaxed. He and Megan filled their small dishes with soy sauce. She liked to put wasabi in hers, stabbing it with her chopsticks until it formed a slurry. Jackson tried that once and couldn't take the burn of it on his tongue and how it made him sneeze. He broke apart his chopsticks and rubbed them together the way Megan had showed him to remove any tiny splinters.

She smiled at him. "This is a feast, J. Check out the Spider Roll. What do you think?"

Megan giggled and picked up a piece of the Spider Roll, where the battered and fried crab legs were poking out of the middle. "Looks like a sci-fi movie, where the food is trying to escape."

"You're right. Night of the Living Sushi."

"Do you like horror movies?"

"I do. Mostly because Kim hates them. I mean, that's how I got started watching them. But now I actually like them a lot. You?"

"Yes. It's been a while since I've been to see one, though."

Her eyes lit up and she leaned forward. "There's this Japanese one that looks terrifying. It's got subtitles, but still. We should go. There is a movie theater here, right?"

"Yes. It's not the nicest or newest. Surf and Cinema. Want to check to see if it's showing? They don't have everything."

"They'll have this. It's been killing it."

Jackson did like horror movies. Maybe. He had liked them when he was a teenager. Probably the last one he saw in the theater was … he couldn't even remember. He used to watch them on VHS. Rented out from the now-closed Blockbuster. He definitely wouldn't tell Megan this or he'd lose more points. Hopefully he could still stomach scary. If he could learn to like sushi, he could do Japanese horror with his daughter.

"We're on. I got tickets already. There were only a few good seats left."

Jackson's eyebrows shot up. Megan had not ever offered to buy anything for him. Did she even have money? He hadn't seen her get out a wallet. She must have some kind of app on her phone. "Thank you. I can pay for it though."

She smiled and picked up her chopsticks and the Spider Roll, which had been soaking in her soy/wasabi combo. "It's the least I can do. Consider it a birthday present. When is your birthday, again?"

"August 15th."

"Happy early birthday, then. Try the Spider Roll. I need to know if you like it. Does Jenna like sushi? We should bring her the next time I'm in town. If she doesn't like it, you'll need to decide if that's a deal breaker. It would be for me. But then, it grew on you."

Jackson absolutely had no words to respond to the ones coming out of Megan's mouth tonight. If he said what he wanted to, which was something along the lines of who are you, it would have ruined the mood completely. So instead he took the other piece of Spider Roll with the legs sticking up. He liked the crunch and the flavor of the crab, mild yet good.

"It's good," he said. "I always feel weird eating crab though. It's not like a chicken breast, where it looks nothing like a chicken. I'm eating legs and it looks like legs."

"I know what you mean. So, you'll ask Jenna then? If you haven't screwed it up somehow before I come the next time." She rolled her eyes.

That was more like it. Jackson laughed. "I'll ask. And try not to screw it up. No promises though. My track record isn't so good, but I'll do my best."

"You're not ugly and you're a millionaire. If you can't keep a woman, then something is definitely wrong with you."

Billionaire. But Jackson didn't correct her. She had given him more in this conversation than in any they'd ever had. He would take it. Even sandwiched between annoyed insults. His long-time crush had kissed him. His daughter was talking to him. That was more than he could have hoped for.

"You might want to keep her away from electronics or heavy machinery, though," Megan said.

"Noted. What brought this on? I mean, why are you thinking about Jenna?" *And why are you talking to me all the sudden?* He wouldn't say that one out loud, but wished he knew.

"You like her. So, I just wanted you to know. That you, like, have my approval or whatever. In case you care."

Jackson felt a rush of emotion and swallowed before he answered, a lump in his throat. "I do," he said, not sure if he meant that he did like Jenna, did care what Megan thought, or both.

It was definitely both.

CHAPTER THIRTEEN

WHEN JENNA CALLED him a few hours before their date on Sunday night, Jackson had to fight back panic. He had been waiting for things to go wrong since they had stepped out of the elevator. He hoped for the best, obviously, but in his experience, too many good things at once meant disappointment. And the conversation and the kiss had been very, *very* good things.

He could hear it in her voice as soon as he answered. "What's wrong?"

Jenna sighed. "Here's the thing: Rachel told the realtor we'd put the house on the market Saturday."

"This Saturday? Like, this weekend. Why did she say that? She's not even here."

"That's what I said. Anyway. I don't want to cancel dinner. But ... I'm also stressed out and up to my neck in boxes."

Jackson could hear the overwhelm in her voice. "I've got this. You stay. I'm going to show up in a bit with supplies:

food, more food, and anything else you need. What else do you need?"

"I don't want to drag you into this. It's depressing. And not fun."

"You're not dragging me into anything. You and I will make it fun—well, as fun as this task can be. Now, what can I bring?"

Her voice sounded relieved. "Besides food, which it sounds like you've got covered, I need some music or something. It's too quiet over here. Everything echoes. Do you have some kind of Bluetooth speaker thing or whatever the kids are using these days? Mom didn't have anything like that. Well, a boom box that still worked somehow. But I donated it to the Goodwill along with her horrendous music selection."

Jackson chuckled. "I'm on it."

"Are you sure? I mean, this is hardly a good first date."

"If we count the elevator as our first date, then this seems like a perfectly appropriate second date. Any food preferences? Cravings? Things you hate."

"I hate pickles. Otherwise? Surprise me."

That wasn't stressful at all—surprising a woman he had liked from a distance for years but barely knew. But if there was one thing Jackson could do, it was rising to the challenge, especially where Jenna was concerned. Even if that meant getting takeout and ordering one of everything. He was going to get this right.

His relationships in the past had been shallow at best. Jackson hadn't even been on a date since he became a Christian, so he didn't know what this looked like in reality. The three guys he trusted as examples—Beau, Jimmy, and Cash—weren't dating anyone. Well, Jimmy was, but Jackson was just waiting for him to announce that he broke up with Amber. He was clearly still hung up on his ex.

Jackson hadn't really seen a great example of what it looked like to date seriously, intentionally, and with God as part of the equation. But he knew that he wanted to treasure Jenna, to woo her, to win her over. He wanted this to end with her walking down the aisle toward him. That thought should have shocked him, but it only got him more excited.

Yeah, it was fast. But they weren't kids with no experience. He hadn't met her and fallen in insta-love. But he knew Jenna had—up until a few days ago—acted like he was gum on the bottom of her shoe. It seemed like he was finally getting the second chance he wanted. And then some. It terrified him, but Jackson felt more determined than ever. Pushing had worked, so he would keep on pushing until he got past all her walls and found his way to her heart.

Jenna felt a giddy, girlish excitement to see Jackson on the porch. She meant to play it cool, especially considering they hadn't talked yet about where they stood. Instead she opened the door and launched herself at him. He took a step back, thankfully not falling off the front porch, and shifted the bags in his arms, doing his best to return the embrace with no free hands. With her face pressed into his neck, she felt suddenly shy.

"Hey," she said, her lips barely grazing against the stubble on his neck. Did he always have that amazing five o'clock shadow? How often did he have to shave? These were questions she wanted answered. If not right now, very soon.

He chuckled. "This is the best greeting I've had maybe ever. Hey right back at you." When Jenna didn't make a move to let go of him, he shifted on his feet. "Not that I'm complaining per se, but these bags aren't getting any lighter. I'd love to be able to hug you back."

Jenna pulled away and grinned at him. "Were all those muscles just for show? You can't lift a few grocery store bags yourself?"

"Oh, you noticed my muscles, huh?"

"No. Maybe. It's not like you aren't aware that you have them."

Jackson just gaped at her while she swiped one of the bags from his hand and darted into the house. She giggled, hearing him chase after her to the kitchen, where they both arrived a little breathless and grinning. Jackson set his bags down on the floor and walked purposefully toward Jenna.

"Now I can give you a proper hug." He pulled her in close, wrapping his arms around her waist and bending his head to the place where her shoulder met her neck. "With my muscles."

She giggled again and he smiled, lips tracing over her skin and sending shivers all the way down her legs. "How did you get in such good shape, anyway?"

He stiffened against her and didn't answer right away. Touchy subject?

"I have a punching bag under the house. And I work out with Beau and Jimmy at the station sometimes."

The answer sounded somewhat innocuous, but Jenna could feel the tension in his body. There was some back story, but she wasn't going to push him for it. Not yet. She rubbed her hands up and down his back. "Ready to get to work?"

Jackson pulled away suddenly. Placing his hands on either side of her face, he was suddenly serious. "I need something from you, Monroe."

Her heart pounded at his intensity. "Anything. Well, within reason. You strike me as a reasonable man."

"I'm pretty unreasonable most of the time, but this one thing should be simple." He paused. "I need a kiss from you in the daylight. To be sure that what happened yesterday in the elevator wasn't a dream."

"I need that too," Jenna said. "I've been afraid you might regret—"

Before she could finish the sentence, his lips were on hers, the sweetest interruption. Where yesterday there had been feverish passion full of unspoken words, this kiss felt languid and unhurried. His lips pressed lightly against hers, never settling for long, leaving her breathless and light-headed.

He pulled only far enough away to rest his forehead on hers, his breath feather-light against her cheek.

"No regrets," Jackson said. "Other than wishing I hadn't waited so long. Sometimes I think—what if I had told you how I felt back then?"

"I'm not sure we were the people we needed to be back then. It may not have worked at all. It's hard to play the what-if game."

"I think you're right. And I'm glad for the time right now. Speaking of right now, I'm here to help. Want to wait on the food or are you ready for a break right now?"

Jenna groaned. "Break. Food. I don't know how much more I can do today. I'm at that point where I just want to burn it all down."

"Dinner, then. Because we can't have Beau and Jimmy showing up with the fire truck for every date." Jackson began to pull things out of bags. When Jenna realized that they were Bohn's bags, she groaned.

"I should have warned you. I don't have pots and pans or anything to cook with."

"Cooking?" Jackson smirked. "I think you have me confused with someone else. I let the café do the heavy lifting on this one. And you should be glad about that. The only version of cooking I do is manning a grill. I flip a mean burger."

"Okay, so you want to address our flaws right now? Well, I don't cook either. I do think I could grill without burning a hot dog, though. Maybe."

"Sounds like a challenge. Next time you're at my place, we'll have a grill-off."

Jenna giggled. "You're on." She leaned against the counter as he continued unloading: a delicious-smelling rotisserie chicken, roasted potatoes, green beans with almonds, a big salad, and a bottle of wine.

She admired the food, but also Jackson. Other than a few lines around his eyes and a much bigger build, Jackson looked like he could have stepped right out of the Sandover High yearbook in his jeans and fitted gray T-shirt.

"Like what you see?" Jackson wiggled his eyebrows at her.

"Yes, dinner looks fantastic." She bumped her hip into his. "No wine for me, though. I know that our first meeting last week was me trying to buy wine at the ungodly hour of nine in the morning, but I've actually stopped drinking. At least for a while. I don't think I have a problem, per se, but it was becoming a crutch. Since we're sharing all our flaws tonight. Might as well share that one."

Jackson studied her. Jenna was afraid that she might see judgment or disappointment there, but instead she saw something like respect. "That's really wise. You've been through a lot, so it's understandable. Actually, other than losing your mother, which is huge, I know very little about what's been happening with you."

She chewed on her bottom lip. It made sense to cover all this early on, but Rachel's warning about moving too fast echoed in her mind. Jackson didn't miss her obvious hesitation and reached for her hand, enveloping her fingers in his. The gesture made her feel at once cared for and safe.

"You don't have to talk to me about this, Jenna. At least not yet. I mean, we're on date two. Or one, depending on how you count."

"You kissed me in the elevator, so I think it has to count as our first date. Or half date. Maybe this is one-point-five. I'd like to talk to you about my disastrous marriage, if nothing else, to get it out of the way. But we definitely need food first."

Jackson gave her fingers a final squeeze before letting go. He turned and fixed them each a paper plate of food. "I totally cheated and texted Rachel for food tips. I hope that's okay."

"How did you get her number?"

"Church this morning."

"Oh." Her jaw clenched. Jenna had refused to go with Rachel this morning, at first saying she wanted to get work done, and then, when pressed, simply snapped at her sister. It had been almost six months since she had been inside a church or cracked open the Bible. She didn't want to talk about it with Rachel, or anyone. But of course, Jackson pressed.

"Out of curiosity, why didn't you come?" Jackson abandoned the plates for a moment and turned to face her.

Tension radiated from her body as Jenna fought to find words. When she met his eyes, they weren't accusing like she had expected. Only curious. Concerned, even. She sighed. "I haven't been in months. God and I are kind of in a fight."

His lip quirked, but he didn't smile. "A fight, huh? Who's winning?"

"Definitely not me. I'm not sure he's actually fighting, so it's a little one-sided." It felt like a relief to say the words, especially to see the way Jackson nodded like he understood. And he seemed to get the fact that this was a hard admission to make because he turned and picked up the plates. "Where are we eating?"

"How about the back deck? It's not as great a view as yours, but still pretty nice."

The wrought iron table and chairs on the deck were covered in a thin layer of pollen, so Jenna wiped them down and Jackson carried out the plates. Jackson jumped up as soon as they sat down. "One more thing! I left it in the car. Eat—don't wait."

He ran down the steps from the porch to the driveway and returned a moment later with a small plastic bag from Surly's, a big box store near the edge of the island that sold everything from clothes to home goods. He set it in front of her plate and sat down again, smiling and looking pleased with himself. Jenna pulled a small box from the bag.

"Excuse the wrapping. It's a Bluetooth speaker," Jackson said. "You said you wanted music."

"I meant for you to bring something, not buy me something."

"I knew what you meant."

Jenna took the small gray speaker out of the box, trying not to look at Jackson. It was a small cylinder that fit in the palm of her hand. Surly's wasn't a high-end kind of store, but the gesture was everything. She very clearly remembered the last gift that Mark had bought for her. Not a Christmas or birthday gift, but a just-because gift. The kind with no occasion.

The memory was clear because it was so rare: five years ago, he had picked up a hardcover book for her from the airport bookstore on his way home from a business trip. A thriller, when she usually read women's fiction. "I thought you might like it. I read it on the plane," he had said. Not really a present at all.

"I can set it up for you if you want." Jackson's voice jolted her back to the present. "Bring me your phone."

Jenna couldn't speak until she had gotten the thick knot of emotion in her throat under control. She passed it across the table and got up to get her phone from the kitchen. When she brought back her phone, he had everything set up.

"It's ready. It should automatically connect to the speaker whenever you're home. If not, just open the Bluetooth settings on the phone and make sure they're on. Think you can handle that, Monroe?"

She grinned at the nickname. It immediately made her feel closer to Jackson. She wanted to ask him to say it again and again. "I think I can handle this."

"Pick a song. Let's see this baby in action." He clapped his hands together.

Jenna scrolled through her music and hit play. The speaker came to life and Jenna leaned back in her chair, closing her eyes with a smile. Despite the pressure of all she still had left to do inside the house, the music instantly relaxed her. She finally stopped hearing the doubt from Rachel's warning and the other worries that had gathered like storm clouds. The song swept them all away.

"Care to dance?" His chair scraped back and Jenna opened her eyes to see him standing over her, holding out his hand.

"Shouldn't we eat?"

"Food can wait. The music's calling."

"I don't really dance. And this isn't exactly dancing music."

"I'm a terrible dancer. I just sway. You can handle that. Sway with me, Monroe."

Taking his hand, Jenna let him pull her up and then flush against him. True to his word, he swayed her in small circles over the porch. Though she had never danced with Jackson, everything about this felt familiar. The feel of his hands on her waist, the way their bodies aligned perfectly, and even his smell. It was not something she could name, exactly, but just *Jackson.*

This was her favorite kind of music—folky and acoustic with rich lyrics. It seemed to wrap around them, blanketing them in peaceful notes and rich melodies. Even though she said it wasn't dancing music, it was exactly perfect for this moment with Jackson. Their first dance, on the back porch of her childhood home, wrapped up in his arms.

"Who is this, by the way?"

"Iron and Wine."

"I haven't heard of them."

"Him. It's a guy."

"I think I like it."

"Let's hope so. That's kind of a prerequisite." Jenna nestled her head closer to his chest.

"We've gone from sharing our weaknesses to having prerequisites. Let me know next time so I'm prepared. Here I thought this was a simple second date."

"You mean one and a half-th date."

"Can't get anything past you, Monroe. Anyway, I'm glad I like the music so I don't get kicked out on date one-point-five."

"It's my soul music," she said, not intending to say it. The words sounded silly out loud.

But Jackson did not laugh and instead kissed her temple, letting his lips linger. "I can see that. Or—hear it, I guess. It's you. Jenna Monroe Music."

"Do you really know me well enough to say that?" Jenna mentally cringed at the words. She hadn't spoken sharply, but they felt too honest.

Jackson didn't even flinch. "Tough question with a complicated answer. I feel like I know you so well and not at all. I told you yesterday that I liked you back in high school. Really, I have since then. Not in a creepy way, but I always watched you." He chuckled. "Okay, that still sounds creepy. I noticed you. I felt like a moth to a flame. If you were somewhere, I noticed. But, obviously, we weren't ever close. I only know what I saw."

"What did you see?" Jenna felt greedy whispering the question, but after Mark, she felt like she needed more commitment before she could fully open herself up to even the possibility of him. This thing with Jackson, it was powerful and fast. Like a riptide, he was pulling her away from safe shores. She needed some assurance of faith that she could really trust him.

His arms tightened around her and his lips moved to her cheek, where his breath fanned over her skin as he spoke. "I saw a girl who loved well and loved hard. Fierce and loyal, funny and unique. A girl far too good for the guy she was with, and far too good for me."

"Jackson—"

"Don't argue, Monroe. It was true back then and is true now. I will never feel good enough for your love, should you ever offer it. But I'm not stupid enough to turn you away if you do. I will simply be thankful for the gift." He pulled back enough that he could cup her face in his hands. "That's what you are, you know. My gift."

She had no words. Jenna wanted to respond in a way that told him how treasured he made her feel. She longed to find a way to tell him the goodness and kindness she saw in him. But the ability to speak escaped her. Instead, Jenna lifted up on her toes and placed a gentle kiss on his lips. Just one sweet, tender kiss.

Sighing, she pressed her face back into his neck. His chin rested on her hair and he lifted a hand to touch her neck, the barest motion of his fingertips. It sent a shudder down the length of her body.

Remember this moment, she told herself, trying to take in every part of it to commit to memory. The warm melody of "Claim Your Ghost" played around them. The night sounds of frogs and insects stirred awake in the marsh woods behind them, what she always thought of as summer sounds. As she continued to sway, safe in Jackson's arms, Jenna began to believe that just maybe, this moment was the beginning of many more beautiful moments to come with this man whose arms felt like home.

CHAPTER FOURTEEN

JACKSON CRACKED his neck and stretched while waiting for Mercer to answer her phone. He had stepped out onto Jenna's back deck so she wouldn't overhear the call. She picked up after a few rings, sounding breathless. "Hey, Mercer. Are we all set for Saturday's first farmer's market?"

"I think so. I've tried to plan for everything, but it's hard to know exactly what you'll need until you've had an event once." She snorted. "Then, of course, you see all the things that should have been done but weren't."

"It's going to be great. I'm sorry I haven't been around this week to help. Not that you need it."

Jackson had spent the last five days with Jenna, helping pack up her mom's house. And talking and kissing. If it hadn't been for the impending deadline, he wouldn't have minded a little less work and a lot more kissing. He knew she needed his help and the task did keep Jackson from pushing her boundaries too hard. He hoped, anyway. Every day it seemed like Jenna opened up a little bit more, her walls crumbling bit by bit. That had to be a good thing, though

Beau had warned him to let things unfold naturally, not to force things too fast.

After all this time, Jackson didn't want to scare her off by going too fast, even if in his mind, he was already there. He knew what he wanted—had dreamed of for a long time—and keeping pace was a constant battle. Jenna's marriage had ended only months before. Though it was clear she had no lingering feelings toward her ex, Jackson worried that jumping into another marriage so soon would send her running, far and fast. But his mind had already moved firmly into the marriage camp. So much of his life felt like wasted time. He wanted to spend the rest of it loving this woman and building a life with her.

And after hearing about her ex, Jenna deserved love and a happy life. Jackson had a hard time keeping his anger in check when she told him about Mark's many affairs. She had looked so vulnerable, lip trembling and looking down at her lap. He knew that he couldn't take away her hurt, but he wanted to show her just how much she meant to him and how much worth and value she had. He struggled with a constant tension between letting all his feelings hang out and pulling back so he didn't rush her. She didn't trust easily. Jackson needed to earn and keep her trust. That wouldn't happen for her in a week.

So he didn't press her for a conversation on what was happening between them. He simply showed up at her house every day with a smile, ready to help, hoping that her desire would unfold to match his. It kept him in a state of constant tension, trying to hold himself back. He kept his internal struggle and his rage toward her ex under wraps, taking it out on the punching bag at home every night.

"What happened to your hands?" she had gasped when

he showed up with bloody knuckles the morning after she told him about Mark.

Jackson had been so mad that he had gone straight from his Jeep to the heavy bag, not taking the time to wrap his hands. "Oh, just some boxing practice." He couldn't even regret it when Jenna fussed over him, insisting on icing his hands and then giving him a hand massage. Which had nothing to do with sore knuckles and everything to do with the fact that she clearly craved being close to him the same way he relished her touch.

Mercer's voice broke into his thoughts. "You will be here Saturday, right? This week has been fine, but I think it's important that you're there."

"Of course. Jenna's house will officially be on the market, which means we'll be done here. She'll meet me there. But I'll be there early and all day to help. She knows I'll be doing work and promised to help as well, or entertain herself if she needs to."

There was a brief pause. "I'm really happy for you, Jackson."

He smiled. "I'm happy for me too." Glancing toward the house, he made sure that Jenna was out of earshot. "I know you'll be busy with the new Bohn's Local stuff, but any new houses to look at? The one yesterday was just okay. Fine, but not great."

Jackson had given Mercer another task: to find a place for Jenna to live. She had been too stressed this week to even think about options. Was this pushing too far? It probably crossed a few lines. Maybe more than a few. But Jackson was working on a way to help without seeming like he was helping, hence the secrecy.

"I agree. An okay option, but not perfect. I've got a few other houses. I'll send you an email with the listings."

He grinned. "You are so fantastic. Thank you."

Jackson caught Jenna watching him through the window, her expression unreadable. Hopefully she hadn't heard him. He dropped his voice and turned his back to Jenna.

"Thanks, Mercer. See you Saturday. Call me before if you need anything."

"Everything okay?" Jenna joined him just as he hung up the phone. He slipped it into his back pocket and pulled her in close.

"Just finalizing plans with Mercer for the Farmer's Market Saturday. I hope you'll still come with me."

"Mercer, huh? I forgot about the Farmer's Market, but I'd be glad to be anywhere but here. Are you sure you don't need to be at the store right now, getting things set up?"

"I have complete faith in Mercer. She's amazing."

Jenna smiled, but Jackson could read something in her eyes. She seemed hesitant or upset. Packing up her mother's life and all the memories was heavy work. He had done his best to lighten her mood, to keep her fed and laughing, but it was still emotionally taxing.

"Everything okay?" He brushed her hair back from her face, letting his hand linger on her neck. She shivered and then smiled again. A better, lighter smile this time.

"More than okay. Because I've got you. I do have you, right?"

"That shouldn't even be a question, Monroe. You've got me."

For as long as you'll have me. He bent down to kiss her when there was a frantic ringing of the doorbell. Jenna pulled back, giving him a rueful smile.

"Later," she said in a low voice. Jackson felt a thrill at the promise as he followed her inside. That was when they started hearing the sirens over the banging on the door.

Jenna flung open the door. An older woman stood on the porch. She looked vaguely familiar, but Jackson didn't immediately know her. The sirens were wailing right outside now, red lights flashing.

"Ethel!" Jenna grabbed the woman in a hug. "What's going on?"

"It's Bob. He fell. The ambulance is here. I just—I couldn't get Steve. He said he was with you earlier this week and I thought you could reach him. Can you tell him we're going to the hospital?"

Steve. Jackson closed his eyes, missing the rest of the conversation. How could he have forgotten that he had lived next door? His heart went out to Steve's mom even as it was also having a mild panic attack about the fact that Steve had been here earlier in the week. Why hadn't Jenna mentioned that?

"Jackson!"

Ethel had gone and Jenna stood in the doorway, staring at him. He had obviously missed something she said. "I'm sorry —what?"

"I need to go. I'm going to lock up their house and follow them to the hospital."

Jackson put his hands in his pockets, trying to channel the compassion for Steve's parents, shoving down the molten jealousy burning a hole in his chest. Behind her, a fire truck and cop car pulled up beside the ambulance. Jackson recognized Cash, Jimmy, and Beau. Great. If he talked to them, they wouldn't miss the fact that he was losing his cool over this. Beau and Jimmy knew about his history with Steve.

"Of course, go. Need me to do anything?"

Jenna gave him a quick kiss on the cheek and grabbed her purse from the front hall. Pulling a key from the door, she pressed it in his palm. "Do you mind turning off the lights and locking up here? I'm sorry to bolt like this."

A joke about giving out house keys died before hitting his lips. Not the right time. He needed to pull it together. He may not like Steve or his past with Jenna, but he should care that Steve's dad was hurt. Jenna certainly did. "I'll call you later. If you need me, I'll come up to the hospital with you."

She waved him off. "I'll be fine. Thanks, Jax."

She was already halfway out the door before he realized that she had used his nickname for the first time. *It had to be now.* Jackson wanted to kick himself for the sour turn of his attitude. Especially as he watched Jenna holding Ethel's hand as the paramedics wheeled her husband out, an oxygen mask over his face. Once the couple was safely in the back of the ambulance, Jenna disappeared into their house.

Jackson went through the house, turning off lights and straightening up a bit. When he locked the front door, Jenna was just dashing across the lawn to her car with a duffle bag over her shoulder. She waved once to Jackson while holding the phone in her other hand. Was she calling Steve? The thought was like poison, making his whole body feel sick. Jealousy was such an ugly emotion, like a poison.

The fire truck and police car were still out front, lights and sirens off now. Cash stood in front of his cruiser, talking to Beau, while Jimmy sat in the front of the truck, door open and legs out. When he saw Jackson, he jumped down and met him on the way to the truck.

"Hey. Jenna followed them to the hospital. Neighbors, huh?"

"And her ex's parents," Beau said. He and Cash joined them.

Jimmy's eyebrows shot up. "Steve? Those are Steve's parents?"

"*The* Steve?" Cash asked. "The one who is always trying to pick fights with you when we see him out?"

"Yep." Jackson rocked back on his heels. It had been a few months since they last saw Steve. But every time their paths crossed, he tried to find a way to provoke Jackson. It was like he never moved on from their high school drama and kept trying to bring it back to the surface.

"Jenna obviously cares about them. She's known them most of her life. I should be concerned and compassionate. But I also just heard his mother saying something about calling Steve and that he was over here this week." The other guys were silent for a beat. "Yeah, exactly my reaction."

Beau spoke first. He usually did. "It's natural for you to be upset. You can ask God for help feeling compassionate, but I don't think one of us would blame you for how you're feeling given your history with Steve and his history with Jenna."

Jackson looked down at the ground. He hated the feelings that were rolling around in his gut right now. They made him feel immature and weak and reminded him of the powerless sway his emotions held over him before he started going to church.

"Things are going so well with Jenna right now. But it's all new, you know? Tentative. I don't know if she's even planning to stay On Island or what's next. I've been afraid to push her, so I haven't told her how I feel or what I want. I know she's vulnerable and I probably shouldn't push things too fast. Knowing that Steve is trying to worm his way back in her life … I feel sick."

"Maybe you should go up to the hospital with Jenna," Jimmy suggested.

Jackson shook his head. "That's the last thing I need. I can't imagine his reaction if I show up there. Jenna doesn't need me going all caveman on her. I can trust her. She was burned by him before and I'm sure she has her guard up."

Beau clapped a hand on his shoulder and grinned. "You're a good man, Jackson. I mean, just as messed up as everyone else, but still. Good."

Jackson chuckled. "Thanks, I think?"

"We've got to get back, Jimmy. Load her up!" Beau called to the other firemen who were lounging around the back of the truck. Jimmy patted Jackson on the back before following Beau.

"Maybe I'm the odd man out, but I wouldn't let that guy anywhere near my girl," Cash said. "For what it's worth. It's not caveman. You're being practical, protecting your woman. Just my opinion. Anyway, see you later and let me know if you need anything."

Jackson got in his Jeep as the cruiser and the fire truck turned around in the small cul-de-sac and headed off. When he got to the entrance to Jenna's neighborhood, he hesitated, hand on the blinker. Left, toward his house. Right, toward the hospital. He wanted nothing more than to put everything on the line. To reassure Jenna that he was going to be there no matter what, not to let his fears and his jealousy and mistrust of Steve affect the way he behaved. Would she feel comforted if he showed up at the hospital or smothered?

With a silent prayer that he was making the right choice, Jackson turned left and headed away from the woman he had no doubt he loved.

CHAPTER FIFTEEN

JENNA HAD FELT like an intruder in Ethel's house. It was one thing talking with Ethel in the matching living room chairs, and another altogether going inside without them. Especially seeing Bob's chair turned over along with the tray table next to him. Her stomach dropped.

Had he fallen right here? Or was this from the stretcher and the team of paramedics? Somehow, she didn't think professionals would be so careless, even in a hurry. There was a dark spot that still looked damp on the rug. Was that blood? Her stomach turned a little, but Jenna found a dish towel in the kitchen and soaked it in cold water, pressing it to the spot. The rag quickly turned pink and her stomach rolled again.

She gave up on the stain, leaving the rag in the washing machine. She needed to get Steve's number and get to the hospital. When she told Ethel that she didn't have his number, Ethel said she could find his work and cell on the refrigerator. Sure enough, there was a typed sheet with contact numbers stuck to the fridge with magnets made from seashells. The sight made her suck in her breath. Her mother had a similar one on the side of the fridge that neither she nor Rachel had taken down. Ethel's sheet looked just like her mom's: a neatly typed sheet that had been taken over with hand-written notes in various colors of pen.

Steve's number was third, below Jenna's mom and Steve's older brother Jeff. Jenna saved both brothers' numbers in her phone and started calling as she hurried through the house, turning off lights. His cell rang and rang. Hearing Steve on the voicemail recording made her jaw clench. Where was he and why hadn't he answered his phone?

"Shoot me a text or something so I know you got this. Or call your mom. I'll probably see you up at the hospital," Jenna said before hanging up. She would stay as long as Ethel needed her, but she really hoped she could avoid seeing Steve.

It wasn't just that he was suddenly unavailable when his parents needed him. Thinking back to the week before when Steve had showed up at her house sent waves of unpleasant feelings through her. A part of her had felt the pull of nostalgia, even as she felt sure she needed to keep herself guarded from him. Though if she had been reading his signals correctly, he might have been tentatively feeling her out for interest. The thought made her shudder. She was with Jackson now.

Wasn't she?

They had spent most of the last five days together. It felt serious, which should have scared her. Especially with Rachel's warning popping into her mind every so often. But the more time they spent together, the more Jackson started to feel like a necessary part of her life. Someone she didn't know if she wanted to live without. And yet, he still hadn't even asked her to be his girlfriend. Every look, every touch, every kind gesture seemed to indicate how he felt, but he hadn't put it in words. Even the way he challenged her—albeit gently—about the way she had shut God out, even that spoke volumes about his feelings.

So why hadn't he said anything? Maybe she had been out of the game too long. She had a terrible track record with men: Steve, Mark, and a handful of guys in college who were hardly memorable. Who's to say she wasn't reading all the signs wrong?

And then there was that mysterious phone call on the deck. Had he really been talking to Mercer? She had caught the genuine smile on his face and the way his body hunched, like he was trying to hide from view. When she had stepped onto the deck, Jackson had immediately gotten off the phone. Though she had missed them with Mark, Jenna knew the signs of unfaithfulness. Furtive phone calls? Sign number one. Mercer was young and beautiful and they worked closely together. Maybe their relationship was more than professional. It wouldn't be the first time Jenna had fallen for a man who had another woman.

Now Jenna's stomach was in knots. This was exactly why Rachel had warned her about Jackson. It was clear even after a few days that he was completely capable of breaking her heart. Because if she was being honest, she had already given it to him.

Focus. She needed to focus on the task at hand. Feeling like she was violating some kind of code, Jenna went into Ethel and Bob's room to pack up an overnight bag. Surprisingly, the room had a minimalistic bent. Whereas the rest of the house had gold-framed paintings and upholstery and drapes, the bedroom had a simple white duvet, wooden plantation shutters on the windows with only gauzy white curtains, and a classic Oriental rug as the only real pop of color or richness.

Jenna grabbed a quilted bag in Ethel's closet and packed up a pair of soft gray pajamas, two pairs of underwear, a few shirts, a cardigan, and a small, matching toiletry bag that she found in the bathroom, already packed with a small bottle of lotion, a lipstick, and toothpaste. Before she left, she grabbed the book that sat on Ethel's bedside table, a cozy mystery with a cat on the front.

She tried Steve's work number as she jogged to her car. Seeing Jackson lock up her front door, Jenna's storm of emotion rose to the surface. He seemed like he belonged there—on the front porch of her childhood home with a key in hand. She wanted him there. Not at this house, but wherever home was. The realization sent a sharp wave of panic through her and she practically sprinted to the car, giving him a brief wave. Later. They could work this out later. She could ask him about the phone call, maybe press him for how he felt about her. No, that felt needy and desperate.

It took ten minutes to get to the new hospital. Well, new to Jenna. As of ten years before, you would have had to go by ambulance to the mainland. Now there was a very out-of-place, shiny glass box of a hospital on the main causeway, six miles south of her neighborhood. On Islanders referred to it as the Cube.

It wasn't hard to find Ethel and Bob, and Jenna had no trouble getting back to see them. Walking through the whishing automatic doors, Jenna was hit suddenly with the loss of her mother and it almost took her breath away.

For her mother, there had been no worried hospital visits.

No late nights. No talks with doctors or slow decline. No warning at all. Jenna had talked to her mom just a few days before she died—a totally normal phone call. Nothing special. After hearing the news, Jenna replayed that conversation over and over again in her mind, trying to remember if she had said "I love you" before hanging up.

When she was just a girl, her mother had spent weeks before Jenna's grandmother passed in the hospital. Her father made frozen dinners for Rachel and Jenna, barely holding down the fort. A few times he drove them up to the county hospital Off Island where her mom had a makeshift bed set up on the plastic-y couch. Her grandmother looked terrifying, like a shell of a woman, her eyes always closed, mouth always open. She remembered her mom massaging lotion into Jenna's grandmother's skin and applying balm to her cracked lips.

Though she felt relieved that she hadn't had to watch her mother waste away, Jenna felt somehow robbed that she didn't have the opportunity to care for her mother the same way. To rub lotion on her elbows, to hold a straw to her lips with water, to read books to her, even as she slept. Jenna did not think of herself as a natural caregiver, but she would have been for her mom. She would have loved that job.

Before walking into Bob's room, Jenna waited in the hallway until she felt like she could talk without tears spilling over her cheeks. Between worries about Jackson, frustration with Steve, and the ache of missing her Mom, Jenna's emotions threatened to unravel her.

"He's asleep," Ethel said as Jenna gave her a hug. In this setting, Ethel looked much older and frailer. Bob, too, hooked up to machines monitoring all the normal things.

"What do they think happened? Is he okay?"

Ethel sighed. "Nothing's broken, but he had a nasty cut on the back of his head. They stitched that up and are waiting for an MRI in the morning. I guess they can't be that concerned if they're not doing it tonight."

That or they didn't have the facilities or ability to do it now, Jenna thought. "I saw the blood on the rug. I did my best to put water on it, but it's probably going to stain."

Ethel waved a hand. "A rug is a rug."

Jenna handed her the duffle bag she had packed. "I brought this for you."

"Oh, you are such a dear. Thank you. I'm stuck here since I rode with the ambulance."

"I'm sure we can get your car up here, or I can drive you home and let you bring it back tomorrow or something."

"Steve can probably help. Did you get ahold of him?"

Jenna shook her head. "I left a message. Did you try him? He probably didn't recognize my number."

"I'll try again in a bit," Ethel said. "Nothing he can do now."

Nothing except be here. Jenna felt anger rise again, clogging her throat. She felt oddly protective of his parents, without having her own to protect. And of all the things causing her emotions to flare, she'd rather focus on this anger than the concern of what was happening with Jackson and the thoughts of her mom.

"Child, go home. You look exhausted. We are fine here. Bob is stable and, thanks to you, I have what I need to stay. Go."

She touched Ethel's arm. "Okay. Please let me know if I can do anything tomorrow. I can bring whatever you need. Or just run you home to shower and get the car if you can't reach Steve. Don't hesitate to call, okay? Just get some sleep if you can."

When Jenna left the room, Ethel was tucked into the hospital-issue recliner next to the bed, a taupe-y faux leather chair that probably was incredibly uncomfortable. Jenna's chest ached. Rage continued to bubble up toward Steve and his brother, Jeff. She had left a message for Jeff, too. He didn't live On Island, but close by and could have been here within an hour. Ethel shouldn't be alone. Here in the hospital, or even in the day-to-day at their house. With Bob's size and his dementia, it wasn't safe or fair.

For a smaller hospital, Jenna struggled to find her way out of The Cube. The emotions pressing down on her didn't help. Jenna ran straight into a wall of a man as she rounded a corner.

"Whoa, there!"

Not just any man: Steve. She immediately tried to back up, but he held onto her arms, a little too tightly, forcing her to stay in his space. She glared. He smiled.

"Where's the fire?"

The crooked grin on his face, the one that used to make her teenaged heart flutter, filled her with rage. "Steve, I've been calling you. Your father is up there in a hospital bed and your mother is sleeping in a chair. Where have you been?"

Of all the things her anger could do, it released her tears. Hot and sudden, they spilled over her cheeks and made her voice tremble. Today—this week—it had all been too much.

Steve's smile disappeared, replaced with concern that only made her more angry and made the tears come faster. He pulled her gently into his chest and she sobbed against him, even as she tried to pull away. After a moment, she gave up and let him hold her. It felt familiar and also wrong somehow, but she didn't have the energy to fight him.

"Aw, Jenna. I always hated to see you cry. I'm so sorry you couldn't get me. I was out on a boat. Can't always hear the

175

phone over the engine. I'm so glad you were able to be here for her since I couldn't. You have always been so good to my mom. Thank you. It means a lot to me."

These last words were little more than a murmur, his breath moving in her hair. Jenna stiffened, and felt a shudder move through her. Finding her strength, she shoved Steve back. They still stood in the middle of a busy hallway near a waiting room. Hospital sounds filled her ears at once and she felt instantly mortified. She stepped closer to the wall and out of the way of a nurse who shot them both a dirty look.

Steve leaned against the wall and ran a hand over his jaw. A pleased smile made her want to smack him. The tan line from his ring looked less pronounced and his cheeks were either sun- or wind-burned. His eyes, now that she was looking, had deep circles beneath them.

"You should get up there and see your parents."

His smile widened. "Always thinking of other people. That's my girl. I'm glad my family means so much to you."

Her brain had short-circuited when he called her his girl. She wasn't a girl. Or his.

"I do care about your *parents*."

Thinking of Jackson, she suddenly felt a jolt of guilt. What if he had followed her up here and seen her in Steve's arms? She had just been obsessing over Jackson's secretive phone call. Here she was with her ex, having what felt and looked like a more-than-friendly moment. She needed to put as much distance between her and Steve as possible.

Drawing back her shoulders, she crossed her arms. "Your dad is in room 241. I told your mom to let me know if she needs anything. She'll be glad you're here. Finally."

Jenna moved to walk past Steve and out the doors just on the other side of the waiting room. She didn't think her car was on this side, but at this point, did not particularly care. She needed to get out of the Cube. What she really wanted was to a take a hot shower and burn off this day.

Steve stepped in her path, blocking her. Her head tipped up and she parted her lips to tell him to move. Before she could even speak, his rough hand cupped her face and he crushed his lips into her.

The shock of it should have made Jenna jump back. But she froze. Which apparently made him think that she wanted this. Only when his hand curled around the back of her head and his mouth pushed more roughly against hers did she jerk away from him.

She stared at him, open-mouthed. "What are you doing?"

A slow grin moved over his face. "Nothing that you didn't want. It shouldn't surprise you, Jenna. We were always meant to return to each other. Childhood sweethearts, you know?"

"No. That's not our story, Steve. I'm with Jackson now."

She hadn't expected a smile, especially not a cruel one. It was a subtle but powerful shift in his eyes and Jenna felt like she saw Steve—really saw him—for the very first time. Not the childhood best friend and first boyfriend. Not even the guy who had cheated on her and dumped her for Anna. She saw what everyone else in her family must have always seen in Steve. With the mask peeled back, it revealed a Steve she didn't know.

"How's that working out? Do you like sharing him with Mercer?"

Her entire body felt like it had been submerged in below-freezing water. The shock of his words literally took her breath away. It was like he had seen inside her head and gone right to the fear and worry she had been obsessing over. But he couldn't have done that. So did that mean there was some truth to her concern about Jackson and Mercer?

Were they really together? No, Jackson wouldn't.

She wanted to bend over and put her head between her knees, but she couldn't give Steve the satisfaction. She straightened her back instead and met his gaze with a hard look of her own.

"Oh—you didn't know about them, huh? I guess that's because you just got back. You've missed a lot of Island gossip. She's young, but not too young. Half your age plus seven. That's the general rule."

Such a pig. How had she never seen this?

"He isn't with Mercer. She's his manager for Bohn's."

Steve rolled his eyes. "Sure. I bet that's why they were out looking at a house together yesterday."

No. But … yesterday Jackson had been busy in the morning. He got to her house in the afternoon, claiming that he had been at work. Had he been acting weird? Could he have been with Mercer? Looking at houses?

"He already has a house."

"He has a lot of houses. I just assumed he was setting one up for his lover. Look, I need to get upstairs and handle Mom and Dad. Call me when you realize that you're done with him. I'll be here."

Steve gave her a final smile that made her shudder and then walked away. Jenna stood in the middle of the hallway, wearing her shock and guilt and fear like a cloak. Steve had lashed out because he was jealous that she rejected him. That's all it was. A rumor. One that cut to the very heart of her vulnerabilities.

Jackson wasn't with Mercer. Not like that. But Steve had been so specific. Too specific for it to have just been a lie.

This moment was too familiar: the pain searing through

her chest even as her ribs felt like they were being crushed. Jenna gasped for breath and stumbled toward the dark parking lot. Her stomach rolled and twisted. Whether Steve's words were true or not, they seeped through her body like a poison, rotting every moment she had shared with Jackson until Jenna was left in nothing but dark and ruined thoughts.

CHAPTER SIXTEEN

JACKSON COULDN'T HAVE ASKED for a better start to the Farmer's Market and the official launch of the Bohn's Local initiative. The weather had warmed and it definitely felt closer to summer than spring in the sun. A gentle breeze lofted the ocean scent over the tables and tents set up in the parking lot. The part of the lot that wasn't roped off had totally filled and parking now spilled over into the strip center next door. People had come early and were sticking around. Mercer had really outdone herself. As if that wasn't enough, she would be singing with Beau and the rest of the worship band from their church in a few minutes.

The only person missing was Jenna. Scanning the crowd again for her, Jackson pulled out his phone and sent her a quick text.

Jackson: Here yet? I've got my eye out for you.

Worry sent beads of sweat rolling down his spine. Since the other night when she left for the hospital, it seemed like Jenna was avoiding him. Jackson had been at Bohn's all day, pulling together some of the details for the Farmer's Market. He had planned to bring her dinner after, but Jenna called and told him that she was too tired. He hadn't thought too much about it. But then she sent a text the next morning telling him that she wanted to work alone. When he had called, she didn't pick up. Now she was fifteen minutes late to meet him.

Had he moved too quickly, pushed her too hard? The last thing he wanted was to hurt her or to drive her away. But Jenna was strong, stronger than she knew. It drew him to her, that inner resilience and the ability to move past what she'd been through without anger or bitterness. When pummeling the heavy bag under the deck with his fists, Jackson wished that he could have just a little of her strength. He always felt like the veil between his emotions and his reactions was so thin, barely able to keep him in check.

Despite her strength, Jenna had been deeply hurt in her romantic relationships. Jackson knew this, had been cautioned by Beau and tried to restrict himself. Yet he must have pushed too far, let her see too much of how he felt. He should have given her more space, held himself in check. That's the only reason he could think of for her pulling away.

As the sound of guitars filled the air, Jackson's fingers curled into fists. If he had lost Jenna, he didn't know how he could recover from it.

"Jax?" Jenna's voice close to his ear sent hope spinning through him.

He turned, grinning. "You used my nickname."

She smiled back at him, tucking a strand of hair behind

her ear, looking a little shy. The breeze blew her hair right back and he fought the urge to brush it back.

"I didn't even notice. Is that okay?"

"Is that okay? I love it." Jackson couldn't help himself. He pulled her into a hug. She stiffened and he almost pulled back, but then she seemed to melt into him. Her hands ran up and down his back in a way that sent heat all the way to the tips of his ears. Maybe he hadn't pushed her away. He was reading too much into it.

They were in the middle of a crowd, so Jackson pulled away before he wanted to and resisted the urge to kiss her lips. Public or no, he didn't think he would be able to keep a kiss soft and sweet. Instead, he pressed his lips to her temple, letting them linger just a little longer than he needed. But definitely not as long as he wanted.

Shaking his head, he stepped back, but took her hand. "Want to walk around?"

"I'd love to. This is really amazing, Jackson. You're so good for the community."

His chest warmed under her words. That's what he wanted and hoped for. Even as he sank money into Bohn's that he didn't think would come back to him. "Thank you. I hope so. I can't take the credit though. Really, this was all Mercer."

"Oh?"

"She was the brainchild behind a bigger campaign we'll be running: Bohn's Local. This is just a part of it. We'll be offering more local things in the store as well. She had the idea and I just let her run with it. Amazing, right?"

"Mm-hm."

Her voice had dropped a few degrees, sounding cooler. But maybe he was imagining that too. He was overthinking everything. Jenna's eyes were on everything and he watched her, finding her much more fascinating than the tables with local fruits and vegetables or even the hand-crafted candles, artisan jewelry, or oil paintings of beach landscapes. The nagging sense that something was wrong filled him again, almost like an internal radar. He tried to shake it off.

When the first notes of guitar and Mercer's voice cut through the crowd over the speakers, it was almost as though a spell had been cast on the crowd. Conversations halted and people stopped moving. Jackson and Jenna both turned to the stage. He got to hear Mercer every week in church, but never got over the richness of her voice. Turning, he realized that Jenna stared at him with a look he couldn't read in her eyes.

"She sings beautifully," Jenna said. There was something wistful in her voice. Had Jenna wanted to be a singer? Or maybe it was sadness. Jackson opened his mouth to ask if something was wrong when she dropped his hand. She gave him a quick peck on the cheek and pulled away. "I wanted to pick up a few things in the store. I'll catch up with you later?"

Before Jackson could respond, Jenna slipped away from him, lost in the crowd and leaving him feeling more alone than should have been possible in a crowd of people. Why had that brief kiss felt like a goodbye?

Jenna wandered into Bohn's, still hearing the music in her ears. Mercer's voice, so pure and beautiful, hanging in the air. A match for her striking features and her ability to pull off something as amazing as the Farmer's Market outside. She didn't feel bitter, just resigned. Hopeless. She could hear the respect Jackson held for Mercer in his voice. She saw the way his head whipped toward her on the stage when she began to sing. His gaze had softened with affection when he looked toward the stage.

Steve's words crawled beneath her skin. Why wouldn't Jackson like Mercer? She had doubted them at first, fought against them the day before as she avoided Jackson. After a day of stewing, she had finally decided that she was reading too much into it and that Jackson wouldn't lead her on like that. He'd looked so furious when she told him about Mark. There's no way he would do that same thing to Jenna. She had told herself that she was being ridiculous. But had they been looking at houses together? What about the secretive phone call? When Jenna saw the way he watched Mercer sing, it felt like a part of her shattered.

Maybe what she needed to do was cut her losses. She couldn't take another heartbreak. If she backed off now, she would have the memories of a week with him, starting in the elevator—had it only been a week? Days' worth of conversations and kisses. Time where she felt herself falling for him in a way that she never had for Mark or Steve.

But it obviously was one-sided or somehow imagined. Jenna couldn't compete with someone like Mercer: younger, more beautiful, so talented. She hadn't been through a divorce or been given an STD by her ex. Jenna felt old and used up in comparison to Mercer, so broken.

No, it was better if she went with what she had originally been thinking—she would move to Burlington to stay near Rachel and be with family. She would go before she fell any harder for Jackson. Forget the future she had started to imagine with him as a real possibility. Rachel had been right to warn her. Too bad she hadn't listened.

As Jenna rounded the corner of the cereal aisle, her steps slowed subconsciously, as though some internal part of her recognized the voice she heard before her rational brain did.

Anna.

Her cart was head to head with Anna's. Jenna knew that she would eventually see Anna, but she still didn't feel prepared for this moment. Not today. Not with everything else.

"Watch where you're going!" Anna snapped, her harsh tone incongruent with her perfect, heart-shaped face. So cute. So pretty. Her hair was cut in a stylish, almost-shoulder-length bob. She didn't have on makeup, but didn't need it with her perfect skin, round brown eyes and full lips. Jenna could only see her from the shoulders up behind Anna's overflowing cart.

Jenna froze, the apology dying on her lips.

"I'll call you back." Anna tossed her phone into the depths of her designer purse. She cocked her head a little and smiled. It felt more like she was sizing Jenna up than anything.

"Jenna. I'd heard rumors you were back. How are you? It's been—what?—ten years? You look...different."

"And you haven't changed a bit."

They stared at each other for a beat.

"How long until you leave? I'm sorry about your mom by the way. At least you'll get some good money for the property. Real estate here really skyrocketed. A lot of us who stayed here did really well."

Jenna just nodded along, waiting for a break in this stream of words so she could find any excuse to extricate herself from the situation. Anna felt like the clichéd antagonist in a movie. You couldn't possibly find a real person who spoke this way or acted the way she did. It was unreal. In movies they had back stories that made their bad behavior okay in the end. Jenna didn't care a single bit about Anna's back story, if she even had one. She just was who she was. And she wasn't nice.

Jenna couldn't get around until Anna moved her cart. At least all the groceries were between them. Any buffer helped.

"How's your life?" Anna just went on. "I heard you got divorced. Marriage is really hard to maintain."

Jenna cleared her throat and swallowed a remark about Anna and Steve's marriage dissolving. She would not be that person. "I did get divorced—how nice of you to say. Probably throwing a party to celebrate soon. I'll send you an invitation if you want to come."

Anna blinked, trying to gauge if Jenna was kidding or not. She gave a dry laugh. "You're so funny. I remember that about you."

"I'm sorry—can you move your cart? I've got to...go. It really was something to see you. Just like old times."

"Just," Anna said in a too-sweet voice.

She pulled her cart to the side so Jenna could pass. As they moved by each other, an orange from Anna's cart rolled out of a bag and to the floor. Jenna bent to pick it up. As she stood and reached out to hand it to Anna, time began spinning off its axis into a slow-motion crawl as her eyes noticed two things.

First: Anna's belly jutting out in front of her, impossibly round and full—*pregnant*—and then: the glint of Anna's wedding ring as she rubbed her hand absently over the swell of her stomach—*married*. Two nights ago, Jenna had kissed this woman's husband.

Jenna dropped the orange into Anna's open palm.

"Thank you," Anna said, smiling sideways at Jenna,

looking like a cat who just ate a pet bird. And then she was gone.

Jenna kept walking but did not feel her legs. Rather, she felt them, but more like they were objects attached somehow to her body, moving forward on their own. Her hands clenched the handle of the cart. She felt a strange detachment to her body and had the sensation that she was both sinking and floating.

She could hear voices around her and an announcement on the overhead speaker, but the sounds were muffled. Outside, Mercer and the band played on, the music one more barb to her heart.

Just like when she got out of the elevator, things started to turn black around the edges. Jenna realized that she was about to lose consciousness, the taste of peaches suddenly in her mouth.

Not here. Abandoning the cart, Jenna lunged toward the two double doors leading to the back of the store. She heard a dull metallic crash behind her as her cart rolled into a display.

To her right she saw an office door and it took everything in her to make it there as the darkness encroached. She flipped on the light switch, her hand slapping at the wall, and barely made it to the wheeled chair. It spun as she landed in it, hard, and just before everything went dark, she registered the photograph on the wall behind the desk: Jackson and his parents in front of his beach house.

This time, she must have been unconscious for only a few seconds. Or that's how it felt when her vision cleared. Sounds slowly returned to normal.

Steve was married still to Anna. That's why his mother still had their family picture, why Anna still wore her ring.

He was with Anna and he had kissed her. A married man had kissed her. She was the other woman.

Having been on the other side of this equation, the guilt was almost heavier than she could bear. It sat on her chest like a boulder. Never mind that she hadn't wanted Steve to kiss her. It happened. She had—willing or not—participated in him cheating on Anna. The kiss was quick, but did it matter? It wasn't sex or an affair or even something she wanted. She should have pulled away quicker, reacted faster. She tried to think back to the kiss, timing it in her mind. A silly exercise that somehow seemed incredibly important right now.

Did she have to tell Anna?

The thought made Jenna put her head between her knees. Anna already hated her. She could only hate Jenna more. This would never be Steve's fault—she knew that. Anna would never believe Jenna over Steve. Would he even deny it? Were there other women? He didn't wear his wedding ring. Had he lost it? Did he need to take it off for work? Was it just a move to try to get to Jenna? The questions felt like gnats, hovering in front of her, touching down and then lingering.

"Jax?" Behind her, a woman's voice called out, approaching the office door. Jenna recognized it as Mercer. Bile rose in her throat at the sound of his nickname on Mercer's lips.

"I thought I might find you in here. Beau had to go answer a non-emergency call so we finished up our set. I think things are starting to wind down. I wanted to tell you before I forgot that I think I found the perfect house. It's just the right size and has a great location. Want to go look tomorrow?"

The stone that had been pressing on Jenna's chest a moment before dropped into her stomach. It felt more like a cinderblock, heavy with rough edges. The pain was just so heavy and so sharp at the same time. She swiveled the chair around and Mercer froze.

"I'm not Jackson."

"Who's not Jackson?" He appeared next to Mercer in the doorway suddenly. Impeccable timing. As always. "What are you ladies doing in here?" His gaze darted between the two women and Jenna tried to read it. He looked more confused than panicked, but Mercer took a big step away from him. Her mouth formed a tight line and her eyes darted around the room. Definite guilt there.

"Mercer thought I was you. I had the chair turned around," Jenna said. "She was just talking about the house you guys were looking at."

Jackson's gaze swung to Mercer. "Sorry, Jax," she said.

He looked back at Jenna and ran a hand through his hair. "Well, I guess the cat's out of the bag now."

Jenna blinked, hoping it would be enough to hold back her tears. So it was true. Married jerk Steve had been right. Jenna could not have hated herself more in that moment. "Why didn't you tell me?"

Jackson sighed and leaned on the doorframe. "I'm sorry. I was afraid that, uh, we weren't that serious yet. I didn't want to push you away."

That hadn't been the answer she expected. It didn't really make sense. Did he want to date them both? Hadn't been serious enough to tell her that he was also dating Mercer? From the guilty look on Mercer's face, she knew all about Jenna.

"Are you upset?" he asked.

Jenna tried to keep her voice level. "Upset isn't the word. I can't believe you're even asking that. You didn't want to push me away? Well, you have. Steve told me, but I didn't believe him. I just thought he was jealous."

Jackson's body practically vibrated with a sudden anger. It sucked out all the air from the room. The heat in his eyes did nothing to dispel the sudden coldness in his voice. "Steve? What exactly did he tell you? And why would he be jealous, Jenna?"

"He saw you two looking at houses and told me all about it."

"When did you see him?"

"Oh, are you jealous now?"

"Do I have something to be jealous about? What happened between you two?"

Jenna choked out a bitter laugh. "Other than him kissing me, absolutely nothing. He's still married to Anna, which he conveniently left out. Now that makes *me* the cheater. Not that I—"

"You kissed him?"

"He kissed me. I wasn't—"

"Jackson." Mercer's voice was a low warning and she turned toward him.

He didn't even seem to hear her. Drawing his shoulders up, he leveled a gaze at Jenna that made her shrink back in the chair.

"After everything you've been through, I cannot even believe that you did this."

The words were like a bullet right to her heart. But he didn't stop.

"I was so stupid. I fell so hard for you, so fast, after years of holding onto feelings, and you were kissing Steve."

"It wasn't kissing. It was just—"

He held up a hand. "I've heard enough." With a final,

searing look at Jenna, Jackson spun around and practically ran from the office.

Jenna could not imagine a deeper, more consuming pain than the throbbing, searing, aching burn in her body. She covered her face with her hands like they could offer any kind of protection. It was too late for protection. She was completely gutted.

CHAPTER SEVENTEEN

JACKSON COULD NOT REMEMBER FEELING rage like this. Hot, piercing, painful. He was practically panting with it. His adrenaline surged, sending sweat down his back and making his hands clench on the wheel.

People often described anger like feeling as though you were going to explode. To Jackson, it felt like his head was trapped in a vise grip that grew tighter and tighter, crushing him with intense pressure that had to release somehow.

You should go home, take it out on the bag.

But he didn't want to direct his fists there. Not today. He had a different target.

He peeled out of the parking lot in his Jeep, hitting the causeway and heading toward the marina where Steve ran charters: yachts, deep sea rentals, sunset cruises, dolphin tours. The kind of thing On Islanders avoided and tourists flocked to. A party boat, where Steve was rumored to party as hard as the guests. The thought of it made Jackson's lip curl. He couldn't shake the mental image of Steve and Jenna kissing. His stomach turned over.

How could she do it? Knowing what it felt like to be cheated on, Jenna was the last person Jackson would have expected to do this. No matter their history. It felt like Jackson had been dropped right back into the middle of high school drama. But this hurt so much more. He had finally dared to hope for a future with Jenna. He'd been looking for houses to encourage her to stay. And she kissed Steve. Of all people, that same guy that had her so fooled in high school.

And his wife was pregnant! Not that it was a surprise that Steve was running around on Anna. The whole island knew. Anna must have known, though she kept her nose just as high in the air as she always had, playing a part. Acting like she didn't know. Maybe she didn't.

Jackson accelerated and passed a slow minivan. He whipped back into the lane so close in front of them that they honked. He sped up.

A scenario played on a loop in his head, half memory, half imagined.

Jenna in his office, telling him that she had kissed Steve.

Steve kissing Jenna, his arms around her waist and her hands in his hair.

Jackson barreling out of his Jeep at the marina and punching the smile off Steve's face in front of a group of Off Islanders.

Each time the loop played, the details shifted. The first part was always short. He needed the reminder to fuel his rage.

The second part sent it blazing. Once, in the scenario, Steve looked at him over Jenna's shoulder, meeting his eyes. Once, Jenna did.

In the third part he felt only sweet satisfaction at the feel of bone crunching under his knuckles. The heat from his anger in full force, burning it all down.

He squeezed the steering wheel between his hands.

Jackson dangerously close to completely out of control. It had been years since he had felt so incapable of calming himself down. He remembered the satisfaction of his fist connecting with Steve's face back in high school, watching the smug look disappear from his face.

That night a bunch of guys had been hanging out at the pier. Jackson had never liked Steve, and not just because he was with Jenna. He felt like Steve had everyone fooled into thinking he was some good guy. But he hadn't been then and certainly wasn't now.

He hadn't meant to fight him, though. Mostly they ran in different circles.

But that night in high school when he punched him—and Jackson felt more fury rising up even thinking about it— Steve had been talking not just about Rachel, but Jenna too. Typical guy talk—the kind that made him feel dirty being a guy.

"Heard you had a good time with Rachel on the beach, Jackson. Guess she puts out more than her sister. Jenna wanted to wait for marriage," Steve had said, shaking his head. A few other guys had groaned. "I got tired of waiting, so I moved on with Anna. Guess I should have picked the other sister."

Before he knew what was even happening, Jackson's fist had connected with Steve's face. It took three guys to pull him off. Jackson had simply lost it. Just as he was about to lose it now. Except they weren't just kids now and this wasn't a spur of the moment thing. The longer he drove, the higher his stress levels rose.

Turn around, man. Not worth it.

The voice of reason in his head sounded very much like Beau.

Who at that moment passed him on the causeway, going the opposite direction in the fire station's red SUV. Beau's head turned as they passed, his eyes hidden behind aviator sunglasses. He lifted a hand in greeting, but Jackson didn't respond. He ground his teeth, hoping that Beau would just keep driving the other way.

But in the rearview mirror, he saw the SUV's brake lights. Beau made a U-turn and sped up behind him. Jackson pounded his hands on the wheel. Beau passed him, then pulled in front of Jackson, hitting the brakes hard. The other lane was full of cars and Jackson was blocked in. Jackson jammed his foot on the brake and stopped before his bumper made contact with the red SUV. But barely. The cars behind him honked and stopped as well, putting on their blinkers to get around.

"Are you trying to kill me?!" Jackson yelled out of his open window.

The SUV put on its hazards and Beau put a tanned arm out the driver's side window, waving Jackson to pull over onto the shoulder. He considered revving the engine and blowing by Beau, but crawled to a stop behind the SUV instead. For a moment Jackson considered gunning it and speeding away, but he knew Beau would just follow, so he pulled over on the shoulder behind him, hearing a few more horns blaring from the road.

Jackson was out of the Jeep almost before it was fully in park, and marched up to the SUV. Beau climbed out of the driver's seat and leaned up against the side of the SUV, almost lazily. Country music still played on the radio, Beau's favorite.

"What are you doing?" Jackson shouted. His fists were clenched and he opened them, palms wide, trying to calm himself. "Weren't you just at Bohn's?"

"We were headed back to the station after a call. False alarm. I saw you driving a little ... fast. Figured I'd save you a ticket. Cops have a speed trap a mile or so ahead. I don't think you would have made it."

"Great. I'll slow down."

"Not so fast, buddy. I'd love to hear about where you're headed in such a rush."

Jackson considered lying. Saying whatever it was that he needed to say to get Beau to leave him alone.

But he knew that one of Beau's best qualities was the worst in this moment for Jackson—his faithfulness. Actually, the word he often thought of in his head was steadfast. It was one of those Bible words that people didn't use much, which is maybe why it carried more meaning to Jackson somehow. Steadfastness was simply faithfulness acted out over time. That's how he thought of it.

Over the past few years, Beau had walked him through his doubts, through the struggle as he began seeing the world through a different lens, through giving up meaning-less (but still pleasurable) relationships with women he didn't care about, and through his struggle to work through his flare-ups with anger. Beau hadn't made him feel judged for his past or the dumb decisions he still sometimes made. He hadn't made Jackson feel like an idiot for asking ques-tions. Beau answered patiently, talked him through things, and did not walk away.

Beau was marked by this steadfastness.

Jackson wished Beau had less of it right now.

"So? Are you going to tell me where you're going or am I going to have to hear it tomorrow when you feel bad about doing whatever it is you're about to do?"

"I'm going," Jackson ground out, "to the marina."

"Let me guess," Beau said. "Dolphin cruise?"

Typically, this kind of light humor helped calm Jackson down. When he started really working on his anger problem, this was something his counselor had suggested. Beau had been able to diffuse Jackson like he was a bomb expert.

"Not on a dolphin cruise … hm. Shark hunting? Romantic sunset cruise?"

Today, this was only making him angrier. His hands moved back into fists again and he did not loosen them this time.

"I'm going to the marina to punch that smug smile right off Steve Taylor's face."

Beau normally didn't react in these kinds of moments, but a flicker of something passed across his face. He had been leaning against the side of the SUV and stood up fully now. A door closed and Jimmy walked around the side of the car.

"Hey, Jackson. Everything okay?"

"We're just fine, Jimmy," Beau said.

Jimmy sat down on the rear bumper of the car, watching. "I'll be right here if you need me."

Jackson needed fewer people between him and Steve, not more.

"Jackson said he's headed out to see Steve at the marina," Beau said. "Want to tell us why, buddy?"

Jimmy snorted. "Steve. Now there's a guy who doesn't deserve a single minute of your time."

Beau casually but intentionally approached Jackson. "How about we head back to the station. We were about to do a pretty intense workout. Get some of that adrenaline out in a healthy way, maybe tape up and do a little sparring…"

"A workout won't fix this."

Beau nodded. He was right in front of Jackson now. "Neither will your fists in Steve's face. Let's work through it. Why don't you tell me what prompted you to pay Steve a visit?"

Jackson clenched his jaw, feeling the vise-like pressure of his anger increasing. He wished Beau would get back in the car and get out of his face. His head pounded.

Beau stepped closer. "You don't want to talk? Okay. Let me try to guess. Tell me when I'm getting close. Let's see— he cut you off in traffic? Shoplifted from Bohn's?"

"Just let me go, man."

"Can't do that. This is what friends do. And I'm your friend, Jackson."

Beau moved even closer. He was almost nose to nose with Jackson, whose anger was flaring the closer Beau got. Short breaths, nostrils flaring.

"Back up, Beau."

Jimmy stood up and shifted a little bit closer to the two of them.

"Not going to back up. I think I've got this now: it has something to do with Jenna. Hot or cold?"

"Cold." Jackson could hear the lie in his voice.

Beau laughed and Jackson felt his arms tensing up, every muscle in his body taut like strings on a guitar. They were wound too tightly. Any minute he knew those strings would snap.

"Here's what I think," Beau said. He took off his sunglasses, so close to Jackson that his hand almost brushed his cheek. Jackson's muscles coiled even further. "I think that you need to get back in your car, turn around, and just go home."

"What if I don't?"

Beau glanced back at Jimmy. "We'll help you get back in the car."

"No."

"If the girl is worth it to you, you'll get back in the car."

"I need to go."

"No one is ever impressed with a bully," Beau said.

"I'm not a bully."

"Then why are you about to get into it with Steve?"

"He was cheating on Anna."

Beau froze. "Do you … did he—do you mean that something happened with Steve and Jenna?"

"It doesn't matter now. Get back in your car, Beau. Don't follow me. You too, Jimmy. I don't need this right now."

"We are exactly what you need, Jax. I want to stop you from doing something stupid that you'll regret later. Let's talk this out."

"I don't want to talk."

"I know you like her, but if Jenna kissed Steve, is she even worth it?"

Snap.

Before he realized what he had done, Jackson's fist was throbbing. Beau had a hand cupped over his cheek, standing back a few feet but still standing. Jimmy right next to him with an arm on his shoulder and the other two guys out of the SUV, all facing Jackson.

All the anger and the vise-like pressure had deflated with the punch. Jackson staggered back a few feet to sit on the front bumper of his Jeep. Cool shame settled over his skin.

He had just hit his best friend in the face.

The weight of knowing this, of seeing just how fast his body reacted without forethought, sank into his chest. He put his head between his knees, panting. His eyes were hot with tears as the adrenaline began seeping out of his body, leaving him with an echoing empty feeling.

A hand touched his shoulder and he startled, knocking it away. But the hand grabbed his own. Jackson jerked his head up.

Beau, cheek already swollen, red where Jackson knew it would later be purple, stood in front of him, holding his hand. His eyes weren't angry, but compassionate. Somehow that was worse. Jackson looked away, toward where traffic passing by was slowing to watch them.

"Do you feel better?" Someone else might have said this sarcastically. But Beau's tone was gentle, his words kind.

"I feel horrible." Jackson looked down at his feet, trying to pull his hand away. Beau would not let him go, but crouched down before him, boots crunching on the gravel. He forced Jackson to meet his eyes. "I can't believe that I hit you. I'm so sorry. I didn't mean to."

"But I *did* mean for you to. Jackson, I instigated you. I pushed you to the edge on purpose. That was the point."

"But why? I didn't want to hit you. I wasn't—am not—angry with you."

"Because I'm your friend. I'll have a lovely bruise later, maybe a black eye if I'm lucky. I hear it can make guys look sexy. We'll see how that works for me with Mercer." He grinned. Jackson couldn't smile back but felt a twitch at the corner of his mouth. "Bottom line is this: I'm okay. And you are too. Now had you continued driving and unloaded on our dear 'friend' Steve, you would most certainly not feel okay. You would feel just as horrible, only you might have a lawsuit too. Or the cops might be putting you in the back of a cruiser. Ladies do not like either of those things."

"But you didn't need to do that. You should have let me go."

"I know. But I'm your friend and corny as it sounds, I love

you. I want the best for you, so I took one for the team. Maybe Steve deserved it—I'm sure he did, actually—but I took it. You see what this is a picture of, right? You see why you can't go punch Steve Taylor in the face. No matter what he's done. This isn't you anymore, man."

Jackson stood and pulled Beau to his feet and into a hug. He pulled him in tight, not caring how all this looked by the side of the road to people passing by. Every so often, a car honked, or someone yelled out the window. Beau clapped his hand against Jackson's shoulder and then pulled back.

"Just so we're clear, you know that I could take you, right? If I wanted." Beau grinned at him. Jimmy snorted from where he stood a few feet away.

Jackson grabbed Beau by the shoulder. "I think you just did. And I couldn't be more thankful."

As Jackson climbed back into the Jeep, a feeling of loss settled over him. Beau had saved him from making a big mistake, but it didn't change the fact that Jenna had kissed Steve. Now that his anger had dissipated, he realized that he had questions. Ones he should have asked Jenna before he stormed away.

She had said that Steve kissed her. She said that she was a cheater. That was about the time his mind grew dark with rage. He didn't even know when Steve had kissed her. Or if she had wanted him to. Knowing Steve, it could have been completely one-sided. Jackson should have asked. Instead, he took her words at face value and threw them back at her in some kind of moral outrage, fueled by his hurt.

His stomach clenched. The words he said were inexcusable. Especially if he didn't have the full story. What an idiot. An irrational, hot-headed, impulsive idiot.

He may very well have misunderstood what Jenna meant.

Now that he was calm, he couldn't imagine her hooking up with Steve.

That morning he had been worried that he had been pushing Jenna away. He didn't need to wonder anymore. His actions and his words today almost certainly had destroyed whatever fragile relationship they had been building.

CHAPTER EIGHTEEN

Jenna sat sobbing loudly in Jackson's office chair. She wasn't just sad, but a big ball of bad feelings: hurt, angry, disappointed. Jackson's final words to her had encompassed every sick and terrible thing she felt about herself after realizing that Steve and Anna were still married. Willing or not, she had been a part of Steve cheating on Anna. Even though she hadn't initiated or wanted his kiss, it happened. She couldn't erase the sick feeling.

Jackson's words only made it worse. And he hadn't so much as apologized for whatever was happening with Mercer. As hurt as she had been about Mercer, she hadn't lashed out at Jackson. He was looking at houses with her, for crying out loud, and Jenna still hadn't been cruel. But one kiss from Steve—an unwanted kiss at that, and Jackson snapped. He had lined up his aim right where Jenna was most vulnerable and taken the shot.

How could she have been so wrong about him? Steve, Mark, Jackson—she really was a terrible judge of character.

Jackson seemed too good to be true: kind, sweet,

thoughtful, faithful. He offered security—financial and otherwise—when she felt adrift. Was that part of the attraction—the idea that he could take care of her with all his money? She hoped that she wasn't that shallow. At this point, Jenna didn't know what she thought about anything. It was all just a big mess.

After a moment, Jenna felt a tentative hand rubbing circles on her back. When her sobbing turned to sniffling, Jenna sat up. Mercer stood beside the chair and handed her a tissue. Her eyes were kind. "I'll be right back, okay?"

Jenna nodded. Any jealousy she had felt toward Mercer had died in the last few minutes when Jackson exploded on her. She had no more fight. The last few days had taken too much out of her. She simply felt limp. If Mercer witnessed all that and still wanted Jackson, she could have him.

Mercer returned a few minutes later with a tea from the coffee bar. Jenna held it while it cooled. Mercer sat in a chair on the other side of the desk. Jenna knew she should feel awkward talking to this woman—the one Jackson worked with, admired, and was looking for houses with. But something about Mercer put her at ease. If she was upset with anyone, it was Jackson. And herself.

A few minutes passed before Mercer spoke. "I'm really sorry about what Jackson said. It was really harsh. That's not like him." She paused and seemed to think hard about her next words. "You know he's got an anger problem? It's something he's been working through for a few years."

No, that wasn't something he had shared with her. One of many things, apparently. She was beginning to feel like Jackson was a stranger. "Not enough, obviously."

Mercer nodded. "I can see where you'd say that. From what I've heard and what he's told me, his main issue was physical. Fighting. Lashing out. He's made strides there."

She grimaced. "I haven't seen him lose it like this. For what it's worth, that's a sign that he cares."

Jenna couldn't even find the words to respond to that. He cared? Funny way of showing it. His bruised knuckles earlier in the week came to mind. That made more sense now. Why hadn't he said something? Oh, yeah—because he had another girlfriend he shared that with.

"How long have you guys been looking at houses?" Jenna asked. Her voice sounded hard and accusing. She didn't care.

Mercer made a face. "He asked me to start looking a few days ago. I'm sorry you found out that way."

A few days ago. That meant sometime this week, while Jackson was at Jenna's house, kissing her and acting like he wanted to build a relationship with her, he was also looking at houses with Mercer.

The pain was so familiar that she almost welcomed it. Not pleasant, but it was comfortable. It was an old friend that she knew well.

"Jackson was going to tell you," Mercer said. "He wanted it to be a surprise."

Was she for real? Jenna snorted. "Some surprise. The guy I thought I was falling in love with has another girlfriend and they're looking at houses."

Mercer's jaw fell open. "Wait, what? You think Jackson and I—you thought we were looking for house for the two of *us*? He and I are not in a relationship. He's my *boss*."

"I'm sorry. I don't understand." Jenna set down her tea and clasped her hands, which had started to shake. "You and Jackson aren't together?"

"No. Definitely not. Is that what you thought?" Jenna could only nod. Mercer's whole face turned red as she continued. "We weren't looking at houses for me and Jackson. He asked for my help with—with properties. It was most definitely not for me and Jackson. We are not and have never been a couple."

Jenna got the definite sense that Mercer still held something back, but her words rang true. Hearing this should have been a relief, but Jenna felt too numb. *It's already over,* Jenna realized. She had let go of Jackson the moment he stormed out of the office. Or maybe the instant his harsh words drove a knife into her heart.

He was probably already done with her too since he thought that she had cheated on him with Steve. Did they even need to talk about it? They had kissed and spent time together, but he hadn't ever said in words what they were building. Maybe it was better this way. They had saved themselves more heartache in the long run.

Now Jenna started to feel something again, dragging her out of the limp numbness. She felt loss. Regret. Defeat. Jenna couldn't open herself up to a relationship when they could hurt this badly. She had lost too much.

"Can I ask why you assumed we were dating?" Mercer took a sip of tea. Her cheeks were still red.

Jenna sighed. "Steve told me. He said he saw you looking for houses together."

"Steve." Mercer made a disgusted sound. "I don't mean to be so nosy, but what happened there? I don't know you well, but Jackson thinks the world of you. I have a hard time picturing you getting swept up in Steve's charms." Mercer said this last word as though she was spitting poison.

"I didn't. We have history, but not one I wanted to restart. I was in the hospital visiting his parents. Long story. They've been our neighbors forever and I stayed close with his mom. He kissed me—I didn't want to or respond. Maybe I didn't pull away fast enough, but I was shocked and definitely didn't reciprocate."

"Not surprising."

"I also didn't know he was still married, not that it would have mattered. I think he was trying to hide it. He was never wearing a ring and deflected when I mentioned Anna. He kind of implied that they weren't close anymore whenever I saw him."

Mercer made a noise in the back of her throat. "I don't know how their relationship works, but he's got a reputation On Island for messing around. He's hit on me before."

Jenna made a face. "Does Anna know?"

"I'm not sure. She's not the friendliest person. Not that anyone deserves that. I just mean that I wouldn't want to be the one to tell her. She seems like the type to shoot the messenger."

Jenna picked up her tea again and took a sip. It was now cold. "She already hates me, so maybe I should tell her."

"You'd do that?"

"I went through this. For years, my husband cheated and I didn't know. Years of my life, given to someone who was with other women. Many other women. If someone could have told me, I would have gotten out."

"You would have left him? Just like that?"

Something in the question made Jenna pause. Mercer stared off behind Jenna with a distant look, like she was suddenly hundreds of miles away. It seemed like less of a question and more of a statement about something else.

She's hiding from something, Jenna realized. *Or someone.* The short, dyed hair and heavy eye make-up were a mask. Jenna didn't know how she knew, but she did, like she recognized a mirrored pain. Different from Jenna's, but still there. If she had to guess, Mercer had endured years of something and now had gotten out. Sandover was her fresh start.

"Leaving is never easy," Jenna said quietly, noting how Mercer's gaze snapped back to her.

"No, it isn't."

They sat in silence for a few minutes, Jenna sipping her tea and Mercer toying with her hands. Leaving. Would Jenna leave Sandover now to get distance from all this?

No. The moment she thought it, Jenna knew that she didn't want to go to Burlington with Rachel. Or anywhere else. Not really. This island—for all its memories and ghosts—held too strong of a pull. Real estate was booming, so she could probably get a job. Hopefully not wherever Anna worked. There were a few offices On Island, so it should be fine.

She could surely find something small to rent or buy if her mother's house sold. Maybe she would need to avoid Jackson for a bit, or ignore the feelings she still had for him and insist on a casual friendship. Could she handle that? The thought of seeing him but not being with him made her chest burn. But she was strong. She had been through worse.

Jenna looked up at Mercer. "Hey, since you've been looking at properties for Jackson, would you want to help me find a place? I mean, if it's not too awkward. I'm going to need a place to rent or maybe buy, depending on what I find."

"Really? You'd want my help?"

"If you'd want to."

Mercer smiled. "I'd like that. And I've seen a few places that might be just what you're looking for."

"Maybe next week, then."

"Sounds good. I'll get your number from Jackson." Mercer paused. "You are going to talk to him, right? Explain what happened with Steve. He obviously has the wrong idea."

"I'm sure we'll talk," Jenna said vaguely. "I don't suppose you'll keep this conversation between us?"

Mercer didn't answer right away. "I'm not one for sharing secrets. That said, if Jackson asks, I won't lie."

"Fair enough."

Mercer, despite being maybe fifteen years younger, could make a really good friend, Jenna realized. She had a wisdom and depth that was surprising and possessed a quiet strength. She seemed dependable and fair. And if Jenna was right about Sandover being her escape, maybe Mercer needed a friend as well.

"Fair enough. Thank you for the tea. And for talking to me."

"Anytime."

Jenna made her way out of the office and out into the store, which was more crowded than she'd ever seen it. She still wanted to make food for Ethel but couldn't bring herself to do it. Maybe she could pick up a meal from a restaurant or something. Lazy, but probably better than whatever she would make.

In the parking lot, people were taking down the tents and packing up their cars with the produce and goods left over from the Farmer's Market. Jenna knew a lot of these faces, these people. Some simply smiled, but a few stopped her on the way to the car to tell her hello or say that they were sorry about her mother. This had been her mother's home. She knew that, of course, but realized that she hadn't really thought about it in that way. Her mom hadn't just raised her children here, but after Jenna and Rachel were gone, after her husband died, she continued to grow roots. It could be that for Jenna too.

Instead of driving home, Jenna went to the beach. She chose a different public access, so she wouldn't have to look up at Jackson's house or run into him. Walking straight onto the beach, she left her flip flops by the wooden steps and didn't stop until the cold waves lapped at her ankles, making her gasp.

The shock of the freezing water temperature freed up her tears. She stood there, the cold on her skin opening her up to really *feel* all the emotions roiling around in her belly.

Anger toward Steve for being the jerk he was and involving himself in her life. Frustration that it took her this long to see him for who he was.

Pain at the thought of letting Jackson go. Disappointment. Regret. There was a tiny sliver of hope too, one that tried to tell her *Maybe if* ... But she shut that down. She had to. She needed to save herself from more pain.

As she stood there, facing the powerful waves and letting the wind toss her hair around her face, another kind of feeling washed over her. It was the memory of being small. The childlike understanding of her place—not just on this beach or island, but her place in the universe. She was a speck. Her problems were tiny in the grand scheme of history. The roar of waves reminded her of the God that she had been pushing away for the last year, out of bitterness and anger and pain.

Jenna was so small. And, as her faith seemed to stretch and unfurl within her, she knew that as small as she was, God cared. He *saw* her, just as he had seen Hagar in the story she loved so much in Genesis. Miserable, alone, suffering. Like Hagar, Jenna may have been tiny in the big, eternal scope of the world. But God knew her and he cared.

As she lifted her arms above her head, Jenna continued to cry. This time they were tears of healing and of joy. The pain was still there and would be for a while. But the peace of God washed over her, making her feel like she had finally come home.

CHAPTER NINETEEN

JACKSON WAS WADING through bills and statements at his desk in the office at Bohn's. It was after hours. He usually didn't stay late unless there was a serious need. Which, today, there was.

He had gotten another offer to sell. A lower one than the last, but still high enough to make sense. From a business standpoint, it would be stupid not to take it. Despite the success of the Bohn's Local initiative they had launched almost a month ago, sales barely picked up. The store seemed more crowded, but not enough to make a dent. The store was still profitable, but the margin continued to shrink. The thought of selling and letting Bohn's become a chain killed him.

Not yet. He wasn't ready to let go yet. It was probably inevitable, but he could keep the store running—for now.

"Knock knock." Mercer stood in the doorway.

Jackson quickly swept the papers into a manila folder, and then stuffed it in a drawer. *Way to hide that, Captain obvious.*

Mercer's eyes were on the desk where he had put the folder. He cleared his throat.

"Hey. I didn't realize you were still here."

"Just finishing up a few things." She leaned in the doorway and crossed her arms. "You know, you don't have to hide that stuff from me. I have a pretty good idea about how things are going with the store. Bohn's Local wasn't the magic bullet we hoped it would be."

It was a statement, not a question. He sighed. "It's a brilliant campaign. Definitely made an impact."

"Just not enough?"

"I wish. Anyway, I got another offer to sell. One that seems stupid not to take."

"But you don't want to take it," Mercer said.

"I don't. This is so much more than a store to me. It's the legacy of the On Island community. One of the last strongholds of the changing island. It gives jobs to many local people. It's also home to me in a lot of ways. I'm keeping it for emotional reasons, not business ones. For now, anyway."

Mercer nodded and gave him a pointed look. "For what it's worth, sometimes we should do the stupid thing that's more difficult."

She wasn't just talking about the store and it wasn't the first time she had tried to push him about Jenna. Jackson ran a hand over his jaw. He needed to shave. His stubble had turned into a half-beard. Not a good look on him, but more and more in the past few weeks, he just hadn't cared. It started the moment he drove away after losing his control and punching Beau. He spent the next few days holed up in his house, too ashamed of his own behavior to talk to anyone.

Beau and Jimmy finally showed up to practically drag him out of bed and back to daily life. "Stop running," Beau had told him. "Whatever you're struggling with, you've got to hit it head on."

"I feel too broken to fix," Jackson had told him.

When Beau had told him that he was being prideful, Jackson had scoffed. Until Beau explained. "Think about it: you saying that you aren't fixable is a different kind of pride. Pride is making you big and God small. If you're saying you are too broken to fix, it's a backwards kind of pride. You think your brokenness is bigger than God's ability to help you."

It made a weird kind of sense and finally got him out of the house. But Jackson was still wallowing. Not only in self-pity, but in thoughts that he knew were self-destructive. He didn't deserve happiness or someone like Jenna. He couldn't trust himself to care for someone because of his anger. He wasn't worth it. She deserved better than a man who assumed the worst and flew into a rage, punching his best friend in the face.

He felt like letting her go was the best thing for Jenna. But was Beau right—was pride the thing that kept him from talking to her?

They'd talked, of course, just not about what happened. He couldn't seem to avoid her. She shopped in the store. She went to his church now and had joined their Sunday school class, sitting by Mercer. The conversations Jackson had with her were polite and sanitized, as though they'd never had a relationship at all. They said hello. He asked how she was doing. She said fine. They smiled and walked away.

She wanted to pretend they were casual friends? Fine. He could pretend.

It was torture. He wanted nothing more than to wrap her up in his arms and beg her forgiveness. Jackson was desperate to make things right between them. He didn't feel like he deserved her, but he loved her nonetheless. That's right—love.

If he'd had a question before, he was sure now: he loved Jenna. Completely. Fully. Foolishly.

Too late. Or, maybe it was exactly the right time. If he had realized it before and told her, maybe it would have been harder to let her go.

He had even more reason to keep his distance. Megan had asked Jackson if she could live with him full-time. Kim didn't fight it, though they'd had a lot of long and unpleasant conversations with each other and with lawyers. Megan would move in at the start of summer.

Would Jenna really want a relationship with him when he came with a prickly pre-teen? It was one thing when Megan was just around some weekends. Living with him would mean being a full-time parent. He didn't even know how that would work or if he could do it. Jenna was starting her life fresh. There was no way she would want to be an instant parent to Megan.

Jackson had thought it all through, again and again. This was the best decision for Jenna. That's what love did, right? It put the other person first.

And yet … Jackson was miserable. When he saw Jenna, she didn't seem happy either.

Jackson leaned forward at his desk, but did not meet Mercer's eyes. "How do you know when it's time to do the stupid thing and when it's time to do the smart one?"

She didn't answer right away. "It's one of those things you just know. Other people will usually tell you to be smart. But that doesn't make them right. You know that song, 'Reckless Love?' "

"How could I forget that heated Sunday school debate?"

Apparently the worship song rubbed a lot of people the wrong way, as they found out one Sunday morning.

"Right. Well, I get why people debate. It sounds on the surface like it's insulting God, calling him reckless. But the song is more of a human picture to show how big God's love is. The way God loves us—well, if it were a friend of yours, you'd tell them to give up. That it's not worth it to chase after someone who's running away from you or rebelling. But God comes after us like that. In the human sense that looks reckless."

"Wow. I don't remember you saying all that in Sunday school."

"Yeah, well. I don't always talk a lot in big groups. But that's what I think about the song and about love. Sometimes real love is reckless. It's foolish."

Jackson had certainly done a lot of foolish things recently, but not the good kind of foolish. Flying off the handle at Jenna without getting the full story. Punching Beau in the face. And then being too cowardly to push when Jenna said she just wanted to be friends.

"So, you'd suggest in this case, that I do the reckless thing?"

Mercer smiled. "Definitely. I have an idea actually. Of a *very* reckless thing you could do."

Jackson laughed. "Of course you do. Can I think about it for a while?"

"Sometimes taking too long to decide *is* making a decision."

"Okay, Mr. Miyagi."

"Who?"

Jackson rolled his eyes. "*Karate Kid*? Ever heard of it? Never mind. I keep forgetting that I'm in a different generation. You are wise beyond your years. And yet you know so little about iconic movies of the past."

"Thanks, I think? Anyway, this is as pushy as I get, but the idea I have is time-sensitive. You probably shouldn't wait." She lingered in the doorway, hand on the frame. "For what it's worth, I really think that you should choose to make the stupid decision. Be foolish, Jackson."

Jackson pictured Jenna's face, remembering the feel of her in his arms as they danced on her back porch. His heart seemed to rocket back to life again, roaring in his chest. For the first time in weeks, Jackson felt like something deep inside him was waking up again.

"Fine. I'll make the foolish choice. Now, sit down and tell me what it is I just agreed to."

CHAPTER TWENTY

"I REALLY THINK you might like this one." Mercer pulled her car into the driveway of a beach cottage set back in the trees, the house up on stilts with space for parking underneath. A hammock swung lazily beneath the house.

Jenna tried not to laugh when she caught sight of Mercer's face, which was pinched. She was already prepared for Jenna to reject it on sight. Which she had done a few times that morning already. And over the past week, though sometimes she actually made it inside the house before saying no. She and Mercer had looked at twenty properties over the last few weeks. The search had been almost lazy at first, but now that Jenna had actually sold her mother's house and had a closing date just a few weeks away, she was feeling the pressure.

She was also feeling indecisive.

Jenna was like Goldilocks—this one too small, this one too large, this one too expensive, this one too worn down. Whether it was renting versus buying, three bedrooms over four, nearer to the beach or on the Sound side of the island, Jenna hadn't been able to pick.

Now that she had a job working for a real estate firm—intentionally *not* the one Anna worked at—Jenna set up the appointment, but let Mercer pick all the listings. Jenna went in blind, with the address and the lock-box codes and nothing else. It didn't matter if she was going about this backwards, the opposite of how she would recommend clients do it. Jenna wanted to find a place that spoke to her.

Mercer had picked a variety. They had looked at fixer-uppers and fully-renovated homes. Even a few new ones, though most of those were out of Jenna's budget. Larger homes, smaller ones. Condos. Houses. Ranches. Beach homes on stilts. Beach side. Sound side. Somehow Mercer kept her patience. Jenna would have tried to pawn off this kind of client on someone else. Maybe the adage about doctors making the worst patients was true also of real estate agents making the worst clients.

Jenna could have done this on her own, but it had been surprisingly fun to have Mercer with her. At least, it was fun for Jenna. If Mercer was still talking to her by the end of this, then their friendship would probably last forever. She had a feeling that it would. Mercer still kept a lot of things close, but Jenna hoped she would open up more over time. They talked almost daily now, but never her past. And never about Jackson.

"I like the look of it," Jenna said. More than like. This house got her blood pumping. It looked like a classic beach cottage, but well-maintained. Possibly renovated.

"About time," Mercer muttered, getting out of the car.

"I heard that!"

Jenna felt a quickening of her heartbeat as she stepped out of the car. The house had the gray-shingled outside she loved, but a bright and cheery coat of white on the trim that looked fresh. It faced north, not east toward the beach, but a swatch of water might be visible from up there. A screened-in porch and big wide deck surrounded the three sides you could see. Underneath the house there was plenty of room for parking, what looked like a little shed, and an outdoor shower with wooden walls and a door. Exactly what you'd want for a house at the beach.

At the top of the stairs to the deck, Jenna went straight into the screened porch instead of the main door of the house. Mercer trailed behind her silently, letting Jenna look. A couch with big blue cushions covered in a print with shore birds sat along the wall, just under a window looking into the house. In the corner there was a tall hanging chair that looked oddly like a birdcage. She sat down in it and found it surprisingly comforting. She wasn't imagining it—she could definitely smell the ocean.

"Is the rest of the place furnished?" Jenna asked. "Everything looks new." And much nicer than what she thought she could afford. Mercer hadn't mentioned cost yet and Jenna was almost afraid to ask.

"It's fully furnished, which should be perfect for you. Especially considering your time constraints."

"Ugh. Let's not mention the deadline, please." Closing was a few weeks away still, but if Jenna didn't find somewhere this week, it would be difficult to get paperwork done and her things moved in time.

The late afternoon sun slanted down and Jenna could imagine dinners around the picnic table, the night falling softly like a shawl. Beau, Mercer, Jimmy, and some of the other friends from church. She had been surprised at how easy it was to walk through the doors of Hope the day after everything went down with Jackson. Something had shifted when she stood with her feet in the cold water on the beach. She was still working through her feelings about everything, but she was no longer angry with God. Instead, he returned to being her refuge he used to be. The way he always had been, even when she couldn't see it.

That first morning at Hope, the worship team sang "Great Is Thy Faithfulness," the old hymn she remembered from childhood. It had brought her to tears. She realized just how much she had stopped trusting in God's faithfulness to her. He was right there all along. She felt his welcome in the songs and the messages. She felt it in the people she was getting to know more week by week. It restored her faith and helped her feel a connection to her mother.

It also meant that she saw Jackson every week. Despite her best efforts to keep an emotional distance, her heart didn't agree. It was a traitor, longing to talk to him, be near him, touch him, spinning her thoughts into daydreams before she could stop it.

You can't let yourself get hurt again, she told herself.

Life is full of hurts. You're making a mistake giving up on him, that other voice argued. It had been getting louder lately, the pesky, argumentative voice. Despite her rational arguments, these thoughts kept coming. Especially whenever she saw Jackson and her body lit up the way it always did. She couldn't help but remember his scent and the feel of his strong arms around her. When he wasn't looking, her gaze still fell to his lips, remembering.

"Do you want to go inside or are we going to hang out on the porch?" Mercer stood by the door.

Jenna retrieved the code for the box that held the key. When she opened the door and they stepped inside, Jenna almost gasped. It was like the kind of beach house she would have designed for herself. It had a casual comfortable, beachy vibe all around. The space had been opened up for a perfect-sized living, dining, and kitchen. Granite counters, white subway tile backsplash, light-gray cabinets that were made to look a little weathered. The main colors for the décor were blue, gray, and sea-green.

Jenna grew worried as she walked back to the bedrooms. This place was fully renovated, had a great location walking distance to the beach, and more than enough space. She always told her clients not to set their hearts on something before signing the papers, but she already had. She wanted this place, no matter the cost. The master bedroom even had a reading nook, with a patterned wingback chair and small table with a book and an empty coffee cup.

"What do you think?" Mercer asked.

"We should go," Jenna said.

"Wait! I thought you liked it."

"I love it. But there's no way I can afford this."

Mercer cocked her head. "You're the agent. I'm just the partner in crime. Didn't you look at the prices or the specs?"

"I like seeing the place first before making a decision based on the listings. I pulled the specs but didn't really look at the details."

"Maybe you should look," Mercer said.

"Just to find out I can't afford it?"

"What if you can? Stop being difficult. Where's the folder?"

"In the car."

Mercer rolled her eyes and stomped out of the house and down the stairs. Jenna took this time to get nosy, looking for a fault that would make her feel differently about the house. But everywhere she looked just made her want the house more. From the homemade chandelier made of driftwood to the art above the couch, which looked more like actual artwork than a print. This was definitely going to be over budget.

Mercer burst back in through the door, smiling. She handed Jenna the folder with the listing. "Good news. It's right where you wanted to be. The high side, but still in your budget. Lease, but with the option of leasing-to-own. If you're interested."

Jenna couldn't stop her smile. "I've got some calls to make, then."

Mercer wasn't the jump-up-and-down, hug-it-out kind of person, but she did give Jenna's shoulder a squeeze. "I'm really, really happy for you. I think that this is the start of good things to come."

"I think you're right."

But even as she said it, Jenna felt the sadness she'd kept hidden wrapping even tighter around her heart.

It was a lovely house, but she was still alone.

"I found a place!" Jenna held the phone up to her ear as she walked through the bare kitchen. Her mother's house was almost completely empty now—a few final pieces of furniture remained just until the day or two before closing. A charity planned to pick up the old couch and a few other pieces of furniture tomorrow.

"Yay! The real question is: can it fit my family when we come to the beach?"

Jenna laughed. "It will be a little tight, but yes. Three bedrooms, two baths. It's one of the old-style beach cottages. Fully furnished and renovated. It's amazing. Five or so minutes to walk to the beach. On the other side of the cause-way, but there's a crosswalk."

"That sounds perfect. I'm so happy for you. Sold the house, found a new one, got a job—everything's coming together." The tightness around Jenna's heart clenched in the silence before Rachel spoke. "I'm sorry, Jenns."

Jenna ran a hand over the empty counter, brushing away invisible crumbs. "Don't worry about it. I'm fine."

"I know you. You aren't fine. You're heartbroken and trying to cover. Tell me again why you aren't talking to Jackson?"

"I'm not *not* talking to him."

"But you haven't talked about your feelings. Or about the fact that you were in a relationship that suddenly went poof for no good reason."

"There were reasons. And he never officially said it was a relationship. It was just a … thing that happened we don't talk about. If he wants to talk, he knows where I live."

"He's being just as dumb and proud as you are. And your reasons are flimsy. So, he assumed something and hurt your feelings. In his defense, you said that you had cheated and kissed Steve. It was a fair assumption for him to make."

"Yeah, I could have worded that better."

"Or explained before he ran out the door."

Jenna had gone over this again and again in her mind. She actually agreed with Rachel in a lot of ways. Her reasons were paper-thin. But she clung to them and didn't know exactly why. Fear? Pride? Though she would never admit it to Rachel, she wanted Jackson to show up at her door. She wanted him to reach out.

She wanted *him*.

But the more weeks went by where they were exceedingly polite to each other, staying at arm's length away, the more she felt ridiculous for thinking that would ever happen. Jenna had been worried about things moving too fast between them, but time and distance gave her more perspective. It didn't feel rushed now. Her feelings weren't flimsy like her excuses. If anything, she was more solid about how she felt now. Things had happened fast between them, but it wasn't a crush or infatuation. Jenna couldn't say the word that accurately described her feelings. She wouldn't. Unless Jackson came back, it was a moot point. And he wasn't coming. She felt more and more sure of this every day, as her heart broke a little more.

"I could have handled it better. But the reality is that Jackson ran out the door. He left. And he didn't come back. I don't want that kind of man. One who runs and leaves. I've had that." She bit her lip to hold back the tears. She would not keep crying about this.

Rachel sighed through the phone. It was a giving-up kind of sigh. "You get your stubbornness from Mom, you know."

Jenna laughed, feeling a slight relief from the pain in her chest. "Yep. So do you. Anyway, back to the house."

"Right."

"Come down anytime. If you happen to want to help me move in, I won't protest."

Rachel groaned. "What about all those friends you've got? Beau and his beefy firefighter buddies. Can't they help?"

"They're *his* friends."

"Oh, yeah. Still. Maybe that would be a good thing. Invite Jackson too. That would—"

"Stop trying to play cupid. I'm impervious to arrows. I actually don't need much help. The house is furnished and I just have the things I came down with. It's sad, really."

"Stop. You aren't allowed to feel sorry for yourself. You're starting a new life. It's going to be amazing."

Jenna kept telling herself that same thing. But it all just felt ... empty. She shook off the thoughts. "There's one kind of weird thing about the house, though. I didn't meet the owner when I was signing the lease, but in the contract, I have to meet them tonight at the house. I couldn't get much more info out of the listing agent."

"That sounds kind of creepy."

"It's unorthodox, but I'm sure it will be fine. The listing agent assured me that I don't need to be worried about it."

"Hm. Can you take someone with you? The girl you've been hanging out with—Mercer?"

"Maybe. I'm not really worried about it. More intrigued. I'm sure it's something like an emotional attachment thing. I'll let you know how it goes."

Rachel was quiet for a few seconds. Jenna steeled herself for what would come next.

"Jenna, I really think you should talk to Jackson."

"I know you do."

"Will you—"

"Nope. Talk to you later, Rach."

After Jenna hung up the phone, she walked out onto the back deck. It was nearing dusk, almost time to leave to meet the owner of her new rental. She leaned her elbows on the wooden rail and sighed, looking out over the acres of woods behind the house. This house held so many memories, ones that she felt so sad to leave behind when she signed the closing papers and locked up for the last time. But the one that hit her right in the gut and the one she hated to leave behind took place just a few weeks before when she danced with Jackson Wells.

CHAPTER TWENTY-ONE

JENNA DROVE to the cottage around dusk. It was beginning to turn the slightest bit of pink toward the west. Normally, a gorgeous On Island sunset would have lifted her mood, but tonight she felt a slurry of unwanted emotions in her belly. She felt sour from her conversation with Rachel, which had riled up all her feelings and regrets about Jackson. Then there were the nerves about meeting the owner of her new place.

The listing agent hadn't even told her if it was a man or woman. What if this was some kind of creepy guy? She had mace on her keychain, just in case. But she couldn't imagine any agent who would agree to something like that in a contract without trusting the person. Still—why all the mystery?

As she pulled up in front of the cottage, the first thing she noticed was the twinkling strands of lights strung up over the deck. And then the reason for the mystery became immediately clear. Her heart began to speed up.

Jackson's Jeep was parked underneath the house.

She pulled in behind it and turned off the engine. The

breeze lifted her hair from the back of her neck through the open car windows. She could hear the ocean faintly and her own heartbeat in her ears. Jackson was here?

Of course. Jackson's family owned properties all over the island under Wells Development. She hadn't seen the name on any part of the contract, but he was a smart businessman. It wouldn't be too difficult with as much money and property as he owned.

Her mouth felt dry and her fingertips tingled. Why was he here?

She had a few ideas—one big one, but Jenna didn't want to hope.

Over the past few years, she had stopped trusting in hope. What she could count on was pain. And then more pain. Sliding back down into the pit when you had clawed your way almost to the top. That's what she knew.

So, as she climbed the stairs to the porch, Jenna tempered the bright gleam of hope—*but what if?*—with more realistic thoughts. Maybe Jackson just wanted to clear the air. They would have an awkwardly polite conversation and he would leave. Or perhaps he didn't know who was renting the place. With so many properties in his family's company, he might not know. Possible, but not likely.

The lights over the deck looked enchanting. Romantic, even. They twinkled and waved slightly over the picnic table, which was set for two. There were blue and white placemats, cloth napkins with blue crabs on them, and a vase of white roses. Jenna tried to swallow down the lump in her throat.

Music filtered to her ears from inside the house. Jenna took a deep breath and knocked at the door.

"Come in!"

Jackson's voice sent nerves flying through her body. Jenna walked inside, her hands trembling on the knob. He grinned at her from the kitchen, where he was stirring something on the stove. It smelled of garlic and something else she couldn't identify. Just the sight of his handsome face made her stomach clench.

Jenna tried to keep her expression neutral as she sat on a stool at the kitchen island. Jackson had shaved. Lately he had grown somewhat of a beard. Jenna had tried not to like it, but truthfully, he looked great no matter what. His current look, with the barest of five o'clock shadows, was her favorite though. She wanted to feel the scratch of it against her palm or against her lips.

"Jenna. I'm so glad you're here."

He was acting like nothing had been standing between them. How was she supposed to respond?

I'm glad I'm here too. I'd love to have your babies.

Sorry for making you think I cheated on you. Whoops!

Can we start over? But also take up where we left off? Because I really like kissing you …

None of the above. Jenna shook her head, as though that would clear her thoughts. She chose to completely ignore what lay between them, just as he was. A smile lifted the corner of her mouth. "I thought you said you only grilled?"

He laughed. "That's the first thing you're going to ask? Okay. Let's go with that. Maybe I picked up a new hobby this past month. I would pour you a glass of water, but I might burn the garlic. No one wants that."

"Burnt garlic is the worst," Jenna said. "I'm glad you have your priorities straight. I'll get the waters."

Jenna found the glasses and got water and ice from the fridge, aware the whole time of how close she stood to Jackson in the modest kitchen. When she had seen him over the last few weeks, it had been from much more of a distance. Enough that she could keep her cool. Now, forced to be alone and close with him, her whole body seemed to vibrate with the longing to fold herself in his arms. She set a glass next to him on the counter and he smiled.

Sitting down again on the stool, she watched his hands as he stirred chicken and vegetables. She couldn't explain the feelings that coursed through her. Too many of them, too intense and tangled. The most surprising of them all was relief. The tension that had been between them, the stiff awkwardness, was gone. At least for now. The conversation was easy, not forced.

"Dinner will be ready in five. I hope you're hungry."

Her stomach made an unflattering sound and she giggled. "Guess I can't say no." He gave her another amazing smile that sent a thrill through her. "Can I ask—why the surprise?"

His smile faded and he looked back down at the pan in front of him. "If I had warned you, would you still have come?"

Jenna knew that she would have wanted to say no, but everything in her was drawn to this man. Even if that made her feel desperate. "Yes. No? Probably."

He smiled. "Understandable. I wasn't sure if you would, so I made sure."

"By making me sign a contract?" She gave him a dirty look.

He chuckled. "Not the most romantic way I've ever asked someone on a date. But very effective."

Her heart flip flopped in her chest: *a date*. He gave her a sideways glance as he plated up steaming fresh pasta, chicken, and vegetables. He sprinkled fresh cheese on top of each plate.

"I've got the table set on the porch," he said.

"I saw. It's lovely."

Jenna hopped down from the stool and followed him out

with their waters. When they were seated outside at the picnic table, Jenna felt suddenly shy. Jackson didn't seem to have the same issue. Without hesitation, he took her hand. "Mind if I say grace?"

"Go ahead." She closed her eyes. The feel of his hand on hers had her thinking about anything but prayer. They were warm and his skin soft, but his grip was firm and sure. She felt safe with him. But she had felt safe before. Tears pricked behind her closed eyes as Jackson began to pray.

"Lord, thank you for the sometimes strange ways that you work. How you take broken things and fix them. Even broken people. Thank you for friendship and for more than friendship. Amen."

He squeezed her hand before letting go. Jenna felt breathless and teary. Sitting here with him felt like too much. Clearly, whatever feelings had been developing between them hadn't gone away. For her, they had gained strength, like a hurricane hovering over the water before making landfall. Jenna wanted this, but she wasn't used to getting what she wanted.

"Are you okay, Monroe?"

Hearing his nickname for her almost pushed Jenna over the edge. A shuddery breath escaped her. "I'm fine, I guess, just … surprised."

"I hope it's a good surprise."

"It is." She stopped all the other questions on her lips and picked up her fork instead, thankful for the food for distraction.

Everything was delicious. Maybe the best thing she'd eaten in months. After a few minutes of eating, punctuated only by the sounds of forks hitting plates and birds calling as they made their way back to roost, Jackson set his fork down and leaned forward, elbows on the table. His eyes crinkled a little with a smile as they fixed on her.

"What?" Jenna wiped her mouth, just in case there was something on her face.

"Hm?"

"You're staring."

"So, what if I am?" His mouth lifted on one side, a flirty look.

"You're making it kind of hard to eat. And the food is excellent, so I'd really like to eat."

"Did you know this cottage is where I grew up?"

She blinked at his words. "Really?" She hadn't ever known where he lived, which was a little surprising given the size of Sandover. But then, she'd never been close with him back then.

"Yep. The back bedroom on the kitchen side was mine. I still remember sneaking out past my parents' room and where the creaky spots in the floor are. Well—were. The renovation fixed that."

The thought of living in his childhood home over-whelmed her. She had loved the house when she saw it but felt even more drawn to it now. "The renovation is amazing. I'm really impressed."

"Thank you. I was happy with how it turned out." He pushed his plate forward and leaned back in his chair, watching her. "This is also the house where I fell for a girl that I couldn't have. First, because she was with another guy —one who definitely didn't deserve her—and then because I didn't deserve her. But I kept her picture in a book next to my bed in that very room. It seems only fitting that she'll be sleeping right across the hall now."

Jenna felt her cheeks flush. "Why didn't you tell me?"

"That I liked you or that this was my house?"

"Both, I guess."

"Fear. Both times, it was fear. But I'm working on that," he said. "Maybe tricking you into dinner wasn't the bravest move, but I figured I'd be all kinds of fearless once I had you sitting here."

Jenna was still processing. "The price of the house—I knew it was too low! You and Mercer were in on this together."

Jackson grinned. "Guilty as charged. Also, for the record, I'm shocked you thought we were together. I would never have done that to you." His voice softened to hold a tenderness that made Jenna's heart flip.

"I'm sorry that I even thought it. I should have known. I think after everything that's happened, I sort of expect to be cheated on or left for someone else. Then Steve said you were looking at houses—"

Jackson held up a hand. "I'm sure he intentionally planted doubt to mess with you and with me. He did see us together looking at houses. Mercer helped me look for the perfect place—for *you*. When I realized this was the place, she helped me decorate with things we both thought you would like. I had some ideas, but home décor is not my strong suit. I wanted you to walk in the door and feel like you were coming home."

"That's exactly how I felt," she said, her voice sounding breathless. She played with her napkin. "You did all this for me?"

"I did. It's not nearly enough, but it's a start."

Her chest felt like it was going to combust. No one had ever done something so thoughtful for her. Not ever.

Jenna gripped the edge of the wooden table. "Jackson. I can't do this." His face fell. Sucking in a breath and trying to gather her own bravery, she reached across the table for his hand. His head jolted up in surprise. "What I mean is that I can't have this kind of conversation without talking about what happened between us. It's too weird. I don't know how you feel, not really, or what you're thinking. We left things on bad terms and then just ..."

"Pretended?" She nodded. He stroked the back of her hand with his thumb. "I owe you an apology. Several, really. I should have done this weeks ago. You know how I am with apologies. I was ... scared."

Me too, she thought. She bit the inside of her cheek to stop herself from speaking. She wanted him to finish, needing to hear these words.

"I've had issues with Steve for a long time, all the way since high school. When you mentioned his name and that he had kissed you ..." Jackson's hand clenched hers almost to the point of being painful. His eyes were focused somewhere in the distance. She squeezed his hand gently. He sighed out a breath and released the death grip. "I just snapped. You made it sound like there was something between the two of you."

"There wasn't, but I know how I made it sound. I was overwhelmed and not thinking how the words came out."

"Mercer explained everything. She said that you didn't want her to say anything, but I had asked her directly what she knew. Why didn't you tell me?"

This was the same question that Rachel had asked and that she had asked herself. "I think I was scared too. And hurt. I felt so guilty when I realized Steve and Anna were still together. Even though I didn't want him to kiss me and I didn't kiss him back, I felt like the other woman. My husband had so many other women. To be put in that position, willingly or not, felt horrible."

"And then I attacked you for it." Jenna couldn't look at

him. He squeezed her hand gently. "Will you take a walk with me, Monroe?"

Jenna nodded. Jackson didn't let go of her hand as they went down the stairs and to the quiet street. The walk to the beach was pleasant, especially with Jackson squeezing her fingers. There was still much to say, but somehow the quiet between them felt comfortable. He didn't speak again until they had crossed over the wooden steps to the sand.

They shed their shoes by the steps and walked close to the water's edge. The night had a bite to it with the breeze. They had been holding hands palm to palm, but as they turned south, he laced his fingers through hers.

Jenna felt his touch from her hands to her hairline, an electric tingle that sent her skin humming.

After a few minutes, Jackson said, "Can we sit? I want to tell you how I feel and I'm not sure I can do it while walking."

They sat in the sand in the small rise just above the reach of the surf. He looked down at their interlaced fingers as he spoke.

"That day, I lost it. In a way I hadn't in years. I started driving out to the marina, intending to find Steve. Thankfully Beau saw me driving like a maniac and stopped me. I was so angry that I ended up punching Beau."

Jenna gasped. "You punched Beau?"

"Not one of my finer moments. Beau engaged me, instigating me on purpose. He thought it would keep me from going to the marina. It did, but it also meant he got a black eye. Not something I'm proud of."

"He's a good friend."

"The best. He knows me well and knows about my anger problem. I've seen someone in the past about it and just started again." Jackson sighed and ran his free hand through his hair. Jenna could sense his shame as it flowed off him in waves. She squeezed his fingers and he continued.

"If Beau hadn't gotten to me, I don't know if I could have stopped at one punch with Steve. That doesn't make what I did okay, but I'm glad Beau did what he did."

Jenna studied Jackson's profile. His face looked beautiful in the light from the half-moon. It was hard to imagine him punching anyone, but she could remember the way his face had looked that day, etched with anger.

"I'm sorry that I pulled away from you, Jenna. I was ashamed of what I did and what I said. I kept thinking that you wouldn't want to be with a guy like me who had an anger problem. *Has* an anger problem. I'm a broken mess."

"Jackson—"

He interrupted her, turning to look full at her and cupping her face in his hand. "Jenna, I'm broken. I am. But if you still want me, I'm yours."

His eyes searched her face, waiting for a response. Jenna wanted nothing more than to close the distance between them and kiss him. But she couldn't without saying some things first. She didn't want to leave any doubt in his mind of how she felt.

"Jax, we're all a little broken. I know that I am. I come with a laundry list of issues. The first of which is feeling like I'm going to be abandoned. When you left that day—" He opened his mouth like he was going to apologize again. She quickly pressed a finger to his lips. She could read the pain in his eyes. "When you left, I curled around myself. I didn't want to get hurt again. Especially not by you. I feel … very strongly about you. That terrified me. Falling for someone has historically always ended with me hurt and alone."

"I'm so sorry I hurt you." He spoke around her finger. She dropped her hand and joined it with his.

"I'm sorry that I hurt you too. Even though I didn't mean to. It was my fault you went off like that. I should have explained."

"I doubt I would have heard you. I was too angry."

For a moment they simply sat, hands clasped together and the ocean crashing behind them. Jenna felt a peace that she hadn't in a long time. "We both messed up. So ... what now?"

Jackson untangled the fingers of one hand from hers and brushed the hair back from her cheek. She wanted to lean into his touch but kept herself still, waiting. He could still break her heart, right now. If he said that he didn't feel strongly toward her. If he said he just wanted to be friends.

"I think I pushed you too fast before. I've liked you for so long. Getting to really know you made me like you even more. You went through a lot this year and even before and I should have slowed down. I just couldn't resist you. I thought maybe we could start again and I could take things slow. But I don't think that's going to work."

Jenna dropped her gaze. He didn't want to be with her. The pain of his words moved through her like poison and she tried to hold it together. When he put his fingers under her chin and tried to lift her face, she resisted at first. But when he said her name, softly, she let him tilt her head up to look at him. His eyes were soft and full of tenderness.

"Jenna, it's not that I don't want a relationship with you. I absolutely do. And I hope you want one with me. I'm not sure it's going to work for me to take things slow. I'm trying. I will try. I don't want to rush you."

"We don't need to take things slow. I mean, I don't want to take things slow. I've let so much of my life just go by when I was miserable and lonely. I don't want to waste any more time. I want you, Jackson. If you still want me."

"There's no question. You're it for me, Monroe."

His words nestled down into her heart. Jenna felt at once breathless and calm, as though an inexplicable peace had settled like a blanket over the surge of nervous excitement and joy. Words came back to her suddenly: *The peace of God, which passes all understanding, will guard your hearts and minds in Christ Jesus.* The passage in Philippians had been about taking worries to God in prayer, not romantic relationships, but Jenna felt sure that the peace she felt now could only have come from God.

Despite her worries and her past hurts and the fears and even the conflict she and Jackson just talked through, peace fell over her. Even with the nervous excitement and the way her heart wanted to fly out of her chest as Jackson leaned toward her.

His lips found hers. He brushed them over hers in a featherlight kiss. As Jenna responded, tracing her hand up his neck to tangle in his hair, Jackson deepened the kiss. He released her hand and gripped her waist, pulling her closer, as though he couldn't stand even the smallest distance between them. His lips swept over hers and Jenna felt like he was assuring her of his feelings. His kisses felt like safety and warmth, but also sparked desire that had answered his.

He pulled back suddenly, moving his hands to her shoulders, holding her close to him, but keeping her back too. They were both breathless and he smiled at her with a brilliance that lit up the darkest corners of her soul.

"Wow," he said.

"Wow is right."

"So we're clear, when I said I didn't want to slow down, I wasn't talking about this. I definitely feel like this shouldn't speed up. Not unless we want Beau and Jimmy to have to put out a fire."

Jenna giggled. "Agreed. But I don't want you to hold back. That kiss was …"

"I agree. And don't have a word either. That kiss *was*." He pressed a tender kiss to the apple of her cheek and it was all Jenna could do not to turn her head and start up the kissing again. As though he could read her thoughts, he tapped her nose. "Let's get you back up to the house. You look freezing."

"I am?" Jenna hadn't noticed the way a chill had entered the air. The heat from their kiss had kept her from feeling the full effects of the wind. But now that he mentioned it, goose-bumps popped up on her arms and she shivered.

Jackson stood quickly and held out a hand to pull her up. He put his arm around her shoulders, tucking her close to him. When they got back to the house, Jenna moved to clear the table, but he waved a hand at her. "Leave the dishes. I'll clear them later. I have one more surprise for you."

He led her to the fireplace. It had a mantle made of rough wood that looked custom-built. Jackson turned and took both of her hands. "I designed the inside of this house just for you. But in truth, I hope you don't live here forever. I've got another house I'd love to decorate just for you. It's got too much of a bachelor vibe going on right now."

She laughed. "Your beach house is incredible. But yeah, it's a little empty."

He looked suddenly nervous. "It is, but it's also about to be more full. Jenna, you should know that Megan is coming to live with me full-time, starting this summer. Things weren't working out with her mother. We're going to see if this is a better fit for her. If that's something you don't feel ready for, I understand."

"I actually feel okay about that. I mean, I have no illusions that it would be easy to just suddenly be involved in the life of an almost-teenager. But I like Megan. I've always wanted kids. Not a deal-breaker, Jax."

"I love it when you say my name like that. Okay, last thing. Did you see what was on the mantel?" He looked nervous again.

Jenna's eyes went to the weathered wood. When she walked over she had missed a small box that looked like—no, it couldn't be. A ring box? Jenna's entire body threatened to shut down when she saw it.

"Hey." Jackson tugged her hand and pulled her closer, forcing her to meet his eyes. "I'm not proposing right now. I know you said you don't want to take things slow, but that look—that panic right there—that's the thing I'm watching for. I can see that you aren't ready for that step. I want to go your speed. Even if you aren't sure what that is or if it changes. Fast, slow, whatever. But that box right there is my commitment to you: I'm in this for forever. I will not walk away from you or cheat on you. I will not leave you. I feel one-hundred percent sure right now, and it's okay if you don't. Yet."

"Jackson, I don't know what to say."

"You don't need to say anything. Not yet. That's an engagement ring. For you. I bought it already because I'm a little foolish like that. And I know what I want. *Who* I want. That's you, Monroe."

Jenna pulled in her breath. She wanted to say something to him, to tell him how she felt, to commit the way he was committing to her, but he was right—she wasn't ready. Yet.

"I'm not opening that box tonight. Not because I don't want to, but because I know you aren't ready. I think I'll know when you are. Or maybe you'll tell me. I didn't quite plan out the details. We can both pray about it. If you want to talk about it more, we can. I think we'll both know when it's time. Maybe that will be a week. Maybe six months. But the ring is here. My heart is yours. I love you, Jenna Monroe. I think I always have, but now that I have you in my life, I love you more than I thought I could love anyone. I want to marry you. Whenever you are ready."

Jenna threw herself into his arms, pressing her face into his neck. She felt the scrape of stubble over her cheek and breathed in the scent of him. Jackson loved her. He bought her a ring.

Though she always struggled to trust, always assumed the worst because of what she'd been through, Jenna trusted Jackson at his word. He came with a daughter—something new that they would both have to work through—and an anger problem. He held shame and guilt and regret. Jenna was just as broken in her own ways, but she felt that same peace quelling her fears and insecurities. Jackson was right. She wasn't ready tonight. But she didn't think it would be long.

"Thank you, Jax." She stood on tiptoes to speak in his ear. Her lips whispered over his skin. "This is the best surprise ever. You are everything I could want and though you're right —I'm not ready tonight to say yes—I have no doubt I will be. Soon."

With this last word of promise, he turned his head and swept her away in the kind of kiss that Jenna felt like had only existed in stories. But this was her life, her man, and she felt sure that they would have their happy ending.

EPILOGUE

THE COOKOUT at Jackson's was in full swing. But not even the amazing preview of summer weather could draw Jenna out of her funk. Above the sound of the surf, music and conversations rang out from the bottom patio, where Jackson manned the grill. Jenna watched him, as he flipped a burger, laughing at something Beau said. Her chest burned with longing. She had fallen for Jackson. Hard and fast. But he had been distant this week and Jenna was worried.

It had been a month since Jackson had showed her the ring on the mantle. Two weeks since Jenna was ready for him to open that box. He had said he would know when she was ready, so she expectantly waited. Nothing. She started dropping hints that seemed to fly right over his head. She wondered if she should flat-out tell him. Maybe he had over-estimated his ability to tell when Jenna was ready.

Now she was glad that she hadn't spoken up. This week things shifted and she didn't know why. Jackson hadn't been ignoring her, exactly, but had pulled back. He was cooler and almost aloof. His smiles didn't reach his eyes. His kisses were brief, lacking all the passion that had been building between them. He seemed distracted.

A yawning distance opened up between them that only grew wider the more Jenna noticed it and pulled back. If he had changed his mind, it would crush her. But he should tell her one way or the other, not drag this out. She was starting to feel like he was just leaving her on the line.

Ugh. Fishing analogies. That's when you know you're thinking too much.

Jenna turned her focus away from the grill. She was currently beating Jimmy at bocce ball, a game she had grown up playing. He had played baseball and apparently didn't know how to throw softly. His tosses continually landed the balls past the tiny white ball they were aiming for. His last one landed in the hard-packed sand and began rolling toward the ocean. Beau scooped it up before it disappeared in the water. He shook his head and lobbed it back. It landed right next to the white ball.

Jenna laughed. "An admirable loss."

Jimmy groaned. "I don't understand this game. You killed me. I think you On Island people invented it as a way of humiliating people who didn't grow up here."

"Where did you grow up?"

"Richmond. Which gives you a very unfair advantage, I'd say."

"Aw, someone's a sore loser," she teased.

"I'll happily take you on in baseball." Jimmy grinned as they began picking up the balls.

"I'll pass and go out on my winning streak. This is probably the only physical game I've ever won. Maybe I should go pro."

He snorted. She dropped the last of her balls into the canvas tote Jimmy had over his shoulder. They walked back toward Jackson's house. He lifted the spatula from the grill to wave at Jenna. She gave him a weak smile back, trying to push down the feelings she was struggling with. Better to think about something else. "Do you think you'll stay On Island or will you ever move back to Richmond?"

Jimmy dropped the bag and got them both bottled waters from the cooler. His girlfriend, Amber, waved from the water, obviously wanting him to join her. He waved but stayed where he was. Maybe Jenna wasn't the only one avoiding relationship issues.

"I'm not sure yet. It's definitely where I want to be at the moment. It's been good for me."

"How did you end up here? I mean, we aren't exactly the biggest beach on the map."

"Definitely not. And that toll booth almost kept me away. I didn't have any cash the first time I showed up here. Packed my car, drove down, and then got stopped with no money. I had to wait for another car to come and beg for cash."

Jimmy had effectively dodged why he came here. She wasn't going to pry. "But you still got on Sandover, despite the toll booth. And then stayed."

"I did. The rest of my family is in Richmond still. My parents, sister, her husband, and their two kids. I miss them all like crazy. But I love my job and I've never had friends like these or such a supportive community. For now, here is good."

Here is good. Jenna felt the same way. At least until this week.

She glanced at Jackson again, but he was deep in conversation with Beau. He caught her watching and turned his body slightly away from her. Beau's eyes flicked to her and he nodded.

Her stomach dropped. Were they talking about her?

Jenna wandered away from Jimmy and settled in a beach chair, watching a family just down the beach. That didn't help. After five minutes of the couple holding hands and laughing with their toddler (who kept trying to eat sand), Jenna felt tears spring to her eyes. She might never have that. If Jackson had changed his mind … she didn't think she could ever open up her heart again. She would leave the beach house that felt so perfect for her and move to Burlington near Rachel. Forget the way the beach called to her. If he rejected her now, she would leave in the morning.

There were sudden shouts and Jenna glanced over to see Beau tossing Jackson—fully clothed—into the ocean. Despite herself, she laughed as he came up sputtering. Beau stood smiling on the shore, grinning with his arms crossed over his chest. "Now we're even," she heard him say.

Jackson made his way out of the water, wringing out his clothes. He was still smiling that big smile and it warmed Jenna. Maybe everything was okay after all. "I'm going upstairs to change. Be back down in a few."

"Okay!"

Snap out of it, Monroe.

Great, now her inner monologue was using Jackson's nickname for her. How had he managed to burrow his way so close to her heart in such a short time? She remembered when she first got back On Island and thought he was a bag boy, insulting him right in the wine aisle of Bohn's. That would make a great start to their story one day, if there was ever a happy ending to share.

Jenna wandered back to the house, wondering if anyone would notice her leaving early. She just didn't feel like good company.

"What's wrong?" Mercer appeared beside her, sipping on a soda.

Jenna groaned internally. She had been trying to avoid Mercer—the one person who would recognize something was wrong and press her on it. "Nothing."

Mercer didn't speak, but simply waited. She was the kind of friend who knew when to push, but also when to wait. Jenna felt stupid being so worked up over a few changes in Jackson this week. It was probably not a big deal. She should just ask him. Tomorrow. Definitely not today.

"Okay, something's wrong. Maybe. But it will be fine. I think. I'm not ready to talk about it."

"You know I'm here," Mercer said.

Jenna smiled. "I do. Thanks. Have you seen Megan?"

Mercer shook her head. "Not for a while. I thought I saw her heading toward the house a bit ago."

"I think I'll go find her. Thanks, Mercer."

Jenna only felt a little guilty for using Megan as an excuse for going in the house and escaping the party. She was learning that Megan needed to be drawn out and engaged. People tended to be scared off by her sarcasm and the way she didn't seem to fear adults. Even Beau and Jimmy, two of the friendliest guys Jenna had ever met, gave her a wide berth.

Jenna had made it her personal mission not to be scared off. Of course, now, if Jackson didn't want to be with her, Jenna would just be one more person letting Megan down.

Megan's bedroom door was open and the room empty. Groaning, Jenna started up the three flights. If she and Jackson did get married, she would have the most amazing calves from all the stair-climbing. She still hadn't set foot inside the elevator since the day she and Jackson got stuck. The first time he had kissed her. Her chest ached.

She pushed aside the negative thoughts, trying to tell herself that she was just overreacting. Just a few weeks ago, she and Jackson had talked about the future, about living in this house together. It would make more sense as far as space, especially with Megan moving there in June. Jenna's beach cottage, as much as she loved it, would be too cramped. Despite its size, this house was starting to feel more comfortable to her. Not as much as the beach cottage, which was where she and Jackson spent most of their time.

Her house, as she thought of it. Jackson liked to remind her that it was his house, a point she refused to concede on. Even though he was right. "You may have lived here longer than me and technically own the house," she liked to say. "But you decorated it for me. I'm paying the bills right now. *My* house. Mine."

"Don't make me evict you to prove my point," he would tease.

But she knew Jackson loved the fact that she had settled in so well in the place that he grew up. She was constantly finding little surprises he'd left for her: blue soaps shaped like seashells in the guest bathroom drawer; a plate that read "You Are Special Today" in the cabinet, mixed in with the others; a hoodie hanging in her closet that smelled like him.

And the ring in the box still sat on the mantel. These days, it felt like a kind of telltale heart—its very presence haunting her, teasing her, reminding her of what she wanted but couldn't have. She couldn't shake the tendrils of doubt, wrapping around her heart. What if his feelings had changed?

Her stomach dropped.

When she reached the top level, Jenna stopped to breathe. It was quiet, Megan nowhere to be seen. Jackson must have still been changing, but the bedroom door was closed. Jenna hesitated, wondering if she should knock and just ask him what was going on. But she didn't have the guts. If he had changed his mind about what he wanted, she would wait for him to tell her. She tried to push the thought from her mind as she walked toward the front balcony. Movement in the tower room above caught her eye.

"Hey." Megan gave her a small wave from the love seat.

"Hey, you." Jenna climbed up and collapsed on the love seat. "Ugh. More stairs." Megan huffed and backed up a little. Jenna smiled. Another thing she'd noticed: Megan moaned and groaned about having her personal space invaded, but it was more of an act. "What are you working on up here?"

Megan had finally started sharing snippets of her videos with Jenna. They were surprisingly good. A little juvenile, sure, but then, she was twelve. Jenna's favorite had been of Megan's classmate, who was your classic mean girl. She had followed the girl for what must have been days, catching her in various insults and bad behavior. The background music was classic horror-movie fare. It was probably a massive violation of the girl's privacy, but Megan wasn't making the video public. "That would just be doing the same to her she does to everyone else," Megan had told her. "I made this for me."

Jenna was impressed by that and by Megan's ability to film and edit and put together a video. She wished that she had a passion like that. Then or now, she'd never had something she'd been that interested in.

When Megan didn't answer, Jenna nudged her. "New project?"

"Oh, you know. Nothing you'd want to see." Megan tilted the phone away.

"That only makes me want to see it more, you know."

Megan smiled. "You're so easy."

Jenna poked her in the side. "Are you going to show me? Or should we argue back and forth some more?"

"Fine." Megan's tone sounded annoyed, but Jenna caught the small smile on her lips.

Megan leaned closer and pressed play. "Claim Your Ghost," the song Jenna and Jackson had listened to that night on the back porch, began while the screen was still dark. The moment the video started, Jenna's mouth fell open. It featured clips of Jenna and Jackson from the past six weeks, starting with the day in the elevator. She watched as Beau half-dragged her up the stairs. It was embarrassing to see herself in that sweaty state, passed out on the couch. But then it zoomed in on Jackson's hand stroking hers. The camera moved up to his face, capturing a look of concern and love that almost made Jenna gasp.

There weren't audible words, only tiny moments of their relationship. Megan had caught Jackson's hand resting on Jenna's lower back. His fingers brushing her hair back from her face. Jenna's laughter at something Jackson said. Her head nestling into his neck, pressing a kiss there. Each moment more precious than the last.

Tears slid silently down her cheeks and she didn't realize that she had grabbed Megan's hand until the video faded to black. Jenna closed her eyes.

"Wait—it's not over yet."

Looking down on the screen, Jenna saw her beach cottage. The music had faded away. She didn't recognize this moment. The camera followed Jackson as he walked to the fireplace and then turned around with a huge smile. He put his finger to his lips, then reached up for the ring box.

Jenna's heart stopped. Jackson flipped open the box and the camera zoomed in on a gorgeous and simple diamond ring. It panned back up to his face, still smiling, but with tears shining in his eyes now.

"I want to ask you something, Monroe. I think it's about time," Jackson said from the video.

The video went black again and Jenna's gaze snapped to Megan. An unfamiliar smile, not unlike the Cheshire cat, spread over her face. "Is that ... it?"

"Down here, Monroe."

Jackson's voice carried up the stairs and Jenna gasped. While her eyes had been glued to the small screen in front of her, Jackson had moved to the bottom of the tower room stairs, surrounded by their friends. He knelt on one knee, and his expression was the same as the video: a huge smile and glistening eyes. Behind him, their friends formed a half-circle around him, all smiling up at her.

Jenna's hand flew to her chest, as though she could still the wild beating of her heart. "Jackson—what?"

He laughed. "Welcome to your proposal, Jenna. I've been waiting what feels like a really long time for this moment. Most of my life, if I'm being honest. I want to spend the rest of my life beside you. I want more moments like the ones in the video, big and small. I love you, Monroe. Will you do me the honor of being my wife?"

Jenna didn't realize that several moments had passed until Megan nudged her, nodding toward Jackson. "Are you going to answer him?" she whispered.

"Oh!"

There were chuckles from downstairs. Jenna stood, suddenly sure that she was going to fall down all seven steps. She gripped the banister so hard that her knuckles turned white. Jackson seemed to read her mind.

"I've got you, Monroe."

She smiled because she knew he did. Jackson took her hand when she reached the bottom. The ring sat in his other palm, waiting. She could almost feel its weight on her finger already.

Jackson squeezed her hand. "Jenna Monroe, love of my life, I promise you my faithfulness and love until death do us part. Will you marry me? Will you be mine, forever?"

This was the moment Jenna hadn't thought to hope for six weeks ago. She had been lost and bitter, defeated and heavy. Love seemed like an impossibility, and love with Jackson Wells would never have crossed her mind. But he had swept into her life like the Nor'easters that sometimes battered the island. God had used him to help heal her, to help her let go and find peace again. She wanted to remember the love in his eyes and the way his smile lifted a little more at the right corner than the left.

"Are you going to answer me, Monroe?" Jackson almost whispered, a smile playing on his lips.

"Yes."

His grin widened, and Jenna knew her own rivaled his. "Yes, you're going to answer me or yes, you'll marry me?"

"Yes to both."

Before she could react, Jackson stood and swept her into his arms. There was cheering and clapping all around them, but Jenna couldn't focus on anything but the man holding her. Jackson slid the ring on her finger and, before she could even admire it, he claimed her mouth in a searing kiss.

Jenna gasped into his mouth, but her surprise faded almost instantly into heated passion and something weightier. In every glide of his lips against hers, it felt like Jackson was promising to love, cherish, and honor her, as though he was already making his vows through the kiss.

It wasn't just her body waking up and responding to the kiss. She felt like Jackson stirred her very soul. He had resurrected her hope. With him, she felt like faith was possible again. Not just a trust in him, because he would let her down sometimes. But a hard-won belief that God held her in his hands. Jackson's love reminded her of how treasured and precious she was to God.

After what didn't feel like nearly enough time, Jackson pulled back. Jenna threaded her hands through his hair, keeping him close, not even caring that their friends were still nearby. They had retreated to the kitchen, where she heard the popping of a cork. After feeling so self-conscious and worried all week, she felt clingy and needy. She didn't want to move even an inch away from Jackson right now.

This close, it was hard to focus on both of his eyes, but she tried, needing this connection. "This whole week I thought you were going to break up with me," she whispered.

His head jerked back. "What? Why?"

"You've been acting so different, avoiding me or just being aloof."

Understanding passed over his features. "That's called me trying to keep a secret and being really nervous. I'm so sorry I made you think that."

"Now I feel really silly for being worried."

"I hope you're not feeling worried anymore. That's the last thing I want you thinking about or feeling right now."

Jenna placed a kiss at the corner of his mouth. "I'm feeling a lot of things right now, but worried isn't one of them." Her voice sounded low and husky, drawing out a brilliant smile that made her want to start kissing him again.

"Okay, happy couple! Time to celebrate!" Beau called.

Taking her hand, Jackson led Jenna over to the group by the wide kitchen island. There were glasses of champagne and sparkling cider.

Beau led the toast. "To love: the kind that knocks us off our feet and changes the course of our life." Jenna didn't miss the way Beau looked at Mercer when he spoke. He raised his glass, and everyone clinked theirs together. "To Jackson and Jenna, and to love!"

"To love!"

As she set her glass on the counter, Jackson wound a strong arm around Jenna's waist and pulled her away from the group to the balcony. When they were alone, his lips found her ear, sending a spark all the way down to her toes.

"I hope it's okay that this wasn't a flashy proposal. I thought about doing something really big and extravagant, but this felt like a better fit for you."

Jenna pulled back enough to look him straight in the eyes. "This was perfect."

A smile tugged up the corners of his mouth. "My other idea was to trap you in the elevator until you said yes."

Jenna threw back her head and laughed. "You might have gotten a different answer if you tried that, Jax."

He kissed her neck, just below her ear and she tried to hold back a squeal. "No way. You can't resist me, Monroe."

She knew that he was right. She couldn't resist Jackson. As she leaned into the warmth of his body and the security of his tender kisses, surrounded by their friends, Jenna was so glad that she had stopped trying.

THE END

Keep reading about Sandover with Jimmy's story, Sandover Beach Week!

A NOTE FROM EMMA

I got the idea for this book while stuck in an elevator at Nag's Head. Not with a handsome man like Jackson, but two girls I had met like an hour beforehand. And, of course, I was the one who opened the door while the elevator was moving. It simply HAD to go in a book!

This is an updated version of my second book, *Sandover Beach Memories*. I was really happy with the book when I finished, but as I wrote more and read more, I realized there were some things I wanted to fix. Originally, there was more of a love triangle. I've grown to hate those and readers don't like them as much either. In this version, Steve is definitely not contending for Jenna and it works much better. I also made a few more tweaks and think it works much better now.

A few real-life inspirations that made it into the book:

- I drink a pot of coffee before bed almost every
  night. I started when I worked at Borders Book

store in the café. I drank coffee constantly through my shifts and it broke me. So now, I do coffee and then go right to bed. I know. It's weird.

- Right before my husband proposed, I went through something similar to Jenna. My mom perpetuated this by calling and telling me that Rob (my hubby) hadn't asked my dad for permission—something that mattered to me. Honestly? I would have married my husband the first week we were dating (long story as to why). So, this was over a year later and I couldn't figure out why he wasn't proposing. Hearing he hadn't asked my dad made me think it was NEVER happening. But my mom was messing with me and the next day my hubby took me on a full day-long scavenger hunt with a ring at the end. I felt foolish being so worried, but it was a real thing.
- Growing up in Richmond, VA, we had a store called Ukrops that was local and family-owned. It was a huge thing for Richmonders to shop there, even though it was more expensive. The kids didn't want to keep it, so now it's gone, but anyone who grew up there might understand how Bohn's took its inspiration from Ukrops.

Thanks so much to my amazing beta readers and proof-reader: Marsha, Judy, Leslie, Vicky, and Patty (who read the book when I was freaking out). I love ALL my readers and appreciate you guys so much!

Want to connect more?

You can get a free book, when you sign up to get my emails. Sign up at http://emmastclair.com/freebook

Join my Facebook group: https://www.facebook.com/ groups/emmastclair/

WHAT TO READ NEXT

The Billionaire Surprise Series
The Billionaire Love Match
The Billionaire Benefactor
The Billionaire Land Baron
The Billionaire's Masquerade Ball
The Billionaire's Secret Heir

Sandover Island Sweet Romance Series
Sandover Beach Memories
Sandover Beach Week
Sandover Beach Melodies
Sandover Beach Christmas

Not So Bad Boy Sweet Romance Series
Managing the Rock Star
Forgiving the Football Player
Winning the Cowboy
Taming the Cowboy's Twin

WHERE IS SANDOVER ISLAND?

I grew up going to Nag's Head, staying at the Sea Ranch and in one-bathroom beach cottages with ten people. We went to Newman's Shell Shop and climbed Jockey's Ridge and ate ice cream at the Snowbird. Once, I had my boogie board broken in half by a wave as a Nor'easter rolled in.

These are some of my greatest beach memories and they absolutely helped me create Sandover Island. But I chose to create fictional island because I couldn't do the REAL Outer Banks justice. They are completely perfect and lovely. For those of you who hold them dear, as I do, writing in any changes would be like blasphemy. I also still see the islands as they were in the 80s and 90s, not as they are today.

We all have our own memories tied up in those real places. Anything in my books that didn't line up with your experiences would jar you right out of the book. I don't want you pulled out of the story by factual inaccuracies or something that might be from my memory, not your own.

No, Sandover isn't real and it wouldn't really fit on a map of the Carolina Coast. But if you love the Outer Banks as I do, when you think of Sandover, know that I'm thinking of Nag's Head and Kill Devil Hills and Kitty Hawk. Suspend belief for a bit and picture one more island with the Sound on one side and the Atlantic on the other. Let those good memories you have fill in the gaps and help you hear the ocean and feel the sand between your toes.

And if you've never been to the Outer Banks?? Oh, my. Let this book help you fall in love and then get ye to the Carolina Coast!

Made in the USA
Las Vegas, NV
17 August 2021

28360651R00163